fall from
FALL FROM

michelle gross

fall from grace

Table of Contents

MORE BOOKS BY MICHELLE.. 7

Part One:.. 10

1.. 11

2.. 22

3.. 31

4.. 35

5.. 40

6.. 46

7.. 51

8.. 58

9.. 63

10.. 66

11.. 72

12.. 77

13.. 84

14.. 88

15.. 98

16.. 104

Part Two:.. 107

17.. 108

18.. 114

19.. 117

20.. 120

21.. 136

22.. 145

23.. 151

24.. 159

25.. 165

26.. 175

27.. 183

28.. 191

29.. 201

30.. 208

31.. 218

32.. 227

33.. 239

34.. 253

Finale: 255

michelle gross

35 256
36 271
37 283
38 308
EPILOGUE 311
ABOUT THE AUTHOR 320

More Books by Michelle

Paranormal Romance: A Grim Awakening Series

'Til Fear Do Us Part, Book One

'Til Grim's Light, Book Two

'Til Death We Meet Again, Book Three

Falling For Fear, Book Four

michelle gross

fall from grace

To the childhood home,

my most favorite person,

the one that introduced me to romance and Patrick Swayze,

that made me into a hopeless romantic,

the fallen one,

the scared one,

the depressed one,

the shell of yourself.

I miss you.

We miss you.

Come back.

It's okay, I get depressed too.

This one's for you because I know, you too, are hopeless to romance.

Part One:

Grade School

1

Grace age 6

Noah age 7

The treehouse is mine. No one has lived in this house for a couple of years… A new family just showed up today. Shit, there's a little girl coming.

Girls are such a pain.

N.P.

Looking back now, it's funny that my parents named me Grace. They couldn't have picked a better name for their only daughter. I was sweet and caring, beautiful everyone told me. Picture perfect, dressed head to toe in frilly little dresses, Mom made me wear. She'd place headbands or bows in my brown hair that added to the freckles splashed across my cheeks. As a kid, I was always the center of attention and I loved it. I knew all the right things to say to make the adults laugh and smile at me more.

It didn't matter how doting my parents were, though, because it was only a matter of time before I started to disappoint them. It wasn't their fault. They didn't know the town we moved to when I was six would be three houses down from a dirty trailer park. And inside one of those trailers would be a wild, lonely boy left to do whatever he wanted day-in and day-out. It wasn't their fault their daughter took a liking to the dirty neighbor boy and became his friend.

If only that was all we became, they would have been happy. If only our bodies weren't made to do the things I did with the neighbor boy.

I met him the same day Dad drove a U-Haul to our new house with Mom and me in her car behind him. The electric and water had been hooked up days before we even got there, Mom and Dad were always efficient in everything they did. Mom was a math teacher and would be teaching at my new school. Dad was an accountant. I didn't really understand what that meant until I was older. I just knew it had something to do with numbers. They met and fell in love in college over their mutual attraction to numbers… Don't ask me, I didn't understand it either.

Our new house was a two-hour drive from our last one, but it was still in Virginia. When I thought of the friends I was leaving behind from kindergarten, it made my heart ache, but the moment my feet touched the concrete driveway at our new place, I couldn't help but feel excited. Everything was new. And for a six-year-old, new was exciting. It wasn't until you were older that change was scary.

"What do you think Gracie?" Dad asked, stepping out of the U-Haul with a smile as he watched me soak it all in. Everyone called me Gracie in an endearing way, and that was another thing that wouldn't bother me until I got older.

I didn't answer his question at first. Instead, I took it all in with my eyes, ears, and nose. This house was just as big as our old house, a two-story, but our old one had been white with a blue roof. This one was white too, but its roof was red as were the windowsills and porch banisters. The air was hot, yet clean as I inhaled. We were in the middle of June so even the breeze was hot. There was another house next to ours, followed by two double-wide trailers. In the distance, I could see a bunch of trailers grouped together. But my eyes quickly fell back on what was ours. The front yard wasn't very big, but the back one was huge. I finally giggled and ran back to answer Dad's question. "I love it!" His hands were there to catch me as he swooped me up and spun me around.

fall from grace

"Okay, you two, we have to unload the last of our things so Dad can take the U-Haul back and pick up his truck." The whole time Mom spoke, Dad mimicked her with a goofy face and it had me laughing the entire time she was talking.

"Steven," Mom clucked at Dad which only made me burst into more giggles.

"Yes, dear," was his sugary sweet reply to her. My dark eyes and hair were passed down from Mom, but my freckles came from Dad who was a redhead with freckles all over his body.

She shook her head and sighed at him. "I give up, I don't know what to do with you both."

Dad sucked in his jaws and looked back down at me. "We better listen to the boss lady." I nodded and agreed completely.

"I'll help," I offered excitedly, already lifting myself in the back of the U-Haul. I bent down for the first closest box and couldn't even grasp it correctly, let alone lift it.

Dad chuckled. "Here, why don't you go check the place out while your mom and I get everything unloaded?"

"Just give me something that I can carry," I protested.

"Gracie," he started, then smiled. "Stop trying to be a grown up and go check out the backyard some more."

I huffed. "Fine."

I hopped out of the back of the U-Haul and made my way through the grass. It needed to be cut, being just above my ankles and making them itch. "And make sure you watch for snakes," Dad hollered. "Better yet, just go inside and look around until I get a chance to cut the grass." I took off running around the house, and I heard his frustrated sigh and smiled.

Glancing at the hill behind the house, I knew I was going to enjoy exploring it but not that day. My eyes lit up when I saw the giant oak tree

13

in our yard. It wasn't exactly the tree that caught my attention, it was the treehouse in it. "Oh, my gosh!" I squealed as I ran toward the tree. My palms and the insides of my legs met the rope in a frenzied rush as I pulled myself up. It wasn't hard for me, gymnastics and naturally being an adventurist kid, I was one of those that thought I could do anything growing up.

My eyes fell on the blankets toward the back of the treehouse before I dropped them back to the floor as I finished hoisting myself up. I smiled to myself once one leg was already on the floor, then the other. Something darted through the treehouse, I paused, my gaze snapping forward. My scream was at the edge of my teeth before two hands clamped over my mouth quickly.

"Shh," a scratchy voice barked out.

My eyes raked over the thin boy in front of me. His dirty hands were cupped over my lips as his blue eyes studied me darkly. They were so bright and blue, even the darkness of the treehouse couldn't hide their color. But the rest of him… was dirty. Even his hair looked dark and matted in such a way I'd never seen before.

Once I saw it was just a boy instead of a monster hiding in the treehouse, I brought my hand to his and pulled it from my mouth. He watched me cautiously as my eyes darted toward the heap of clothes and blankets behind him. "Do you live here, boy?" I asked him quickly.

A flash of color hit his cheeks so quickly, I probably saw wrong. "No, but this is my treehouse, *girl*," he snapped back with venom.

I lifted an eyebrow. "Maybe." I gave him my battle smile. I always got what I wanted, but in this case, this treehouse was already mine. "But, not anymore. My parents bought this house and *this* land, and that places this treehouse as *mine.*"

His eyes held a gleam to them that made my smile falter for a fraction of a second. "Wanna know what happened to the last family that lived here?" he asked me, and I leaned in for what he was going to tell me. "They moved away because of me, I scared their son so bad he begged them to move!"

I blinked a few times before I burst into giggles. "You're a liar."

"Ask anyone," he hissed. "His name was Jeremiah, and they moved seven months ago. This treehouse has been mine ever since."

"How old are you?" I asked. "Six, like me?"

"No, seven." He grinned smugly. "And don't think that just because you're a fancy little girl that I'll let you have your way."

"Fancy?"

He pointed toward my dress. "What kind of creature wears polka dots? You look like a unicorn shit on you."

I gasped, my hands flying over my mouth. "You said a bad word. You can't say that!"

"What?" He genuinely looked confused at first then an evil smirk claimed his lips. "Shit. Shit. Shit. Shit."

I gasped again. "You're such a foul and dirty boy!"

He laughed at my choice of words, and my cheeks warmed. "And you're such a bratty girl," he argued back.

"Get out of my treehouse." I stood up, twisted my body halfway, and pointed toward the exit.

He turned around and grabbed a couple of clothes from the pile. "Like I'd want to stay here and fight with a loud-mouthed girl anyway," he told me.

I dropped my hand finally and just watched him slip past me. My eyes fell back on the blankets and clothes he was about to leave behind. Even at age six, I looked too deeply into things and saw them for what they truly were, not how a normal child would. I glanced back to him as he was tossing his clothes on the ground. "Do you have somewhere to go?" I couldn't help but ask. "Where're your parents?"

He turned around, a dark storm brewed in his eyes. "I wasn't living here!" he yelled. "Stupid girl!"

My eyes grew wide. "I was only—"

"You were only being nosy."

I practically blew steam from my nose as I glared at him. I brought my leg out to kick him but he saw what I was about to do, and jumped. I hurried to the edge and looked down to see him scooping up his clothes. "Don't come back," I said haughtily like I had done something great to make him run off.

He smirked. "Oh, I'll be back." And it was a promise because the very next day, he came again. I guarded the treehouse like it was a treasure trove. I just knew from the looks of him he was going to be a persistent pain in my butt. When I wasn't in the treehouse that day, I was looking out the kitchen window eating a popsicle. That was when he came back. He snuck in the backyard through the hills so that told me he knew his way around the woods. I hopped off the counter and headed for the door.

"Where're you going?" Mom asked me.

"Treehouse," I replied. I didn't want to give away the boy. If my parents knew of him, that might ruin the fun I was sure I would have with him.

"Be careful."

I stopped at the door and ran to the fridge, tiptoeing to get another popsicle in the freezer. "You and popsicles," Mom laughed, shaking her head.

I grinned at my own secret as I hurried outside. The boy let out a frustrated sigh the moment my head peeked above the treehouse where he sat. "You should stop wearing those dresses if you plan to keep climbing up here," he pointed out.

fall from grace

I couldn't respond to him just yet with my popsicle wedged in my mouth. I gripped the wood and tossed the extra popsicle to him as I finished hoisting myself into the treehouse. Once I was inside, I walked over to him and sat down, bringing the popsicle out of my mouth with a *popping* sound. He watched me cautiously then glanced down at the popsicle in his lap. "I brought it for you," I told him.

His eyes widened. "This is why girls are strange," he muttered.

"How so?" I asked, leaning on my hand as I spoke.

"One minute, a girl will be mad at you for saying something, then the next, she's trying to be sweet." He shook his head and sighed, ripping into the wrapper before sticking the popsicle in his mouth. "It's so annoying."

"What's wrong with trying to get along with you despite our first meeting?"

He shrugged his shoulders in reply. "Are you going to tell me your name?" I asked him.

"Noah," he answered. "Noah Phillips." He lifted his gaze. "And yours?"

"Grace," I chirped. "Grace Harper."

He snorted. "Figures."

I gave him a hostile look. "What?"

"Even your name sounds prissy."

"I am not prissy," I protested.

He nodded his head like he wanted to say, *sure, sure.*

I lifted my chin up, remembering the way he entered the yard. "You just reminded me, I saw the way you entered the yard… You look like you know your way around the woods."

He smiled smugly. "I know these woods like the back of my head."

I rolled my eyes before smiling. "Good." He lifted a brow in question. "Take me on an adventure."

His reply was the lift of his eyes and mouth as he moved across the creaking wood in a hurry, shimmying down the rope. I got up and followed after him. I looked over to the house before following him into the hills where he spent hours testing me with steep places, high tree branches, and small creeks. The only thing that he managed to get a reaction from me was when he lifted some sort of bug in my face, and I jumped back screeching. He grabbed his stomach and pointed at me as he lurched over and laughed.

I huffed. "Put it down!"

He lifted himself up and nodded. "Yes, Miss Priss."

"Don't call me that, either."

When he smiled at me this time, it was different than the times before, more relaxed. "Ya know, you're not so bad for a girl."

His smile was contagious. I tucked my hair behind my ear. "I guess that makes you my first friend here."

He rubbed a hand down his dirty shirt, almost like he was as self-conscious as a seven-year-old could be. "I guess having one girl as a friend won't hurt," he said slowly.

I stepped closer to him. "Then it's a promise."

He frowned. "What is?"

"That I'll be the only girl you spend your time with," I giggled innocently, not understanding the true gravity my words placed on him that day. "I'll always stay with you as long as you promise something."

His eyes searched mine. "What?"

"That you'll always take me on an adventure."

18

He smirked. "I can do that."

I nodded. "I think so too."

"Gracie!" In the distance, my mom's voice rang loud.

"Oh no," I whispered, "it's my mom."

I took off running as quick as I could down the hill, occasionally scooting on my butt and leaping over branches and puddles of mud. Noah stayed right behind me, and soon I was laughing as we made a game out of it.

"Quick, the giant mutant spiders are right behind us!" Noah screamed.

I looked behind him and gasped. "Noah, duck!" He did and I sighed in relief. "It almost had you."

He jumped right next to me, knocking into me. He grabbed my arms and I his as we twisted around each other to keep our balance. "I got you, Miss Priss," he said to me in a princely tone that had us bursting out in laughter.

"Grace!" Mom yelled, snapping me out of our game.

Noah jerked his hands from me and stepped away quickly. He suddenly looked nervous, tugging on his dirty shirt, and looking down and around, anywhere but at my mom as she stared him down.

"Mom, this is my friend Noah," I told her quickly, not wanting him to feel uncomfortable and look so unlike that confident boy I had first met.

"How'd you make a friend when we've only been here two days?" she asked me curiously. "So, you live around here, Noah?" She looked to him.

He finally met her eyes. "Yes, ma'am."

19

"That's great." Mom gave him a smile. "You'll have to introduce us," his face paled at her words, "but, Grace, you can't just run off into the woods like that. It's dangerous," Mom cautioned.

"Mom, Noah knows his way around."

She sighed. "I'm sure he does." Mom looked at him again. "Noah, would you like to come in and eat with us?"

Something about the shine in his eyes and the hard swallow I watched slide down his throat told me he liked the idea, but he still looked hesitant. "Umm…"

"Do you need to go ask your parents?" Mom asked about his parents again.

He straightened quickly. "No, they won't mind."

He ate with us that night. I'd never seen someone eat so much food. I smiled proudly that day, thinking his appetite was because of Mom's cooking until he left, and Mom stood by the door watching him dart over toward the trailers.

That night, I listened in on my parents as she told Dad about Noah. "I know how dirty a kid can get while playing outside during the summer, but Steven, he looked as if he hadn't had a bath or a decent meal in God knows how long. And as soon as he saw me, he started fidgeting with his clothes like he was used to grown-ups commenting about how dirty they were and was self-conscious." Mom sighed. "It bothered me."

"Don't think too much of it," Dad told her. "You're making assumptions when he might just be *that* dirty from playing outside, unlike you thought."

Mom's voice softened, "You're right, I do tend to get ahead of myself."

I heard Dad kiss Mom's forehead and slipped back upstairs into my room from the hallway where I was peeping outside their door.

20

fall from grace

Only Mom hadn't been wrong that day. Noah's parents were far different from mine.

2

Grace age 6

Noah age 7

Girls are frustrating, I don't understand them... But Grace isn't so bad. She's super girly when it comes to things like bugs and stuff, but she's not afraid to have fun and get dirty even in the ugly dresses she wears... I guess it's not too ugly because she's not bad to look at and the longer we stay in the sun, the more freckles she wakes up to the next day. I like her freckles, even the gap in her teeth... Grace is pretty, I suppose... looking at her... I sort of understand why adults want to kiss and touch.

I wish she wasn't so nosy, though.

I'm embarrassed and I don't like to feel that way. I don't want her to find out about the house I live in. The parents I was born to. The way my Dad gave Mom the drugs she wanted that slowly chipped away at her life. I don't want her to find out how unimportant I am, not when she looks at me like I can show her anything...

I'm not needed, perhaps I'm not loved more than a drug in this family. She doesn't need to know that though.

N.P.

The next day, and the one after that, and every hour of daylight that summer, Noah came to play with me. He became my friend within a day's time, but the extent of what we became rapidly grew with age, and even though it started out innocent, it couldn't stay that way.

When he came back over that next day, I was so surprised to see that his hair wasn't brown like I had originally thought. Now that it was

22

washed, it was blond. He wore the same clothes he did the day before, though, and I still wore dresses. Mom cooked for us every day, often scolding us for sneaking off into the hills when she told us not to. Noah behaved around Mom and Dad, always. It was when he was alone with me that he let his cheekiness show.

Two weeks into living in our new home, I experienced a taste of what Noah's life was like. He had been taking too long to come over, and I was so impatient and tired of waiting. Mom had made me promise not to go over to the trailers where he lived, but I couldn't obey the rule that day, much like how I couldn't stop myself from playing in the hills when she told me not to.

I knew which trailer was his. I made sure to watch the evenings he ran off to his house when the sun was setting in the sky after we had played all day. Out of all of the trailers, his was the dirtiest. The once white trailer was colored with green mold on its side and trash littered the ground around it like his parents were hoarders of scraps and metals. By the time my flip-flops hit the first step on the porch, I was a little wary about testing the steps. The porch was a lost cause and barely reached the door, there was a gap of at least half a foot between the two.

The door was open except for the screen door. I peeked inside and tapped my tiny knuckles onto the glass. I was moments from running inside when I saw the woman lying on the stained yellow sofa passed out. Her legs were spread eagle and her arms were sprawled out at her sides. Her mouth was wide open and her eyes were looking upward, completely void of life. It was the scariest thing I'd seen. Fear and worry for the woman clawed up my stomach, chest, and throat in a rush.

There was movement inside the trailer. My eyes widened and reached for the handle; my thoughts were running back and forth between going inside to check on her or rushing back to the house to get my mom who was an adult.

The coffee table was littered with needles, cigarettes, and pills. Was this Noah's mom? Was she sick?

23

A man stepped to the door and I recognized this man as Noah's dad immediately. There was no mistaking the color of his hair and eyes that were so much like Noah's. Even before I discovered his parents were addicts, his dad would have been a handsome man before his addictions prematurely aged his skin and destroyed his teeth.

Behind him, I saw Noah go to the woman on the sofa. He hadn't thought that I would be the one knocking on the door. He started tapping her shoulder. "Mom," he waited. "Mom. Mom!" He sounded both worried and annoyed. "Why did you let her get this way again?" he yelled, and I thought it must be his dad he was yelling at. "Dad! Get over here and check on her. Or don't, I'll call 9-1-1."

Noah's dad looked down at me and smiled, flashing yellowish teeth before stepping in my line of sight so that I could no longer see Noah. "You know how your mom gets when she's resting… stop being overdramatic."

"She's not—"

"Eh, Noah didn't tell me he had a little girlfriend." He turned his head. "Is this where you disappear to at night?" He gave away another secret of Noah's in that moment.

Noah rushed to the door with wide, fearful eyes. When he saw me, he grabbed his shoes and rushed out the door. "Noah?" I whispered nervously, but he took my wrist and led me down the steps, out of the trailer park, and across the road back to my house. "Noah, is your mom okay?" I asked but I got no words from him until we were tucked away inside the treehouse.

"Don't go back to my house," he told me. The look on his face scared me. I'd never seen him look so serious before, even when we first met arguing over the treehouse.

"Sorry," I mumbled, "you were taking so long…"

fall from grace

"Just promise me not to go back over there, okay?" He propped his elbow on his knee and looked at me so earnestly that I dropped my eyes. "Bad people show up at my house, it's not safe."

He said things I couldn't comprehend. "What do you mean, bad guys?" I shook my head softly. "Why would bad people go to your house?"

"Not everyone's parents are as put together as yours, Grace!" he snapped, then his eyes widened in realization. He spoke softly this time, "If I tell you, you can't tell your parents."

My stomach knotted. "Why?"

"Because I could get taken from my parents if anyone decided to call and report them… and even though… they're still my parents," he said begrudgingly.

I grabbed his hand. "I won't, I promise." I was telling the truth. The thought of him going away and leaving me, I hated the thought.

"My parents are addicts."

"Addicts?" I knew what the word meant. Mom often said I was addicted to popsicles. I just didn't know what was so bad that his parents were addicted to.

"Just leave it at that, Grace," he told me. "Pretend you don't know, I didn't want you to know."

I realized how little I really did know about life that day. I saw my friend differently. He was more than a boy, maybe a man in a boy's suit, but that wasn't entirely right either... Maybe somewhere in between a kid and having to grow up faster than he was supposed to.

I did the only thing I knew to do. "Noah." He lifted his head. "Where's my adventure?"

He smiled. We were once again as we'd been for the past two weeks.

That night, with his dad's words ringing in my ear, I sat by my window flipping through pages of a book as I watched the treehouse. Noah had gone home around eight. I had bathed and gotten ready for bed. It was a little after nine and all I could think about was how I had thought Noah had been living in the treehouse… and with his dad's words from earlier, I waited.

Thankfully, the moon was full that night, and the porch light didn't reach out to the treehouse. My heart soared the moment I saw his thin form darting across the lawn. I slammed the book shut and got up. My parents were still up watching TV, which was the very reason I had told them I was going to bed earlier than I normally did so they wouldn't come upstairs to check on me. I tiptoed across the house and slipped out the back door easily. The moment my bare feet touched the cold, wet ground, I grinned and took off sprinting toward the treehouse.

A flashlight beamed down at me as I climbed the rope. "What are you doing?" Noah whisper-hissed at me.

I slung my legs over and pushed him back so I could move past him. I smiled lightly and took his flashlight, pointing it at him. He sighed, shielding his eyes with his hand. "Do you sleep here every night, Noah?" I asked softly.

He ran his hand through his matted hair. "Not every night," he whispered with a shrug.

"It's kind of chilly," I told him. "You don't… in the winter, do you?" I feared for him if he did. When he didn't answer, that was answer enough.

"It's nothing," he grumbled. "Stop being nosy, Grace."

"You do things that make me worry for you," I said, flicking his nose.

I could barely see him as he grabbed his nose in the darkness. "I'm rethinking this friendship," he told me.

26

"Sure, sure."

I flopped down, pulling him down with me. "What are you doing?" he grumbled.

I laughed. "Too bad we can't see the stars inside the treehouse." I placed my hands behind my head. He got comfortable next to me. We lay there in silence for several seconds as he pointed the flashlight toward the ceiling, turning the light on and off. "You won't be lonely anymore," I whispered in the dark space around us, trying my hardest to make the words sound as if we were older. We were there together, but why was there such a vast amount of difference between us? Why did I try so hard to make sense of things at only six-years-old?

He made a sound in his throat. "I'm not lonely," he muttered.

I turned my head and smiled. "Not anymore."

No summer was better than this one. The nights Noah went to the treehouse, I slipped off and stayed with him. His blankets had an odor to them that I could never get used to but that didn't matter. I didn't even care that he was dirty and even the days when he did bathe, he rarely put on clothes that were washed. Mom took notice too, and a lot of days I wanted to ask her to wash his clothes, but the fear of something bad happening because of my meddling, I let him be. I wanted him around more than wanting him to be clean, and the fear of Mom calling the people Noah was afraid of taking him away only made my choice easier.

I discovered so much about Noah, he didn't fear hardly anything. He picked up bugs, frogs, and a black snake that he swore wasn't poisonous. His favorite food was meatloaf, and Mom made it for us once a week. He liked popsicles like me, but when I discovered his love of chocolate ice cream, I started making Mom buy that for me instead so that I could share it with him.

I cut my foot on a piece of glass while playing in the hills with him, and he had carried me on his back all the way down. I could still remember how surprised I was that he could, his shoulders were no bigger than mine, and we were the same height. After that, he never let me go into the hills with flip-flops. Mom had scolded me too, and he stood right by her nodding and agreeing, causing her to shake her head and smile at him.

Then school came that August. Luck was on our side that day when I stepped into my classroom and saw he was in the same class as me. Mom taught sixth through eighth so it would be few years before we had her for a teacher.

I noticed his clothes were ones I'd never seen him wear before. His parents must have bought him new ones just like my parents did for me. I was so happy until I approached him while he was talking to two other boys. "Hey, Noah!" I beamed at him only to get a cold glare in return.

"You know the new girl?" one of them asked him.

"Since when do you hang out with girls?" said the other.

"I don't!" he yelled.

"Hey, I'm Sara," said someone stepping to my side seconds before I could yell at Noah. My cheeks felt like flames, and I was embarrassed. My stomach hurt with his need to ignore me.

Sara pulled me away and I shot Noah a glare. He had the decency to look worried before he crossed his arms and gave me an arrogant smirk. "You're new here so you don't know that those three dweebs are jerks. They're mean to all girls—"

"It's only because they like us," another girl interrupted Sara. "Hi, I'm Tiffany." Tiffany was shorter than both Sara and I, but Sara was the only blonde out of the three of us.

"My name's Grace," I told them.

"How do you know Noah anyway?" Tiffany asked. "He's the biggest jerk of them all."

fall from grace

"We live in the same neighborhood," I answered, sneaking a glance over my shoulder at him. He was laughing with the others, but he met my eyes for a fleeting moment. "I thought we were friends."

Sara and Tiffany laughed. "Guys suck," Tiffany said.

"Girls rule and boys drool," Sara added, and they both laughed again. I quickly followed with a fake one as I turned around to see what Noah was doing.

That evening, I drove home with Mom as she asked me how my first day was. I sat on the porch and looked toward the trailers. When the bus dropped Noah off, he didn't even go inside his house. He started running toward my house. I slipped inside and ran out the back door. I managed to make it inside the treehouse before he did.

When his head popped up first in the treehouse. I brought my knees to my chest and glared at him. "What do you think you're doing?" I asked him.

"I can't be friends with you at school, Priss," he told me right away.

I puffed my cheeks out. "Why not?"

"Because you're a girl!"

"You're right, and you're a boy, so I don't want to be friends with you at all." I stood up. "Not even when we're not at school!"

"You don't mean that," he said plainly.

"Yes, I do." I started going down the rope.

He poked his head out. "But, I'm the only one that can give you an adventure."

I paused, looking up. "Fine, but just so you know, you're my enemy at school."

"Now you're getting it." He watched me walk away. "Wait, where are you going?" he sounded depressed that I was leaving.

29

I turned around and stuck out my tongue. "I'm too upset to play with you today. You're lucky I need you for adventures or else—"

"Or else?" he challenged.

Mom opened the back door. "Come and eat you two!" She looked up at Noah. "I made brownies."

Noah jumped down and ran past me. I puffed my cheeks out in frustration then it turned into a smile as I followed after him.

fall from grace

3

Grace age 7

Noah age 7

Being around Grace is the easiest thing in the world to do, pretending not to be interested in her at school is hard, especially when I know Dustin only picks on her because he thinks she's cute. I pick on her to keep her away from my friends, and it's become a game where we tease each other at school (mostly me teasing her) only to go home and play together.

I like her more than I like Dustin and Mark, only I'll never tell anyone that.

When I visit the treehouse at night, I always secretly wait for her to come to me.

This might be what it feels like to have someone care about me.

I like the way Grace makes me feel sometimes, no... I just like her.

I'm going to call her my best friend...

I'm glad she's my best friend.

N.P.

Our first school year together was spent playing the part as mortal enemies at school while rushing to play together the moment we were home. It wasn't hard to pretend not to be his friend at school, he had a way of crawling under my skin, and he would say the meanest things in front of his friends. Which I was no different, I fell into Sara and Tiffany's world rather easily, and it became fun to talk bad about the boys like they did us.

31

michelle gross

I turned seven November eleventh, and it was that night I discovered Noah in the treehouse again. I checked for him every night, and that was the first night he had gone to the treehouse to sleep since the summer months. It was cold outside, too cold for him to be sleeping in a small boxed room up in a tree with no door. My parents were asleep as I slipped on my coat and boots and made my way to the treehouse. My fingers were burning by the time I climbed up the ropes. I didn't see how Noah could handle this cold.

I saw him huddled up in a corner. Every blanket he had was on top of him. I couldn't even see his face. I crawled over to him. "Noah," I whispered.

He startled immediately at the sound of my voice. "Grace?" he sounded half asleep. "Go back, it's too cold."

"No," I told him. He pulled the blankets down from his face to look at me. "Why are you here when it's this cold outside?"

"Too many people at the house," he answered. "I can't stand being there when they're smoking and being loud."

"Come on," I said, pulling the blankets off him. "You can sleep in my room."

His eyes widened. "No," he said quickly. "I don't want your mom or dad to get mad at me for being there without asking."

I smiled. "Then it will be our secret. Come on, you can slip out in the morning. You're good at that kinda stuff."

He shook his head again. "No, Grace, really. I don't want them to hate me." I just looked at him. He didn't talk or give praise to his mom or dad, but he always tried so hard to be polite and good around mine. I never called him out on it or asked why he did it.

"There's gonna be nothing for them to hate if you get sick and die out here!" I yelled. He sighed and looked away from me. I reached out for his hand and gave it a tug. "Please, Noah, I'll wake them up and let them know if that's what you want."

32

fall from grace

"Fine," he muttered, jerking his hand away and standing. I smiled and followed him down the rope. We didn't wake my parents. He slept on the floor of my room with a blanket and pillow I gave him. I felt pleased that he listened to me and glad he wasn't out there freezing.

He was already gone when Mom woke up the next morning and neither her or dad had a clue he spent the night.

On the days it was too cold to go outside and play, Mom made us stay inside. Noah let himself in that evening after sleeping on my floor the night before. He hopped onto the bar stool next to me and immediately tossed something on the countertop. I picked up the piece of wood and turned it around. On the other side was a carved bear. I looked to him.

He looked away from me quickly. "It's a birthday present," he muttered quickly. "I didn't know your birthday was yesterday."

He carried a pocket knife around with him all the time, but the only thing I had ever seen him do with it was cut up sticks when he was bored. "Did you make this?" It was far from perfect. It might not even be a bear but that was what it looked like to me.

He shrugged his shoulders. "Yeah."

"I love it," I told him. "It's a bear, isn't it?" He nodded.

Mom leaned over the counter and took it from my hand. "Did you really do this, Noah?" Mom smiled at him. "It looks great." She handed it back to me. "How'd you learn to do that? Looks complicated. With a knack like this, Noah, you will make good use of those hands when you're older."

Noah looked to me with a smile full of Mom's praise. "It's just something I do when I'm bored. I'll get better, and when I do, I'll make you another one."

"This one is perfect." And it was for me. "But, I'll look forward to more from you."

michelle gross

"Do they ever act like seven-year-olds?" Dad asked, stepping into the kitchen. He placed a kiss on Mom's lips before rubbing Noah's head with a smile. "Hey, kiddo."

"Hi, Steven," Noah replied.

Mom shook her head. "I know, I wouldn't think they ever played if I didn't see it with my own eyes every day."

And maybe that was our problem, we should have behaved like kids.

4

Grace age 8

Noah age 9

I'm just a kid, but I think I know my future. It starts and ends with Grace.

She doesn't realize we are meant to be more than friends, but I'm starting to. One day, I'm going to grow more than I am now, and when I do, I'm going to kiss and touch her when she lets me. I know what adults do. I know all about sex because I've seen it during my parents' parties when everyone's so high they don't care that they're getting it on right in front of a kid. It's why I disappear to the treehouse to get away. I hate the noise, I hate the smell, but most of all, I hate the way my parents look when they exit real life and disappear into whatever place they love so much. Sex doesn't look all that great from what I've seen in person, but at the same time, I want to try it with Grace.

I'm waiting to grow up. I'm waiting for Grace to as well.

I want her to know about this part of growing up like I do. I feel like with her, everything will be a little more beautiful… Because it already has been a lot brighter since she came into my life 2 years ago.

N.P.

Noah never celebrated his birthday with me. He didn't even tell me when his birthday was or if he celebrated his new age with his parents every year. He didn't seem to care. What kid didn't get excited for their birthday?

There was something downright crooked in his grin that day when he brought the VCR tape his cousin had gotten him for his birthday. I couldn't share his excitement because all I could think about was still not knowing his birthday like he knew mine.

I crossed my arms and feigned disinterest in whatever he wanted to show me on the tape. He tilted his head at me and sighed. "What is it, Priss?"

"When are you going to tell me your birthday?" I pouted. "I can't believe you've already turned nine and I'm just now finding out!" I studied him a moment. "Is it today? And you're a May child?" I smiled, knowing I at least knew the month he was born.

He shook his head. "It's not today, and don't worry about it." He looked around the living room. "Where's your mom?" he asked quickly.

"Cooking," I answered and watched as the devilish grin returned to his face.

He took my hand. "Come on, we can't let your parents see," he said as he led us up the stairs. I studied the color of his ear as it grew red. Noah was up to no good, too bad I didn't care. Once inside my room, he shut the door and hurried to the TV.

"What are you up to?" I asked.

After pushing the tape into the VCR, he turned around and looked at me. "Promise me you won't scream or tell your parents what I'm about to show you?"

The question in his eyes unnerved me. I swallowed. "Just what's so bad on the tape that you are acting so sneaky?"

He smirked, turned the volume almost completely down, then pressed play.

Adults. A woman. A man. Her legs spread open while the man… inside.

A felt nauseous, scared, freaked out, disgusted.

36

fall from grace

Thankfully, I made no promises about not screaming. Because I did.

He quickly stopped the tape and ran to cup my mouth. He stopped my scream and said, "Turns out there's a lot more to being an adult than you realize, huh, Grace?"

I jumped away from him. "Why would they?" I squinted my eyes. "Why would you show me that?"

His eyes widened momentarily before glaring. "Don't worry, I would never want to do that with you. You don't even have boobs!"

My mouth fell open. "I'm only eight!" I hissed. "Like you have that big 'thing' between your legs, either!" I felt a pang of fear just bringing it up again, but Noah always made me so fighting mad that I talked about it aloud.

His face turned bright red. "You have—"

"Is everything okay?" Mom peeked her head inside the door and asked.

"Yeah," I said immediately. "Noah was just leaving, weren't you?"

"Yeah," Noah hid most of his grumble in front of Mom as he walked back over to the VCR and took the tape out, then left.

Mom tilted her head at me. "Did you two fight?"

"Yeah," I mumbled. "Boys are stupid."

Mom snickered. "I give you guys a day before you make up."

———

Mom had been wrong. Noah and I were at odds for weeks after that. I no longer knew how to hold a conversation with him without thinking of the redhead's bouncing breasts and her privates being 'invaded' by that guy's 'thing'. What was worse was I couldn't even look at my parents normally anymore without thinking that they did that to each other. Adults were suddenly a mystery to me when I was so confident I knew a lot as a kid.

I was wrong. So wrong.

I blew Noah off every time he came over to the house. I was lonely and bored the month of June because I didn't want to give in and play with him even though I wanted to. I hated that he showed me that tape. I hated that it changed the way I looked at people, especially adults.

I was never going to do any of those things when I grew up. It looked disgusting and how would it even fit… I shook my head. *Don't even think about it.*

The only problem was even though I was upset with Noah, I missed him. School was out for the summer and I was lonely, and he was my best friend.

So, when he tapped on the door that day, I was more than ready to put the tape behind us. Mom answered the door and greeted him. "Gracie, Noah's here!" she called through the house. I moved from the couch and slipped on my shoes before heading toward the door.

"I'm going to the treehouse with Noah," I told her.

Mom looked at us with a smile before shaking her head. "It's about time," was all she said.

Noah followed behind me quietly. That was another thing that changed after seeing those few seconds of the tape. I stopped wearing dresses. I was extra glad as I climbed up the rope with Noah behind me. I was suddenly fearful of everyone seeing my body through a pair of eyes like mine—one that suddenly saw everything anew. I knew I shouldn't feel this way over a tape. I was only eight, but that was my problem; I saw too much. I thought too much. I felt too much.

I turned around to face him, the silence eating away at us as I pressed my knees to my chest. He looked just as miserable as I felt. "I'm sorry, Grace. I shouldn't have shown you the tape," he said right away.

38

fall from grace

"Why did you?" My voice wasn't laced with accusation or guilt. I just wanted to know.

"It's just something I already knew about, and I don't know, you're smart. I guess I thought you would have already known about doing it." He shrugged his shoulders. "I wanted you to know about it like I did."

"How would I know about that?"

"I've seen it at my house before, okay!" he blurted. "I don't know why I showed you! I guess I was just being a boy and wanted to scare you or something, but I didn't imagine it would freak you out this much." He covered his face with his hands. "I'm sorry, Grace, I won't ever do something like that again so please don't hate me, and please stop ignoring me." He lifted his eyes from his hands and pleaded with me.

The tears fell down my cheeks. "I don't ever want to talk about this again," I whimpered. "I'm never doing that when I grow up either," I hiccupped. Noah steadily scooted closer to me. "I missed you—don't ever show me that kind of stuff again!"

He nodded as I rested my forehead against his. He stiffened as I calmed down with our small contact. Just like that, the tape faded from my thoughts as the need to be normal with Noah again became more permanent

"Don't worry, I'm just a boy," he whispered between us. "I won't even try to touch you that way even when I become a man."

When he spoke those words, I knew he was willing the words to be true, and they were true words… that was until puberty hit us both.

5

Grace age 9

Noah age 10

I made a promise that I'd keep, but it doesn't mean that it's not one that I hope she will someday let me break.

I care about her too much to hurt her, especially when I fear her hating me, but when I'm alone with my thoughts, the need to grow up and steal her heart gets even stronger.

Will her eyes ever discover me in a way that I picture her getting old and being mine?

I'm not a normal kid. Grace is far from childish some days, too… Except today. She can't be left alone. She needs me to look after her. It's okay because I want to.

N.P.

"Don't even think about it, Grace," said Noah before I even did anything.

"I'm just taking it some food and water," I mumbled as I opened the gate and stepped inside the fence of one of our neighbor's yard. "He's clearly hungry and I just want to pet him."

"You clearly need your own pet," Noah hissed behind me. "Seriously, Grace!" He grabbed my wrist and yanked me backward. I turned and glared at him. "This is trespassing."

fall from grace

"I'll come straight back out as soon as I give him the bologna and water!" I promised. I slipped from his grasp and left the gate cracked. Bruce, the Pitbull tied to the porch jumped and barked as I moved closer. His tail wagged as he watched me. Before I even squatted, he jumped up and stole the bologna from my hands. I laughed and petted his stinky fur. "You are such a good boy," I told him as I poured the bottled water into his bowl. "It's too hot to be going without water, ain't it boy?" I cooed and went on.

"Okay, you gave him the bologna, now come on," Noah barked, and I tilted my head to see him looking around anxiously.

I turned my focus back to Bruce. His collar looked a little too tight. "Hold on, I'm fixing his collar."

He exhaled a frustrated breath. I ignored him though and focused on holding down Bruce so I could loosen his collar. Once I was finished, I gave him another rub down his back before walking around. "About time," Noah complained as he opened the gate for me. "And you stink now," he added. Bruce was barking and whining. He didn't want me to leave him. "Now he's throwing a fit because of you." I rolled my eyes.

"He'll enjoy that water here in a bit," I replied.

Then, a boo-boo happened. Not really a boo-boo. More like uh-oh.

It's like Bruce waited until the moment we had our backs turned to slip out of his collar, and since we hadn't noticed until he was running out of the gate between us, it kind of made it impossible to shut the gate before he got out.

"GRACE!" Noah yelled my name, and I felt the fear race through my veins. This wasn't my dog, and his owner was such a turd.

I bent down to grab him but he was long gone. "Bruce!" I screamed. "Noah, what are we gonna do?" I looked to him and asked.

"We?" Noah gave me a horrible look. I knew Noah though, despite his anger with me, he wouldn't leave me alone even when I was

41

the one at fault. Dogs were my weakness. I couldn't help it. "Let's try to catch him," he said hurriedly.

We took off running after him. He was always visible in sight, going house to house, trailer to trailer, peeing on everything, but we couldn't get close. He'd spot us and take off running like a bolt of lightning. We kept at it for a long time, often cornering him on both sides, but he somehow always got the better of us.

It wasn't until I ran inside and grabbed some more bologna that I was able to coax him into coming to me, but by then it was too late. We watched from behind another neighbor's house—where we caught Bruce—as Bruce's turd owner pulled into the driveway. And when he stepped out of his truck, placing his hand on his hat, the first place he looked was the spot Bruce was supposed to be, then I just knew he saw the opened gate next. I held Bruce by the collar and turned to Noah nervously as we led him over to his house.

Noah and I were both covered in sweat and exhausted, but now I was scared of what Bruce's owner was going to say to me. "It's okay, Grace," Noah told me. Maybe he knew I was on the verge of crying. "We got him, he's safe, and we are taking him back."

I nodded but when I looked up, Bruce's owner was heading toward us with an ugly scowl on his face. "Mind telling me why you kids have my dog and my gate is wide open?"

"I saw that his bowl was empty—"

Noah prevented me from talking any further. "I just went to give him some food and water since it's been hot today, and his collar was looking a little tight—"

"Kid, are you trying to say I'm not feeding my dog?" He seemed angrier now.

I was truly scared because I knew I shouldn't have. "No, sir," Noah started.

fall from grace

"You little shits are starting to make me angry." He looked to me and pointed. "I should have known you would eventually make your way over into my yard, always hanging around the fence and calling for Bruce."

Tears were in my eyes. "She just likes your dog, sir," Noah sounded angry now, and I hated that I got him into this.

"I'm sorry," I started.

"Give me my damn dog," he yanked Bruce from my hold, and even his pet whimpered and hunkered down. My heart broke.

He looked at Noah again. "Your John's boy, ain't ya? No wonder," he spat the words out, and I immediately turned to see how Noah would react. His parents were his sore spot. He gripped his fists but otherwise held it in.

"Everything okay out here?" Noah's dad, John, hopped off their porch with no shoes or shirt on. Just his jeans and a cigarette in his hand. He sauntered on over to us.

"Yes, your son and his friend came over into my yard and let Bruce out."

"It wasn't on purpose," I said quickly. "It was an accident."

"My son?" John asked, looking back and forth between us. "Doesn't sound like something he'd do." I felt my cheeks color. Somehow, I knew he knew this was because of me.

Bruce's owner placed his hands on his hips and huffed. "Shit," he said in disbelief. "With parents like y'all, it's no wonder... I'll have to check and make sure nothing's been stolen."

"Say whatever you want about me, but my son's not a thief. He's a good kid." It was weird hearing his father praise him when Noah refused to talk about them. "Check your shit, just leave the kids alone. You got your dog, and y'all won't go back into his yard, will ya?" I shook my head immediately. Noah looked like he was about to explode.

43

Maybe he didn't like his dad helping us. There was so much I still couldn't figure out about Noah.

"The next time it happens, I'll call the cops. Y'all staying up and partying all hours of the night, keeping everyone up is getting out of hand too," he huffed before jerking Bruce by the collar. "Come on, boy."

John blew out a stream of smoke as he watched him leave before turning back to us. "You didn't really let that dog out, did ya?" he asked Noah.

"Not on purpose," Noah replied.

"You weren't even the one in the yard." John smiled at me, and my eyes widened before I averted his gaze.

"Yes, I fed the dog and loosened his collar because it was too tight. He got out before I finished closing the gate."

"Noah," I whispered, but he ignored me. Why was he taking the blame? The worst part was over. He didn't have to go that far.

John didn't look like he believed him anyway though. "Mm-hmm," he said through another cloud of smoke. Then he threw the cigarette on the blacktop and ruffled up Noah's hair. "Well, well," John said through a yellow smile.

"Stop it." Noah pushed him away.

"So, you have something you want to protect, do ya?" John asked him. Noah looked to me then immediately turned back to his dad with a hint of red across his cheeks.

"Just leave me alone," Noah huffed. I stood there quietly, observing their interactions. I was glad that Noah's dad had come outside and diffused the situation, but most of all, this weird feeling warmed my chest at the thought of Noah protecting me when he could have done otherwise.

fall from grace

A few months later, Bruce died and that fear of his owner only turned to hatred. Maybe I should have left him to be a stray. Maybe he would have still been alive.

6

Grace age 10

Noah age 11

It's the little things I notice about Grace. Like the way she blushes when you say the word **kiss.** *I know she's thinking of the video I showed her every time someone brings up the things she's so desperate to forget.*

I want to grow up already.

I need to be a bigger man than Dad so I can stop the hurt Mom does to herself. She thinks it feels good to fade away, but from the outside, I see that her addiction is slowly stealing everything from her.

I'm tired of shaking her body, wondering if I need to call the ambulance and hide while they come get her so they don't know a kid lives here. I'm tired of being sick with fear that I'm going to lose someone that's not even present in her own mind most of the time, let alone in my life.

I can't give up on her. Not even Dad, who's more present than she is, which is what makes it worse. He lets her go into the darkness, then follows her soon after. I wish I was an adult already. There are too many things that I need to be but can't as a kid.

N.P.

Entering fifth grade was like stepping into a new world. Things began to shift in girls and boys. Girls were picking boys they liked and calling them "mine" or their "crush", and boys were doing the same—of course, there were some that had always done this since the first grade but now it was openly discussed. Friends were running and confessing to their other friends. It could be very confusing. It's amazing how fast someone could have a new crush every week in a repeated cycle.

I didn't mind it though. Just one little part of this new world irked me. Girls were noticing Noah in a way that I had from the very beginning. Noah was still a jerk, as always, at school, but now girls seemed to crush on him even more because of it. He started playing football last year for the school. During football, Dustin's parents always dropped Noah off from practice every day and after ballgames or he rode the bus for away games. I was bored a lot because of it so I had no choice… I signed up for cheerleading this year. My friends, Tiffany and Sara were already on the team, and they were so happy that I finally joined them. Although, they were a little suspicious as to why I suddenly wanted to join this year.

"It's because of Noah, isn't it?" Sara smiled, nudging my shoulder with a goofy grin. "It's okay, we all have a crush on him so don't be shy."

"You have the best chance at being with him since you live next to him," Tiffany added. "He's so cute." Tiffany started wearing lip gloss. It made me want to do the same.

"Why are you guys crushing on him?" I mumbled. "I thought you hated him?"

They both laughed. "How can you hate him now? Look at him," Tiffany said, pointing her head toward the boys in the back of the room. Noah was one of them. He never wore the best clothes but for some reason, he just stood out from the rest. His blond hair was shaggier now and his blue eyes still shined bright. I placed my hand on my chest and looked back to them. "I'd kiss him!" Tiffany said a little too loudly while covering her face.

My face felt red. I must have been feeling the embarrassment for her. "Kiss?" I whispered. "Why do y'all keep bringing that stuff up all the time now? Cooties, remember?" In my mind, I was thinking back to the video Noah showed me. Kissing led to…

47

"Oh, come on, Grace," Sara pushed my shoulder playfully and they were both laughing. "Don't pretend you wouldn't kiss Noah."

My cheeks reddened. "I wouldn't!" I told them.

The whole class heard us because Dustin laughed in the back of the room and said, "Hear that, Noah, Grace says she doesn't want to kiss you."

"Read. Not talk," Mrs. Fleming, our teacher told the class.

Oh, my gosh. I was so embarrassed.

I dared to peek over my shoulder at them. Noah had his chin resting in his palm as he leaned over his desk staring my way. "Grace is afraid of stuff like kissing," he said with an evil smirk.

The whole class laughed. I turned back around in my seat.

"Okay," Mrs. Fleming stood up, "since you guys want to keep talking, I guess we'll read together." This time everyone groaned.

"Your face is so red," Sara told me, almost like she pitied me.

Mom stayed at school planning and grading papers the evenings I had cheer practice, like today. We always practiced in the gym. Even though I didn't get to spend time with Noah during practices, I knew I would get to cheer at all his games.

He was a pain at school but he was still the most fun to be with, and that made him my important person. Besides, I knew I was the only girl that he cared anything for. I didn't want to kiss him or anything like the other girls, but I didn't want him kissing anybody else either.

After practice, I hurried to Mom's classroom at the "middle school" part of the school. We'd get her as a teacher next year. She was closing her door when I rounded the last corner. "I was heading your way," she told me with a smile. "You ready?"

I nodded, grabbing my hands and squeezing them. "Let's go see if Noah's practice is over with. We can give him a ride so Dustin's mom doesn't have to." I walked by her side down the hall. "Now that I'm on the cheer team, we can just wait on him the days we have practice on the same days."

She gave me a weird smile. "Oh," Mom dragged the word out with a laugh. "Now it makes total sense."

"What?" I looked up at her, still fidgeting with my fingers.

"You wanted to cheer so you can cheer for Noah?" Mom bent down and smiled all goofy in my face.

I smiled and pushed her away by her shoulder. "Mom, stop, no. Not exactly… just got boring last year with him gone all the time because of his sports."

She nodded. "Come on, let's go see if he's still outside."

He was. They were walking off the field as we walked through the parking lot. Dustin saw us first and tapped Noah's shoulder. The thought of Dustin running his mouth to everyone made me a little nervous.

Noah raked his hand through his sweaty hair self-consciously before holding it up to tell Dustin to give him a minute. Dustin nodded but watched us the entire time.

He messed with his hair again once he stopped in front of us. Mom looked at me like she expected me to ask him but for some reason, I couldn't stop thinking about the classroom incident earlier. He looked at me. "Hey, y'all looking for me?" He shook his head quickly. "Did I do something wrong…"

Mom laughed. "Noah, stop worrying." He finally smiled and relaxed. "We came to see if you wanted to ride home with us, right Grace?" He looked at me again and I smiled.

"Yeah, I just got out of practice too," I told him.

He messed with his hair again while looking down. "Yeah, let me go tell Dustin." He took off running. He grabbed his backpack on the bench after telling him. It felt like he was getting the stink-eye from Dustin as he made his way back over to us.

I normally sat in the front seat with Mom on the way home, but I hopped in the back with Noah instead. I caught Mom's eyes in the rearview mirror, and she was grinning again. I ignored her, though. Noah and I were always together. Why was she acting like things were different?

Noah pulled a water from his backpack and drank half of it. "Do you want a drink?" he offered.

I wasn't thirsty but I was happy that he offered so I said, "Yeah," and he handed me the drink. Once I handed it back, he immediately took another drink. His lips lingered for a while before he covered his mouth with his hand. His cheeks looked a little red, and there was something sheepish about his smile as he looked ahead.

"What are you up to Noah?" I asked right away.

He shrugged his shoulders.

He chose not to answer me until we were walking side by side inside the house. He made sure Mom was several feet away before leaning over and whispering into my ear, "You said you didn't want to kiss me, Priss, but you just gave me an indirect one."

He tapped his empty water bottled and laughed. He went on ahead of me.

My cheeks were hot. Noah made me feel funny that day.

I guess it wasn't funny… more like a small burst of warmth spread through me.

Was Noah changing, or was I?

7

Grace age 11

Noah age 12

Grace's body is changing. I'm always with her, I always notice. She's tall but I'm taller now. It shouldn't make me happy but it does. I'm the only guy that's lucky enough to be close to her. I'm not afraid to hint around that no one's to mess with her to the other boys in our class. It doesn't mean that they'll listen.

I wouldn't listen if I were in their shoes either.

But my relationship with Grace, no one will ever compare.

I'm only a boy, but I know already with every new moment I spend with Grace, she's my future. I just have to be someone that can take care of her. I'm my father's son, instead of teaching me how to be a man, he's taught me every way not to be.

I can't give her wings, but I'll make her heart soar, the moment she lets me.

I'm still waiting... to grow up.

N.P.

Everyone was talking about "it". The "it" I was referring to was the things that went on in the video I could never forget.

Sex.

michelle gross

Most of the girls in our grade were starting to get boobs, me included. I hadn't started my period yet but Sara had already. It was getting awkward to be around Noah when we were alone anymore. All I could think about was the things everyone whispered about at school.

Why was everyone so curious about something like that?

Noah was at a weird stage himself. I kept remembering how we used to be the same height. Now, his inches were leaving mine behind. He often slipped into my room at night to shower and sleep on my floor the nights his parents held parties. He was becoming increasingly more self-conscious about the way he looked and smelled. I often teased him the same way he did me, but sometimes I remembered the moments he made me feel strange and I was at a loss for words.

I still didn't want to kiss Noah.

I didn't—

I didn't want him to say yes to any of the girls that asked him out either.

Luckily, he always said no.

———

"Here," Dustin muttered, slapping a folded piece of paper on my desk. I jumped, and some giggled as he walked off. Sara whispered my name from across the room but I ignored her.

"All right, settle down you guys," Mom told the class. A lot of the boys had a crush on her. It made me even more proud of her. I haven't met a person that didn't like my mom.

As she wrote on the chalkboard, I opened the paper.

Will you be my girlfriend?

Yes or No

fall from grace

Dustin liked me? That seemed impossible with how much he picked on me. I grabbed my pen and circled no, and gave it to him when the class was over. I hurried away because I didn't want to see his face when he saw that I turned him down.

After lunch, everyone was talking about Dustin and me, saying we were a couple. I looked for him at recess because Tiffany and Sara said he was the one going around telling everyone I said yes.

He stood next to Noah and some other boys from class, leaning against the snack machine. He smirked when he saw me approaching. "There she is. Come to hold my hand?" he asked, and everyone laughed but Noah.

"Why are you telling people I'm your girlfriend?"

He tossed the paper in the air. I barely caught it in time. It was the same question, but the yes was circled instead of the no. "You said yes," he lied.

"No, I didn't," I crumbled the paper up in my hand. "You obviously changed my answer. Why are you such a jerk, Dustin? Who would date someone so mean?"

Noah smiled then Mark jumped in and said, "So that's how it is..."

"It's okay, I know you're embarrassed about it," Dustin went on, clearly not wanting to give up his lie.

"Enough, Dustin," Noah finally said before casting a somewhat devious look my way. "You know, Grace doesn't like boys and things like kissing..."

Dustin rolled his eyes. "Give her a few years, I can change her mind."

Noah looked unimpressed. "She said no, so leave it."

"I knew you'd be this way," Dustin hissed then laughed. "You always make sure to drop hints so that none of us will crush on Grace.

She's not your girlfriend. Stop acting like you're any different than us just because you live close to her."

I threw the paper in his face and he turned to me surprised. "Noah's clearly different than the rest of you!" I screamed then looked at my surroundings. Everyone heard me. "He doesn't worry about those kinds of things like the rest of you idiots!"

I stormed off but not without seeing the expression on Noah's face and Dustin's words, "If that's what you think…"

———

We didn't really get to go on adventures anymore. My favorite time of the year used to be the warm months so that he could take me hiking in the mountains where we'd let our imaginations run wild. Now we didn't do that either.

Noah played basketball and football while I cheered, which took up some of our time. When we weren't at ball games or practice, we were in the treehouse sitting next to each other reading silently, or in the house where we fought over our favorite characters in TV shows, and played video games.

Sara and Tiffany always wanted to spend the night, but I wasn't ready to share Noah with them. They knew he came over sometimes. They just didn't know that our lives were constant with one another's. That's something I knew I'd never grow out of.

He didn't come over after practice today, though, and I wondered if maybe it had something to do with my outburst at break. Tiffany said everyone had been talking about it, but when she said, "You shouldn't put Noah on a pedestal. He's still a guy and his thoughts are most likely no different than the others," I chose not to say a word.

Truthfully, I knew more than anyone how much Noah was like the others. He thought like the others or he wouldn't have shown me that tape… And little things he'd do, like share his drink with me or touch my hair like it held a hypnotic hold on him sometimes, or just the way I'd catch him staring at my legs and chest that was growing.

I wished I could keep pretending I knew nothing. Even lately, I wished Noah wasn't my favorite person in the entire world. I didn't feel like myself sometimes. Someone new was taking the place of the old me. I was afraid of her. Afraid of what I'd continue to feel around Noah.

I couldn't stop tossing and turning that night. If Noah would have come over today, I knew I would have been fine but he didn't, so I was left thinking of him.

He was filling every part of me. Soon, I wondered if I would be able to think a thought without it being of him.

But, for me, it was always about Noah, whether I was six or eleven.

With the light off, I got out of bed and ventured to the window, and there my heart raced with both fear and excitement. The glow of a lantern drifted through the window of the treehouse. Why didn't he come inside to sleep if his parents were keeping him up? He was avoiding me after today. With the press of my toes burying themselves into the carpet, I just knew with everything in me, he had to be.

Like I knew Noah, he knew me. He should know that I didn't like to be pushed away, especially when it came to him.

My parents weren't asleep yet. I heard their hushed voices talking with the TV on. I was careful as I tiptoed out the door and into the damp September night. I ran once I was outside, only taking a few seconds to make my way up the rope. He turned off the lantern once my knees were up. "Noah," I groaned.

"Afraid of the dark, Priss?" His voice was raspy. It had a gruffer tone to it lately. My stomach swam with butterflies.

"Turn it back on," I sighed, afraid to move it was so dark. I heard him shuffle around before he flicked a lighter and relit the lantern. "Why didn't you come inside and sleep?" The lantern played shadows on his face. He didn't answer. "Why didn't you come over today?"

"Do I have to come over every day?" he asked, lying down and placing his hands behind his head. I crawled over and did the same next to him.

"Yes, that's what we do, Noah," I whispered. The only days we weren't together was when my family went on vacations every year.

"We're getting older, Grace," he sighed, staring at the ceiling as I made shadows with my hands. He tilted his head and I did the same. His expression made it seem like he was hurting somewhere. "Why did you lie today?"

When I went to raise up, his hand shot out to stop me. My skin heated. "Because you promised," I barely managed to mumble.

He leaned closer. "I remember, but Grace... I'll grow up. One day, you're gonna look at me and you're gonna see what I've always seen."

"Noah..."

He scooted his head closer, closer... I was too surprised and nervous to do anything but watch as he placed his lips against my forehead. Then he slowly raised up, "You should go."

I raised quickly. "What was that for?" I placed my hand on my forehead.

"Because you're you, and I'm me."

I smiled because somehow, it made it perfectly okay.

As I slipped down the rope, I said, "Come stay in the house."

"I'm heading home," he replied, coming down the rope next.

"No one's at your house tonight?" I asked.

He nodded. "Nope."

"Then why…"

He grinned. "And Priss, don't get too close to Dustin. He wants to do bad things to girls already."

How long would Noah continue to stay safe before he stopped trying?

Or was the kiss already proof that we were changing?

8

Grace age 12

Noah age 13

I flirt with Grace every second we're together, she's so used to the things I say to her, I don't ever think I'll break through and let her see me as more than a friend. She says I'm different than other boys but I think she knows better.

I'm the boy that thinks of her most. I'm the boy that's waiting to be a man, but the growth in my body only makes me hope that she sees it too. That I'm no longer a kid. I'm a teen, and all my thoughts are forever filled with her.

N.P.

I awoke to womanhood. When I yelled at Mom that morning, she came upstairs and I told her that I had started my period. She covered her mouth and started crying, saying something about her baby growing up. What was even more embarrassing, she told Dad as he was eating his breakfast. He stood up and hugged me then stepped out of the room where I was sure he went to cry in private. I was the offspring of overly sensitive, gooey, lovey-dovey people.

It was embarrassing but I was lucky to have parents like them.

---

fall from grace

I hated when I started my period. This was my third month since I started, and I did nothing but worry that I would bleed through my pants at school to the point that it was all I thought about every time I stood up from my chair after each class. I'd wait to leave class most of the time, except today of all days, I didn't. Sara was rushing me and Tiffany since it was lunchtime.

Only when I stood up, Tiffany gasped. Immediately, I covered my butt with my hands thinking that was what it had to be. Everyone was staring as they walked out the door, and I was afraid Tiffany was going to say it aloud. I looked down at my seat and thankfully there was no blood.

"What's with you guys?" Mark stopped at the door. Dustin was next to him, straining his evil eyes extra hard to find a weakness. Dustin was a jerk, but with hair and eyes as dark as his, he kind of started to pull me in over the years. The boys were starting to look different now, including Noah.

Tiffany scooted closer to my backside so that no one could see the blood stains. I felt somewhat relieved but wished the boys would hurry up and leave the room. "You coming?" Mark called to Noah who was still idly sitting in his chair not really doing anything.

"Yes, go on ahead, I'm coming," was his reply. Mark shrugged his shoulders and left with Dustin. Noah stood up when they did and he took me by surprise when he took off his hoodie. There wasn't even a need for a hoodie right now but he always seemed to be wearing them lately. He walked over until he stood in front of me.

"What?" I mumbled, keeping my hands over my butt.

"Move your hands," he told me right before placing his arms at my sides and wrapping his hoodie around my waist. Once it was tied in the front, he turned and walked away. "Go to your mom's class and get her to run home and get you a different pair of pants if you don't want to keep wearing the hoodie like that all day." He left the room.

My face was burning. I never told him I started my period. That was too mortifying. How did he even know?

Sara and Tiffany squealed the moment he left. I was sure he probably still heard them though. "O-M-GEE, does he always treat you like that when you guys are together?"

"No wonder you don't want us to ever spend the night," Sara nudged Tiffany's shoulder and said.

"You're so lucky," Tiffany sighed. "With the way he acts with the rest of the boys, I would have never expected him to have that side to him."

"Is he really always like that?" Sara asked this time.

He loved to tease me, but I did the same to him. Only this time, he didn't. I thought of how he carried me on his back more than once when I had twisted my ankle or the way he took the blame when I had let Bruce loose by mistake, or the way he always treated my parents with respect, and all the other little things he did for me on a daily basis in between our teasing and time together. Noah was different than anybody else.

"Let's go," I told them, ignoring their question.

And it was the reason why I never wanted to share him with any other girl.

Mom went home and brought me another pair of jeans to wear that day but I didn't give Noah back his hoodie. That night, I checked it for blood but there was none. When I slipped the hoodie on and stood in front of the mirror in my room, I didn't know what came over me. He was bigger than me already. How much more would he continue to grow? I brought the hoodie up to my nose and breathed in. It smelled like him too. He didn't stink like he used to. He showered more and he wore some sort of cologne now.

fall from grace

My stomach felt a little weird and tingly. I grabbed my flat stomach before quickly tearing out of the hoodie. I dropped down on the bed and cradled my head in my hands.

I felt a little sick, maybe. I didn't know.

I washed his hoodie that night and the next day after school, I handed it to him.

I whispered, "Thanks."

He smiled. "I borrowed a new book from the library today. Wanna go in the treehouse and read?" he asked, something that was always normal.

I grabbed my stomach. That feeling was there, along with the unease of my nerves.

"I think I want to play a game of HORSE. Do you want to?" I was afraid to be alone with him.

"Yeah, I can read tonight. Do you know where we last put the ball?" he asked, and I felt relieved.

"I think it's next to the ball goal."

"You didn't have cheer today?"

I shook my head. "No practice for you either?"

"Nope," he answered. "We got a game this Friday though."

I laughed. "I know, I'll be cheering at it, remember?"

"I know," he groaned. "Grace?" I looked over at him as we walked around the house. "Your uniform looks good on you this year."

I blushed. "Noah," I groaned. "That's a little embarrassing." He laughed. "You look the best on the field, too. Even I can't help but think you're cool."

He covered his smile with the back of his hand. "I'll win for us this weekend, just watch," he said with a wink.

I felt myself blushing again.

I was starting to realize Noah was not the one that's changed.

It was me.

That Friday, Noah scored the winning touchdown.

9

Grace age 13

Noah age 13

I want to kiss her, touch her, see what else my hands can do. The way that Grace is a little more nervous and wary of being alone with me tells me that she's thinking of the same things I do.

I shouldn't... But I do.

And I will because she's Grace.

I think I can un-promise now.

N.P.

I turned thirteen today. It was a Saturday and I spent the morning waiting on Noah to arrive. I looked over all the wooden pieces he had gotten me so far. Every year, he carved me a new animal. I had a bear, two cubs wrestling, another more improved bear, a wolf and his mate that I got the following year, and an eagle from my 12th birthday—that was his best work yet. His hands steadily improved over the years. I kept them on my desk.

There was a knock on my door. I raised my chin up from the desk and smiled when Noah cracked open the door. He saw what I was looking at and smiled back. "Happy Birthday, Miss Priss."

I rolled my eyes. "I can't believe you still call me that," I told him. I finally figured out his birthday last year, and the only reason I found out was by snooping in his backpack the first of the school year and seeing where he filled out his information on the paperwork that had to be returned to school. May 5th. I grinned thinking about how Mom and I bought him a pair of shoes this year for his birthday. He treated them like they were amazing and only wore them for basketball.

"I'm forever going to call you that," he teased with a smirk as he dropped down on my bed. He held my new piece to add to my collection this year. It was wrapped in a grocery bag. I got up and flopped down beside him on the bed.

"What animal do I have this year?" I asked as I took the bag from his hand. He watched me open the bag with as much eagerness as I felt. It was a little bigger than the other ones. I was at a loss for words when I saw it. It was a wolf's face with an eagle sitting atop its head with its wings stretched out as it was about to take off. "Noah... it's beautiful. The best yet," I turned my head and told him.

"What color stain are you going to get your mom to get for this one?" he asked. In order to preserve the wood, we started staining them last year after my first bear started to mildew.

"Don't know." I placed it next to the others before sitting back down on the bed again. I glanced over them all with a smile. "I want bigger versions of these in my yard when I get my own place."

He leaned over a bit. "I can do that, I'm sure."

"I know, I can't wait to see what you'll be able to do when you get older."

He reddened. "You have a lot of faith in me."

"Of course! You're so different than other guys our age," I said then remembered a couple months ago and stiffened.

He remembered too. "I'm not all that different than them, really." I couldn't read his expression. His hand found mine on the bed and

64

covered it. My eyes felt a little heavy, my chest a little strange, and my stomach a web of warmth.

He leaned in. "I promised I'd never want to do those things to you, Grace… Can I un-promise now?"

I licked my lips while staring at his. He saw and closed in. He met my eyes once more before I shut mine. And Noah kissed me. His lips were a lot warmer, a lot softer than I thought they'd be. It didn't make me sick and I didn't think of the video. Instead, I felt myself smiling when he pulled away, and when I opened my eyes… *I just shared my first kiss with Noah.*

Noah swallowed then he came for my lips again. This time, his fingers wrapped around the back of my head and his lips were a little harder, clumsier, and his hands were shaky.

"Come eat some cake," Mom said right next to my door. We pushed apart right before she opened the door. Her eyes narrowed, missing nothing. "You two are looking a little weird," she muttered before turning around. "Come on downstairs. Y'all are getting the age where you shouldn't be left alone."

We glanced at each other quickly before jumping off the bed and following Mom out of the door. My stomach was in knots. That was our first kiss and Mom already caught a whiff of it… Wait a minute, was I thinking there was going to be more of them?

My eyes widened when I felt Noah's fingers slide through mine briefly. I glanced at him and he smiled ruefully, then he let go and stepped down the stairs.

10

Grace age 13

Noah age 13

I wonder what Grace would say if I told her how much my mind stayed on her. Not just her body, it was her mind, her smile, her laugh... her future.

I wanted it all. Which meant I had to figure out mine. I had to have a future. Something better than the trailer park kid that I am. Something that gave me the chance to have her.

Grace is my destination, my goal.

I have two very important people to impress if I wanted to reach the future I picture every night. If I show my parents how to do right, I can save them from themselves too. Mom needs help. Dad needs motivation. I've never seen him work, but he gets a check every month that keeps the lights on. This body of mine is made for moving, these hands can't ever stay still. Maybe if I show him how to be, he can be a better husband to Mom. I won't ask for them to be better parents, just to be better to themselves.

N.P.

It was like I was seeing the world anew after the kiss I shared with Noah. I couldn't even fall asleep that night and spent most of it looking out the window waiting for him to come. I didn't know why. He only ever spent the night on my floor the nights his parents had people over.

fall from grace

The next morning, the waiting began again the moment my eyes opened. I was putting on my shoes by the door when Mom asked, "Where are you going?"

"I figured Noah would be here already, so I'm going to go see if he wants to come over and play games."

"Wait for him to come over. You know your dad doesn't like you going over there," Mom said, and I sighed. I already knew that but it wasn't like I didn't sneak to get him anyway. I couldn't with Mom knowing now.

"I hate waiting though," I mumbled, and she laughed before dropping down beside me on the floor.

"Grace, about yesterday…" Mom drifted off. I knew this conversation was coming, I just didn't want it to happen so soon.

"What?"

"I'm sure you know already… you and Noah are getting older and I just don't want you two to make any of the wrong choices." I didn't say anything, I just looked down. "I know you two have something special, and I know Noah would never intentionally hurt you, Grace, but he might feel things and you might feel things."

"Mom," I covered my face up. "I'm not dumb, stop."

She smiled. "I know. I'm a teacher at your school, remember? I know just what kind of conversations kids are having at your age… just don't rush into these things, okay?"

"Mom, I don't want to lie, so I'll be honest. I want to kiss Noah, and I'm still going to even though you want me to wait."

Mom closed her eyes and sighed. "Grace… kissing always leads to more."

"Noah would never force me to do anything I didn't want to do!"

She nodded. "I know, but little Noah has always loved you, of course he's going to want to try—" she cut herself off when she realized where she was going.

My eyes widened. "Noah loves me?" Mom covered her mouth with a smile. "And he's not little," I told her.

That only seemed to depress her more. "I know, don't remind me. I can't believe he's already taller than me, and you too!" she whined.

"You're acting so uncool right now, Mom, I can't help it you're short."

"I'm 5'4, that's an average height for women in America!" she huffed then pointed at me. "You're the one that's going to be super tall like your dad. It's a good thing Noah seems to be outgrowing you."

My mouth fell open and I pushed her. "Mom, how can you say that to your daughter? You're gonna give me height issues!"

She hugged me and started planting kisses on my cheek. "You know you're beautiful."

I tried shoving her away. "Ugh! Mom, stop! So embarrassing." I couldn't help but smile.

The front door opened in front of us and Noah stopped halfway in and glanced down at us. "Uh… what are you two doing?"

Mom finally let go of me and stood up. I did next. "Noah, you got something to tell me?" Mom asked, crossing her arms. Noah glanced my way before meeting Mom's penetrating gaze again. "Something about k-i-s-s-ing—"

I didn't know whether to cover my eyes or ears. She was being so embarrassing. "I don't kiss and tell," was Noah's answer.

Even Mom's jaw dropped with me. "Noah Phillips, did you just sass me? You never speak out of line, unlike my ungrateful daughter." She pointed at ungrateful daughter—me.

fall from grace

He cracked a smile. "I'm sorry, Mrs. Harper."

She shrugged. "Don't call me that, we aren't at school." She turned around and I gave Noah a look that said, "She knows about the kiss!"

His facial expression was something along the lines of, "No kidding!"

"And bring the PlayStation downstairs to play it," Mom said with her back turned. I gave another wide-eyed look to him. "He-he-he," Mom started wiggling her shoulders around with her evil laugh as she turned back her head. "You didn't think I'd make it easy, did you?"

"That means a bigger TV. Sounds good to me," Noah played it cool. "I'll go get it."

"I'll come with you," I said quickly.

Mom narrowed her eyes at us as we trailed up the stairs. Once we inside my room, Noah closed the door silently. I met his eyes anxiously and he blew out a breathy laugh. "I always thought I'd have to worry about your dad, not your mom."

"You've thought about this stuff already? Getting caught before the kiss—" I covered my lips.

He ran his hand through his blond strands. "Not getting caught, just getting their—never mind," he said quickly, a tint coloring his cheeks.

"We better hurry before she comes and gets us," I told him, hurrying to the TV stand. I got on my knees and bent my head through the cubby to unhook everything.

"Here let me," Noah squatted beside me.

I moved my head and let him do it. Just being next to him in silence had my stomach a mess. When he leaned back and saw me, he kissed me right away. Whatever my expression had told him, he replied with, "You looked like you wanted to be kissed."

Then he stood up with the game. He was almost out the door before I convinced my feet to move and tugged on his shirt from behind him. He turned his head just as I wrapped my arms around him from his back. I let my palms press on his chest that was so much wider than it used to be. Not yet a man, but not a boy either. "I don't know why, but I've wanted to see what you felt like now."

His gaze swallowed me whole. "And?"

"Indeed," I inhaled. "I was right. It's different now. We're different. I thought we knew everything about each other... I guess there's still so much to know."

"Maybe you've thought that, but I've always been waiting..."

"Waiting for what?"

"To grow up, so that I can discover you in a way I never have before."

I was wrong. It wasn't a storm brewing.

It was an abyss that I was falling into.

If only I cared.

fall from grace

11

Grace age 13

Noah age 13

This isn't the first time Mom's OD'd and we've had to rush her to the hospital or call an ambulance, but it doesn't change the fact that every time it happens, I think I'm finally going to lose her and my heart falls to the floor and I freak out on Dad every single time. This woman I call Mom has done nothing other than give birth to me, yet I can't give up on her.

I don't know the meaning of give up. I don't give up on myself and the things I want, and I don't give up on the people I care about, no matter how messed up they are.

Grace is going to worry. She gets afraid a lot and tends to worry more than a normal person. I'll go to her as soon as I can. I'm scared too, and I feel like she's the only person in the world that can make me better.

N.P.

Noah wasn't at school the next day. It had me worried that maybe he came down with something bad because he never missed school unless that was the case, unlike me, who could just tell Mom my throat felt a little scratchy and she'd call into work so that she could take me to the doctor.

fall from grace

After the back hug I gave him yesterday, we spent the rest of the evening playing video games until Dad got home. Noah had gone outside and helped him cut up some firewood because Mom and I liked using the fireplace in the winter. It was November, but I didn't think yesterday had been too cold. Was that the reason?

I could tell even Dustin and Mark looked a little bummed out that he wasn't at school. Sara and Tiffany always asked me about him. This time was no different but I didn't have an answer to give them.

On the way home, I said to Mom in the car, "I'm going to go check on Noah." I didn't want her to tell me no.

"You've got one minute." I jumped out the moment she put the car in park. "Grace, I'm serious. After you check on him, hurry back. He won't feel like coming over today if he's sick anyway."

I nodded then started running across the street to the trailer park but slowed down when I saw that his dad's beat up car wasn't in the driveway. Did something happen? I tiptoed around the holes on their porch and knocked on the door. When no one answered, I jumped off the side and ran to where I knew Noah's room was. I'd only been to his house a handful of times but every time I came to get Noah, his dad just told me to come on in like he didn't care that the house was a mess or his mom was passed out on the couch. I was old enough now to understand the things his parents did, and it scared me so I could only imagine what it must feel like for Noah, watching his parents destroy themselves over a high—an escape from reality. Noah still didn't like talking about them. Sometimes I wanted to just hug him and the days I encountered what he lived through, I hoped for his parents to get better and to love him more than their drugs.

I peeked into his window. He wasn't lying on his bed and his light was off. No one was home. Now I was more worried than I was before. I walked back home in a slump. When I stepped through the door, Mom asked, "How's Noah?"

"I don't know. Nobody's home."

"I'm sure everything's fine," Mom told me. "You're too young to worry this much." That was the thing about adults. They thought being young meant your uncertainties weren't worth the anxiety you felt.

I knew something was wrong. It wasn't a feeling I could make go away, at least not until Noah came home and told me everything was all right with him.

He didn't disappoint me and somehow, he must have known I was waiting for him because he cracked open my window silently about ten that night. All that anxiety slowly poured out as I got up out of bed and helped him with the window. He used my old playhouse that was kept next to the house to climb onto the roof so that he could reach my window. Even without the playhouse, he was tall enough now that he could probably climb up from the porch.

Just one glance at him and I could tell he was tired, even in the dark. The way he moved through the window and the slouch in his shoulders. "Noah..." I was caught off guard when he wrapped his arms around me and hugged me like his life depended on it. "What's wrong?" I whispered, my lips pressing into his collarbone.

"I'm scared, Grace." My heart dropped as I felt the first tremble rack his body, seeping into mine. Noah didn't cry. Noah never cried—but he was crying now. "I'm afraid I'm going to lose her."

My throat constricted and my eyes burned with the need to cry. "Who? Your mom?"

He nodded, still holding onto me. "She overdosed again today. The doctor told us her heart wouldn't withstand another one—how do I make her stop, Grace, when death doesn't even faze her?"

"Shh," I tried to soothe him. "Where is she now?"

"Still at the hospital. Me and Dad just got home. She might get to come home tomorrow." He leaned away from me. I watched in fascination and awe as he pulled himself back together after briefly falling apart in a way I had never seen before. "Do you care if I stay here and sleep tonight?"

I shook my head in reply and he walked over to the closet where I kept the covers he used to sleep with. "No, I want us to share the bed tonight." I didn't feel embarrassed or ashamed when I said it. I hadn't meant the words to mean any more than what I said.

I crawled under the covers and patted the other side. He walked over to the bed, slipping off his shoes and jacket. "I won't do anything," he told me quietly as he slipped under the same covers as me.

I smiled into the darkness. "I know."

If I said, *touch me, Noah,* I knew Noah would.

If I said, *no,* I knew Noah would listen.

If I said, *I want you to kiss me,* then decided I'd rather not, I knew Noah would accept that I changed my mind.

Because that was the kind of boy Noah was, and the kind of man he'd stay.

"I want to kiss you goodnight then maybe you can hug up to me while I fall asleep," I whispered toward his darkened face. I couldn't see but I felt and heard as he moved in to kiss me. His lips were dry this time around, and it made me wonder how little Noah drank and ate today.

When he pulled back away, he said, "Turn around and I'll hold you."

And he did. It started out as the most comfortable position, having his arms around me, but quickly became the worst. I was sure his arm was numb underneath my head because my neck was killing me yet I didn't move because even though our bodies were uncomfortable, our souls were at ease.

Noah was gone before Mom woke me the next morning, like he always was.

Only this time, it was so much more different than all the times before… And it was only the beginning.

12

Grace age 13

Noah age 13

I feel like Mom's going through a new change, a much scarier one than I'm used to. The doctors said her heart was too weak to handle much more but the very next day, she's already reaching for the pill bottle, and begging Dad to go out and spend our last dollar on whatever drug she's craving. I feel like my hands aren't big enough to get a hold of this life and what's happening with Mom. She needs help. I can't help her. Dad doesn't try to, and she certainly doesn't want it. Instead, I think she's begging to leave this world.

And she hates me for making her stay.

I want to be with Grace, but here is where I have to stay until I know she's safe from herself again.

N.P.

Monday morning was another new beginning for Noah and me. Instead of sticking to our friends, we sort of just gravitated toward one another. I didn't ask him to spend time with me at school, nor did he, but he stepped up to our table that morning and sat down with us. Sara and Tiffany held in their questions that I knew they'd save for later. With Noah there, Dustin and Mark also ended up with us. It was like that the entire day, in between our classes and at lunch, he chose to stay with me.

I wondered what we were now? Did kissing make him my boyfriend?

77

But Noah did something shocking that day. He quit the football team, something he loved. At first, I didn't understand but as I stayed behind for cheer practice and he was walking out to catch his bus. He took my hand in his and leaned in to whisper, "I won't get to see you until tonight. I don't really want to leave my mom alone any more than I have to if she really came home today." I nodded, and he left.

Noah was terrified of something happening to her. I wiped my forehead and tried to ease away this awful feeling but I couldn't. Noah was scared, so I was too.

Noah didn't come that night. He didn't come to school the next morning, but he did come to see me the following night and I rushed to the window the moment I saw him. I had been watching for him like a hawk.

I probably saw wrong… I waited until he stepped into the room before I grabbed ahold of his face and looked closer. "You have a black eye," I gasped.

He didn't pull away, but he did try to shrug it off like it was no big deal. "She threw an ashtray at me when I wouldn't let her take what she wanted, that's why I didn't go to school. I didn't want anyone to report anything…"

"You quit the football to stay at home more, didn't you?" He nodded. I tugged him toward my bed and flopped down but instead of sitting down next to me, he dropped down to his knees in front of me. "What are you…" He placed his chin on my knees and looked up. I smiled and ran my hand over his dirty blond strands. "You need a bath."

"Do I stink?" He lifted his arm.

"No."

His fingers made circles across the side of my bare legs. I always slept in shorts and tank tops. The only thing I added in the winter months were socks because my feet stayed cold. Chill bumps broke out over my legs as he continued his circles. It was weird… It kind of made me want him to touch me more. "Grace…" Noah had an intense look about him.

"You can," I whispered breathily.

He looked a little taken aback. "Can what?" he asked, and I realized my mistake. I still tried to hide my face even though it was too dark to really see much more than our eyes. "Grace…" his voice held a tease. "Do what?"

"Nothing," I muttered.

"Are you giving me permission to touch you more than this, Priss?"

The answer was in the silence. He moved his chin and started pulling at my socks. "What are you doing?"

I saw the shadow of his smile. "Where can I touch? What can I see?" He pulled my other sock off. "Show me."

His words sparked something in me. I was both nervous and curious of the feeling I got in the pit of my stomach from his words. I thought my curiosity was sure to win. "Um… This is a little embarrassing."

He rubbed the bottom of my foot and I jerked. "Stop!" I hissed through hardly controlled giggles.

 He pulled me down onto his lap so quickly, my laughing stopped before he even put his hand over my mouth. "Shh." His face was inches from mine. "You're gonna wake your parents." Only I wasn't thinking about my parents, I was thinking of the ache that clawed into my stomach. Completely foreign, a little scary, maybe I could explain it by calling it "tingles".

His breath tickled my chin. "I feel weird, Noah."

"How do you feel?"

"I don't want to explain it, it's embarrassing."

79

"Do you still have your nightlight?"

I thought about it. "It might be underneath my bed in a shoebox."

He moved me off his lap as he started reaching underneath the bed for the box. A few minutes later, he found one and plugged it in the wall. It lit up the room enough that I could make every part of his face. He looked a little different right now. Maybe it was the shadows of the night playing tricks on me, making it feel like we were older than what we were.

On my knees on the floor, I watched Noah move across the carpet back to me. Somehow, he looked like a panther coming at me. "Why'd you want the light anyway?" I asked as he backed me against the bed and pulled my feet out from underneath my butt.

"Can I, Grace?" he asked. I blinked then nodded my reply. He moved in for the kiss. I closed my eyes and took in the way he moved as he kissed. When his tongue slid over my lips, the kiss became something new. The moment my tongue met his, he groaned and something about the sound of him and the taste of him inside my cheeks had me wrapping my arms around his neck. He pulled away briefly and watched my expression as he tugged at the bottom of my shirt. When I lifted my arms up, he pulled it over my head and his eyes widened as he took in my ordinary white bra.

I covered myself with my arms. "What is it?"

He dropped his head in his hands and sighed. "They're just... big, so much bigger than I imagined them to be." His eyes looked a little glazed when he lifted them back up to look at me. He pulled my arms down and brought his hands around my back to unhook my bra. Now it was a lot more nerve-wracking to think of him seeing me without a bra.

He kissed my forehead and waited for me. I slowly uncovered my breasts but before I could see his reaction, I grabbed the bottom of his shirt and pulled it up over his head. His eyes fell back on my chest afterward. Noah was wider than he used to be. His body was harder now while mine was softer.

fall from grace

I spooked a little when his hand cupped my breast, then he did the same with the other, sliding my nipples between his index and middle fingers. It felt ticklish but I also thought that it kind of felt good.

I realized I was letting Noah do things to me I said I'd never want to do. How funny growing a few years changed not just our bodies, but the way I felt and looked at Noah.

I leaned in to kiss him and he pulled me on top of him as he fell back onto the carpet. My warmth touched his warmth, I liked the way my chest felt against his. I felt *it* against me. In my head I was trying to recall how the guy's thing had looked in the video. I knew it changed and got hard like Noah's now. I wasn't scared because I had no plans on doing it with Noah right now. I just wanted to enjoy the way it felt to just *explore* him and let him *feel me.*

I gasped when he kissed my neck. "Noah," I exhaled.

His hands slid up my legs and slowly slipped underneath my shorts until they were cupping my butt. It was a little harder to breathe quietly now, my stomach was so feathery and tingly, it started to get the best of me.

He rolled us until he was on top of me. "Grace," he whispered hoarsely. "Have you ever touched yourself?"

I didn't know what he meant. "What do you mean? Yeah, how do you think I clean myself?"

"No, I mean have you played with yourself? Got yourself off?"

"Oh," I mumbled. "No, I haven't."

"Let me show you how to make yourself feel good," he told me with a kiss before he slid off to my side. Propped up on his elbow, he looked down at me as he ran his hand over my stomach.

I sucked in. "That tickles."

Then he started to move his hands toward my shorts and I grabbed his hand to stop him. "If you don't want me to touch you, let me

81

show you with your hands," he whispered. I brought my hand over my stomach where he placed his over mine, then he started dragging our hands inside my shorts. I lifted my head to see but Noah's eyes were on mine, observing my reaction.

He lowered his lips to my ear. "Now… I'm going to press my fingers over yours to show you how to move your fingers."

"Did you learn this from the videos?" I asked him. He nodded and pressed his fingers down. I gasped as he began making circular motions with mine and his fingers. It felt weird but a good weird, and when he nibbled on my ear, I felt it down there with our fingers. "I think I want you to kiss me, Noah," I breathed just as his hungry mouth consumed mine.

Noah pressed his body into mine as we kissed and touched. He pulled away and lowered his mouth over my nipple before taking it in his mouth. I bucked when he did. His fingers slipped through mine and we both froze when he touched my flesh. Heat soared through me. Noah's fingers were better than mine, I decided, and slowly pulled my hand out and when Noah began to do the same, I gripped his hand from doing so.

"I want you to," I whispered.

He slipped his fingers back into my underwear and the sound that rose from his chest was louder than my own. "Grace…" But that was all he said before his mouth covered my nipple again and his fingers swirled circles over my flesh.

I moved my hips as Noah rocked into my side and kissed and teased me in ways that built something inside me. The closer it got, the more anxious I felt until it was too much. I grabbed his hand. "Noah, stop!" I cried softly. "Something's coming—" My feet jolted when it did happen and I let my head fall onto the carpet as the aftershocks tickled my body until I jerked over and over until he finally stopped.

He kissed me when it was over and I smiled through the kiss. I felt like laughing because it felt so good but we had to be quiet. "Noah, that was…" I said through kisses.

He smiled then slowly raised up. "I know, you were beautiful, but I've got to go." He stood quickly and I frowned. He covered his pants up but not before I saw the shape of him or the wet spot against his jeans.

"Did you not like it?" I stood up and covered my breasts.

He flicked my nose, something he constantly did after that one time I did it to him, and I grabbed it. "That's the stupidest thing I've ever heard you say, of course, I did."

"Then…"

"Because I need to change… and check on my mom. Dad won't stop her from taking anything." He opened the window and stepped out into the night air. It was cold. "Come here." I listened and grinned after he gave me another kiss. "Goodnight, Grace."

"Goodnight, Noah."

13

Grace age 13

Noah age 13

Life is steadily falling apart. I fight my own sleep to keep an eye on Mom. Every time I do sleep, I wake up to find her passed out somewhere and my blood feels more like ice as I shake and jerk her until she finally stirs. It's only a short bit of relief because I know I'll fight her same demon tomorrow.

I don't like when Grace cries, especially when her tears are for me. I don't ever want to be the reason for her tears.

N.P.

Noah didn't come back to school until his black eye was gone. He hadn't visited me anymore at night since the night he touched me last week, but he made some time to come over and talk to me for a few minutes every day. It wasn't nearly enough but I didn't want anything bad to happen to Noah's mom either.

But I wondered how long he could keep her from her choices?

That Monday when he came back, Noah dodged and answered questions like a pro about why he hadn't been at school. He didn't tell the truth. Even when he told my parents, he made it sound like his mom hit him by accident. Neither of them said anything about it but the way my dad watched him that day sent a bad feeling in my stomach, like maybe he waited for the day to Noah to end up like his parents.

fall from grace

It had been seven years since we moved to this town and it hadn't taken half of those to learn the reputation of The Phillips. They lied, they stole, and they did drugs. When Dad's weed-eater was stolen last year, the first person he had assumed it had been was Noah's dad. And if I really looked closer, I saw the way he watched Noah since then. If I hadn't begged Dad that day, I knew he would have gone over to their house and confronted them.

Maybe it had been since then, or the day that Noah became a teen, that Dad occasionally watched him with a penetrating stare. I wondered if Noah sensed the way he watched him sometimes.

That evening at dinner, Mom said, "Noah hasn't been coming over a lot this week."

I took a bite of my mashed potatoes. "He's been busy." I wouldn't say things behind Noah's back.

Mom frowned. "I just hated to see him quit the football team. He was our best player."

"Noah quit football?" Dad interjected, taking a little more interest than I liked. "Why did he do that?"

"He's just… trying to be there for his Mom," I managed to say.

"You mean, keeping her from OD-ing again," Dad muttered under his breath.

"Steven!" Mom hissed.

"Yeah, actually." I lifted my head. "No matter what, she's his mom. Of course, he'd want to save her!"

"You can't save someone that doesn't want to be saved," Dad told me. "Noah's a good kid, but I'm afraid with the way things are going, he's going to turn out just like his parents."

"Steven," Mom sighed.

"Dad!" I snapped. "This is Noah! My best friend, Noah, you are talking about. The boy that carries the groceries in for Mom every single Sunday and the one that helps you carry in wood in the winter and the boy that cuts our grass in the summer. Heck, he cuts everyone's grass in the summer and gets paid for it! Don't belittle him when he's genuinely good and chooses to love his parents despite what little they do for him."

I stood up to leave. "Sit back down, Grace," Dad barked. He placed his fork down and looked at me. "Why don't you invite your friends from school over Grace? Why don't you hang out with girls your age instead of a boy? It's not normal."

"Enough, Steven," Mom was angry now. "I don't know what's gotten into you but there's nothing wrong with Grace hanging out with Noah. He's a good boy."

Dad snorted, even I was taken aback by the way he was acting. "How do we know he's not making her keep to herself with just him and her." He looked at me. "Is that it? Is he jealous and doesn't want you to have any other friends over?"

"What are you talking about? I don't invite my friends over because I don't want to share him!"

Even Mom looked surprised by my answer. My cheeks were hot and I regretted the words the moment I said them.

"Is that so? Then time to start learning."

"What do you mean?" I asked him.

"I mean, you aren't kids anymore. I've ignored the way he's always looked at you before because you were kids but I won't anymore."

Mom covered her face with her hand. My lungs burned with fury. Did Mom perhaps tell Dad what I said? I wouldn't think she would do that to me, but then again, Dad was her husband and I was his child. It was so infuriating to be a kid. I held my tears as I studied both my parents before running upstairs.

fall from grace

Of course, Noah finally came that night and as happy as that made me, I knew I had to tell him to leave. Noah could tell something was bothering me the moment I met him at the window. He didn't even step into my room.

He frowned. "What's wrong, Priss?"

Just because it was Noah, I couldn't hold in my tears. I covered my eyes up and he pulled me in. The November air was cold, but Noah was so warm. "For now, it's best for you not to come up into my room." He tilted his head. "My dad, he's being weird. I think he knows our relationship has changed and it makes me feel guilty, but I don't want you to stay away because of it."

"He's not being weird Grace. You're just finally picking up on what I've always felt." He wiped my eyes and smiled sadly. "He's just getting to the point to where he can't hold it in... You hanging out with someone like me."

"There's nothing wrong with you," I whimpered.

He smiled. "I know, silly. I'll see you at school tomorrow, okay?"

I nodded and fell into a better place when he left me with a kiss.

14

Grace age 13

Noah age 13

When it comes to succeeding and life in general, I already know that the odds are stacked against me. I don't have the right clothes and shoes. I'm judged first by my poor outer appearance, then I'm judged second by my parents. I'm not expected to succeed but that's exactly why I will. The thing about being born in my world, I already know not to expect things to get better because they don't, but I have the motivation to crawl out of the mess I'm in.

I don't want the world. I just want the ability to give the one I love a peaceful living.

I'm always picturing a future with her, I hope one day she starts to do the same.

Just a little longer… I'm slowly getting older.

N.P.

"What's with you and Noah?" Sara asked Friday morning at the table before Tiffany or Noah had arrived by their buses. I always rode to school with Mom.

"What do you mean?" I pulled my hair back into a ponytail.

"He's always with us now, and so is Mark and Dustin." She slurped her orange juice through the straw. "Are you two dating?"

"No…" I thought about it. "Noah and I are…just us."

"Huh?" Her eyebrows shot up.

"I don't know how to explain it."

"Explain what?" Tiffany said, sliding in next to Sara as she scooted over. "Hey."

"Hey," Sara replied. "Just trying to get Gracie here to spill the dirt on her and Noah."

"Don't call me Gracie," I grumbled.

"Really, though," Tiffany sighed. "You guys act like you're together."

I smiled and shrugged my shoulders and they both started squealing. "I knew it!" Sara slammed her palm against the table and said.

"What about you, Sara?" I squinted my eyes at her.

"What about me?"

Tiffany laughed, "Don't even pretend, we see you crushing on Dustin." Sara threw a napkin at her and we all laughed.

"Like you don't think he's hot either," Sara protested.

"Oh yes, me like the way he looks a lot," Tiffany sang the words out. "Besides, Noah's never been up for grabs because of a certain someone..." They both turned toward me.

"Y'all are lively this morning, aren't ya?" Dustin crept up on us without us noticing him. He did a little chin tip to tell me to scoot over and I did. "Waiting on the boyfriend?" he asked and I blushed.

Sara and Tiffany started their oh's and ah's again. "Is that what Noah's saying?" Tiffany asked quickly

Dustin shook his head. "No, but it's not hard to tell with us hanging out with you losers." Sara threw the same napkin she had thrown at Tiffany at Dustin. He picked it up and threw it at me. I knocked it away and smiled when I saw Noah stepping through the door. His eyes were on our table before I even found him. He smiled back and Dustin got up and let him in as I scooted to back of the booth so all three of us could fit.

"Hey," he said with a smile aimed at me.

Noah came over all week for a few minutes despite my dad's unexpectedly outburst Monday night that I had told him about. Other than that though, Dad hadn't said anything to Noah.

I was used to spending hours with him every day and now I was only getting minutes with him before he'd go back home.

"You guys are totally dating," Tiffany mentioned.

"How about it, Grace?" Noah smirked. "Are you my girl?"

I rolled my eyes and they widened when I felt him move his hand over mine underneath the table. I flipped mine over and our fingers entwined. I smiled but otherwise said nothing.

―――

I found myself staring at Noah in class all the time. He also caught me staring, but I didn't care. All I could think about was how I wanted to kiss and touch him. The closer it got time to go home, the more depressed I felt. I wouldn't see him much this weekend if I didn't let him visit my room again at night. I was feeling more comfortable again now that Dad was back to himself… Or maybe Noah was right and he was satisfied that he hadn't been coming over much the past two weeks.

I hated thinking about it that way.

When the last class ended, Noah waited for me by the door before he ran to catch the bus. I didn't speak to him this time around, I

90

just slipped the note into his hand and hurried to Mom's classroom. It was a little embarrassing to stick around and wait for him to read it. I had asked him to come to my room tonight and smacked my cheeks as I ran down the hall and grinned at my own bad thoughts that involved Noah and what I wanted him to do to me.

———

I didn't think Noah was going to come once it hit midnight. He still hadn't shown. I waited by the window for the longest time before slipping back under my covers where it was warm. It had to be close to one when he startled me awake by sliding in next to me. His shirt and skin were chilled from the frosty night. I propped myself up on my elbow and leaned over him. "I didn't think you were going to come."

He breathed from his nose, "I wasn't going to miss the chance to spend some time with you since we haven't gotten to lately."

"How's your mom?" I asked.

He shook his head. "I don't know how I expected to prevent her from doing what she wants. She takes whatever Dad brings her while I'm at school because she's passed out on the couch when I come home. She has a new hiding place and I have no idea where they keep it... She only just now fell asleep, but I wonder if I'm even making a difference? Maybe I gave up football foolishly thinking that my parents might care if I'm right in their faces all the time instead of over here or at practice..."

"Maybe not today... But maybe one day, you'll make a difference."

"What do you see when you look at me?" I arched my brow at him, and he added, "Do you pity me? Is it because you thought I was living in the treehouse when we first met that you became my friend? I was always embarrassed eating over here for the longest time because I thought your mom fed me because she thought I didn't have any."

I placed my hand on his cheek. "I don't know how to answer that question because the only thing I see is Noah when I look at you. I don't

91

see anything else. I just see my best friend. The one that promised me adventures." I felt his smile against my palm. "As for Mom, I remember clearly how she talked to Dad about you when we first met, and you're right, she did question and worry, maybe even pity you but," I whispered quickly, "that is not the case with her now."

"And your dad?" he asked slowly.

I laid back and sighed. "That's the strangest thing, Dad seemed to be the one that wasn't being judgmental about your appearance, yet... I don't know what he thinks now."

"It's okay," he replied quickly as if to dispel the bad vibe this conversation brought in the room. "I'll prove he's wrong about me."

"You don't have to prove anything to no one, Noah, you're not your parents."

"I do," he whispered. "I have things I want in this world and if I want something, I need to know I can protect it, unlike my dad."

That made me remember the conversation he had with his dad in front of me.

So, you have something you want to protect?

Was I the thing Noah wanted?

It made me all warm and fuzzy but at the same time, I could be acting self-centered, thinking that I was that important to Noah. He could be talking about life in general, or maybe a job he wanted when we grew up—

"Priss, you got quiet on me." He loomed over me.

"Sorry, I was just thinking."

"About what?"

"About..." I peered around the dark room. "When you're going to touch me again."

fall from grace

"Have you touched yourself any since then?" He ran his hand over my stomach.

I nodded. His eyes should have been adjusted enough to the darkness to see that I did. "I tried, it's not the same as when you do it. I just don't really feel anything."

"Sounds like you're not trying very hard." He bent down and blew into my ear. I laid my hand on his shoulder and pulled him in. He grabbed my breast and groaned. "No bra," he confirmed.

"Thought it would be easier this way…"

He kissed my lips only once then dragged them down my chin onto my neck. My breath quickened as he continued downward while his hand slipped underneath my shirt and cupped my breast. I opened my mouth but no sound came out. "The light," he said, climbing off the bed to turn on the nightlight. He climbed back on the bed and stopped himself at my knees. Instead of asking, he placed his hands at the waistband of my shorts and waited for my approval. When I nodded, he pulled them down slowly taking my panties with them.

I studied his reaction before I said, "What is it?"

"I just can't believe I'm getting to see you like this." His eyes burned through me.

"It's just me."

"There's no such thing as 'just' when it comes to you for me, Grace."

"We're different than other people our ages, aren't we?" I found myself asking.

"We're just us," was his answer as he lowered himself between my legs.

My eyes widened. "What are you doing?"

"I'm going to look then I'm going to place my lips there."

My mind told me that it was weird, but my body awaited what he'd show me tonight. I couldn't keep my butt still when his breath tickled the inside of my thigh. "Every inch of you is perfection. How is that?" he swore.

"Can I see yours?" I asked him.

He looked up at me. "You want to?"

I nodded and he placed a kiss on the inside of my thigh before raising up. I sat up and watched as he unzipped his jeans and pulled them down enough so that it sprang free. I jumped back and he couldn't contain his grin when I did. My stomach dropped and filled with heat at the sight of him. Guys were so different than girls. Theirs went into ours… What used to be scary was still, now that I was face to face with one. I couldn't even imagine how it could go inside… "It's kind of scary looking, isn't it?" I voiced my opinion aloud.

He covered his forehead with his palm. "You're blunt even in this situation, I should have known." He smiled. "I don't know whether to be offended or not."

"It also gives me the tingles when looking at it." I leaned closer. "Scary tingles, like I'm afraid of it, but I also want to get to know it."

He covered his mouth this time to stop himself from bursting out into laughter. "I can't do this." He threw himself over me and we bounced on the bed together, the springs creaking to our weight. "You're too cute."

Only I wasn't smiling. I felt Noah bare against my own flesh. His skin was like fire compared to mine. It felt good. The mood was thicker when I leaned my face up to kiss him and he dived his tongue in my mouth. The heat in my stomach burst through me like lightning. This was what Noah could make me feel.

The feeling he gave me all but died into panic as I heard someone coming up the stairs. From the look on his face, I could tell he heard it too. "Noah, someone's coming," I whispered as he slid off the bed, zipping up his pants. As soon as I get my shorts slid back up, Dad opened my door and the fear I felt was the most potent I'd ever experienced. He took in Noah standing at my bedside and became enraged.

Noah didn't even say anything to defend himself. I guess he knew there was nothing to explain that my dad wouldn't already know. "What the fuck are you two doing in here? What are you doing to my daughter?" Dad said right before he swung at Noah.

Noah turned his head to ease the brunt of Dad's fist. Mom stepped in behind him and gasped. "Steven, you can't hit a minor!" Despite the fear pulsing through my veins, I finally stood up and moved closer to Noah.

"Dad, please," I cried.

Noah pushed me aside and gave me a look that said, *it's okay Grace.*

"Like hell I can't, he's in my house doing God knows what to our daughter!"

I covered my face and cried. I made a mistake. I was scared for Noah and afraid that Dad wasn't going to let me see him ever again.

"I'm sorry, I didn't mean to make either of you mad," Noah started, "Grace is everything to—"

"I was a kid once, I know exactly what boys are thinking." Dad grabbed Noah by the shirt collar and shoved him out into the hallway. "I won't let you ruin my daughter's life just so you can satisfy your curiosity of her."

Noah blew from his nose. "You know it's not like that, Steven! Grace is more than my best friend. I'd never hurt her!"

I followed them out of the room crying. Mom was next to me. I didn't know if she was more disappointed or if she was going to burst into tears as she looked at me.

Dad nodded. "I know you think you know how you feel right now, but those feelings are going to change and the one thing that's certain is my daughter will be the one left hurting." Noah shook his head. "Go, boy, I don't want you back in the house. Do I need to go to your worthless parents and tell them what happened? Or would they even care?"

"Dad!" I screamed.

"I'll go." Noah lowered his face before lifting his head back up to face Dad with a piercing stare that even surprised me. "One day, you're going to know that my feelings for Grace surpasses even what you feel for her as a parent!"

"Why, you little punk!" Dad yelled.

"Steven," Mom hissed beside me. "Go, Noah before things get worse." Noah looked to Mom slightly embarrassed before he nodded.

He met my eyes and I started crying again. "Don't be upset with Grace," he couldn't help but say before he walked down the stairs and out the door.

I stepped backward the moment he was gone not knowing what my parents were going to say to me. Only Dad didn't even turn around to face me. He got to the steps before he fell to his butt and cried. I was frozen in place and couldn't believe I was watching and listening to my father cry. Mom was still beside me but even she was crying. I wondered if her tears were for the fact that she was disappointed in me or that she was sad to see my relationship ruined with Noah because of these new feelings I had for him.

"How could he?" Dad yelled through his tears. "You're my baby, Gracie."

"Dad," I whispered, crying with him. "We didn't mean to make anyone upset."

fall from grace

He turned his head and looked at me. "It's the fact that you're only thirteen Grace and you're still growing! You can't make decisions like that with your body randomly or even under my roof!"

"Nothing you're thinking happened," I told him. "I'm sorry, I'm truly am."

I was. I felt terribly guilty and sad that I disappointed them like this. I had two parents that looked at me like I could do anything, which was one of the reasons I excelled in school. My parents gave me everything and I returned it with heartache.

Even now, I wanted to beg them to forgive us so that I could keep spending time with Noah out of school. But I didn't because I knew now was not the time. The damage was done. I would just have to wait and see what tomorrow held.

"Go to bed, Grace. I don't feel like talking about this tonight," Dad said, standing up and going downstairs.

"Mom," I pleaded as she started walking.

"I know you and Noah care for one another, but understand your dad, and understand me, it hurts because you're getting older and there's nothing we can do to stop it."

15

Grace age 13

Noah age 13

When it rains, it pours.

N.P.

I slept in that Saturday morning and didn't wake until something slobbery and warm slid over my cheek repeatedly until I opened my eyes. A black puppy with blue eyes wagged his tail at me and I raised up. "Oh God, where did you come from?" I asked and scooped him up in my arms. He kept trying to get to my face and I laughed until I saw Mom standing in the doorway watching me.

"Your dad picked him up at the shelter today and brought him home for you," she said, stepping into my room and sitting down at the edge of the bed.

"I don't understand." I kept petting the little black monster. "I did something I shouldn't have and you guys finally let me have a puppy?" I asked in disbelief. I'd wanted a pet my whole life and this was how I got one?

Dad stormed in my room next. "I'm sure this little guy will bark his head off when we get unexpected visitors at night." I sighed, so that was what he was for. My guard dog. "They said he was most likely a Husky and German Shepherd mixed," he added before leaving the room. The puppy's ears made him look like a German Shepherd. I rubbed my thumbs on the inside of them.

fall from grace

"His puppy pads are downstairs. It's your job to teach him how to use them until you can train him to go outside."

I nodded quickly. "Um, Mom." She sighed as soon as I said her name. "Do you think you and Dad are going to let Noah come back over again? He's spent half his life over here at our house!"

"Stop trying to make us feel like the bad ones, Grace."

"I know." I looked down at the puppy. "I'm sorry. It's just… I feel like Noah needs me in his life, especially right now…"

"I don't know, your Dad's really upset. Give him time."

———

My heart hurt. My stomach protested to food. I felt guilty that I hurt my parents. I felt lonely and sad that I couldn't just walk over and talk to Noah, who I knew I'd feel at ease next to. I'd sit on the porch with Gus—the name I gave the Husky mix. I couldn't stay outside more than a couple of minutes at a time because it was too cold out. Noah wouldn't come over today. He wouldn't make things worse for me, and for someone that had always cared what my parents thought of him, I knew this must be making him feel guilty too.

Which meant I probably wouldn't see him until Monday at school.

Only that wouldn't be the case. Sometimes things happen that you'd least expect, then there were the things that happened that you tried to prevent. The ones that kept you up at night in fear of them becoming a reality.

That night, the sirens pierced through my dreams. Normally, nothing could hardly wake me but the sound was deafening through my room. The first thing I thought was it was going to Noah's house. In my head, I told myself I was wrong, and in order to prove myself that, I just had to see which house the ambulance pulled into.

Being next to Noah for so long, maybe I slowly tapped into his same fears because I thought briefly that hearing sirens, seeing cop cars, or random strangers pulling into your driveway where all things to be afraid of. His fears were somehow mine now.

I needed to know Noah was safe tonight. One more night.

I ran downstairs, Dad was already out on the porch. The cold air crawled up my bare legs as Mom stepped into the hallway. She watched me skip the last few steps and dash for the door. Dad stepped into the doorway. "What are you doing up?" he asked.

"I heard the ambulance. Whose house?"

"Go back to bed." He wouldn't let me get by him.

"Whose house!" I snapped.

"Whose house is it, Steven?" Mom asked this time. "It's not Noah's, is it?" I felt a small bit of relief knowing that Mom still worried for him.

Dad leaned his head out the door and sighed. "It looks like it's near the trailers."

"I have to go check on him. What if it's Noah?" I panicked.

"You know who it's gonna—", Dad sighed, "Let me put on my shoes and I'll go check." The moment he bent down, I slipped through the tiny space between him and the door and ran out. "GRACE!"

I was already running down the road, feet burning against the frigid blacktop. I didn't care that I was in my tank top and shorts. The cold didn't bother me, knowing that Noah and his parents were okay was all that mattered.

Yelling broke out in the distance. My heart sank. I recognized Noah's voice and he was angry, he was upset. I could tell he was crying. I saw the ambulance in front of his house and slowed, taking in Noah and his dad next to the porch. Noah pushed his dad. I was close enough now to make out their words. "You killed her!" Noah yelled at him and I stopped, eyes widening.

Killed...?

"I didn't kill her," his dad cried out. "She kept begging me, Noah, begging me to give her just one more, one more. I've never been able to say no to her!"

Noah reared back and punched his Dad in the face. He staggered back. "You could have gotten her help, but you didn't. You just fed her the drugs she wanted!"

"What about you?" His dad moved into Noah's face. "You could have told someone. Maybe got someone to help her, but no, you let her just as much as me!"

I covered my mouth. How could he say that to Noah? How was it Noah's fault?

Noah stepped back, tugging his hair with a face so broken, my feet started moving again. "Because I didn't want to lose her! But I lost her anyway!" Noah was furious again. "And now you're dead to me!"

"Grace!" Dad yelled behind me.

Noah and his dad turned to look at me. His eyes were remorseful. He wished I hadn't witnessed what I did.

Our eyes broke contact when two men carried out his mom on a stretcher. My throat filled with bile when I saw that she was covered completely up. No...

Another man stepped up beside them. "I'm going need you two to come in with me." Noah looked like his worst fear had come to pass while his dad simply dropped his head and nodded.

I felt Dad's hand come down over my shoulder. "Come on, let's go home."

How could he say those words so easily after what he just saw? After what we knew Noah was going through. Noah wouldn't even look my way. He started following the guy to the ambulance. "Noah!" I screamed and he finally looked at me. He stopped and I ran to him.

What was even scarier was how Dad didn't stop me. I should have known that wasn't a good sign. I already saw where this was heading for Noah, and I was truly afraid that if he got in the back of the ambulance, I might not see him again.

I started shaking my head frantically and he couldn't look at me again. "It's going to be okay, Priss. I'll be seeing you soon," he lied.

"Noah," I cried. "Wait!"

But he didn't and Dad pulled me aside as one of the guys nodded toward us before getting in the front seat and driving away.

Dad led me back to the house where Mom took one look at me and cried herself. I ran upstairs because I knew Dad would tell her what just happened.

Noah's mom died from an overdose. His dad came home the next day alone. He buried his wife without a funeral. I didn't know if Noah got to say goodbye or where he was. Our teachers—Mom being one of them—informed us that Noah was transferring out that following Monday. Everyone asked me questions at school like I would know. He didn't even have our house number because he never had a phone and we were always seeing each there every day so there had been no point.

Life was all wrong. A terrible imbalance to what used to be. I'd adapt, but I'd never forget Noah or the way just the thought of him made me feel.

A week later, Mom found me in my room where she sat down on the bed and told me, "If Noah is the kind of boy you think he is and the kind of man I know he can be someday, then this will be nothing for him. He'll be okay. He's been taking care of himself his entire life. And if he's meant to be a part of your life, he'll make his way back when he's able."

At school, Tiffany asked, "Did you tell him you loved him?"

It was then I realized Noah and I never said that to each other once. It wasn't something I ever had to hear him say. It was in the way he called me Priss, or in the way he always looked out for me, or in the way he scolded me when I did wrong and smiled at me differently than he did for everyone else.

Some things didn't have to be said in order to be known.

I loved Noah. I thought he must know that the same way I knew that he loved me.

Without my parents' permission, I would start to sneak over to Noah's dad's house and ask if he heard anything about Noah, in which the answer would always be no. I knew his dad didn't care as much as I did, but that didn't mean I wouldn't stop bugging him.

Life without Noah was…

16

*I'm welcomed into a stranger's home. I lost everything within twenty-four hours. The couple that takes me in, I'm sure has heard all the dirty details since they are there to pick me up and take me to their home so quickly. I'm so angry. All this bottled up rage has slipped out now that Mom finally let go. Dad knew, **he knew**. The same way I did. The way she was searching for an end and he didn't try and stop her.*

This hateful person that I'm not, takes a hold of me. I lash out on the couple that takes me in. I keep expecting the curtains to fall and their peaceful smiles to warp into the reality that was my life...

———

All I can think about is getting in touch with Grace. I need to hear her voice. I wish she hadn't come out that night. I wish my parents didn't ruin even that part of my life, the one with her in it. I sink to the floor and cover my face with my hands. I'm crying, snot and all when I see Janet staring up at me from the bottom of the stairway. Her and her husband, Dean, are the ones that took me in. She's always watching, always waiting, always smiling with a sorrowful expression as she watches me. I get up from the stairs and disappear into the room they gave me where I cry for Grace in private.

I'm not ashamed to cry. Grace is something worth crying for.

———

fall from grace

I lash out some more. Dean and Janet are ever patient. It makes me feel horrible. But it also makes me afraid. I can't be so lucky… not me… to end up with two people that actually care.

———

I don't know Grace's number but it is easy to call up the school and ask to be transferred to her mom's classroom… Only I don't like the reality she gives me, but I accept it because I know it's not going to change how I feel.

Nothing ever will.

———

Dean and Janet… are good people. The nights where I couldn't sleep in a stranger's home slowly eased into being normal. My anger fades, but the hurt stays. I still miss the mom who wasn't really one. I still think about the dad that I spent hating.

But my future is still there. I'll make it because I'm not my parents. I'm not where I came from. Some people might say otherwise, but I'll prove them wrong.

Life without Grace was… waiting to see her again.

N.P.

michelle gross

Part Two:

High School

17

Grace age 16

Noah age 17

I realize I can be no different than any other guy. I can hurt a girl without knowing, without caring. I had sex with a girl for the first time and it wasn't Grace, but the entire time I was above her, it's Grace who I wonder about. It's Grace that I miss and crave as I explore and map her body, learning all the ways that make her feel good, learning all the ways that I'll do to Grace. Then I slept with her a few more times until she wanted more. She wanted what I already gave to someone else a long time ago. She knew where my heart stood when she came onto me, but she tried at my heart anyway, so she was left crying when I walked away without much feeling at all.

I tried to picture a life without Grace. I tried another body other than Grace, and it leaves me missing her more.

The only thing I find out is that I'm not a good guy unless it's next to her.

I call up Grace's mom once more…then I wait.

I wait… I wait while driving by her house, hoping to catch a glimpse of her. I place myself where I might run into her sooner. I wait… but I'm losing patience.

N.P.

Dustin pulled his truck—that his parents paid for—into my driveway and when he turned the engine off, I groaned inwardly.

"Your parents aren't home yet," he said it like it was an invitation for him to come inside. He had passed his driver's test over the summer and loved to show it off. I only had my permit because I was a bit nervous behind the wheel—okay, big-time nervous.

"Mom will be home anytime," I told him in hopes that he'd stop looking over at me like that.

He didn't. "Do you want me to come inside?" I was beginning to understand that most guys couldn't read body signals or they just didn't care. I could think of one boy that read me better than I read myself, but Dustin wasn't him… But he had been my boyfriend for the past few weeks now. I finally gave into him after he truly seemed like he cared about me in some way. He even stopped flirting with other girls because I had told him I hadn't believed him when he said he liked me because he was always dating someone. And I craved the idea of touching someone intimately. Kissing Dustin wasn't that good at first but with time, I'd truly grown to enjoy the feel of his lips on mine. He was very handsy too but I made him keep it PG because I wasn't ready. Maybe I wouldn't be ready for anyone if they weren't Noah. But I was giving in to the idea and even seeing Dustin for the attractive guy he was, if only he wasn't so pushy.

"No, I'd rather you didn't," I told him nicely. "Don't you have football practice today?"

"Not 'til six." He rubbed his head before looking over at me. "What made you want to start cheering again this year?" This was something he kept asking since I decided to go back on the cheer team the first of the school year. We would be cheering at their first game of the year this Friday. "You quit the year Noah moved." I never told anyone that Noah didn't exactly move, he was placed in a foster home somewhere, but maybe they knew and just pretended not to know. None of them knew his parents or that his mom passed away, only I did.

I looked down at my hands. "Yeah, that's why. I always did like it and when I realized I only have two years left of high school, I decided to…"

"Be normal again?" He laughed and I shrugged my shoulders.

"If I'm honest, it was because Mom kept bugging me about it, saying 'you won't regret gettin' back on the team but you will regret it if you let these moments pass you by'," I mimicked her voice.

He chuckled. "I'm really glad you gave me a chance, Grace. I was beginning to think you were never going to get over Noah."

I rubbed my eyes and smiled weirdly. "Yeah… Call me tonight, okay?" He pulled me in and kissed me.

His lips were against mine and I still dreamed of Noah.

Once inside, Gus attacked me at the door. "Hey, Gus." They had been wrong about Gus being German Shepherd and Husky mixed. He obviously had one of the two in him but his growth was stunted to the size of a Chow Chow and his eyes that were once blue were now a gorgeous golden color. I rubbed his snout before he followed me into the kitchen. I pulled out Sunday's leftovers from the fridge and peeked out the door to make sure Dustin was gone before opening the front door. "Come on, Gus, let's go make sure he's still alive this week."

I tried to visit Noah's dad, John, every week when Mom and Dad were both gone. They'd kill me if they knew I was taking him our leftovers occasionally.

The screen door was unlocked—like always—with the door wide open. I rolled my eyes when I saw him and the young man that had been frequenting his place lately passed out on the stained sofa. Gus rushed in when I opened the door and I covered my nose from the smell. Good Lord, how did it keep getting worse? "Wake him up," I told Gus but even my poor dog was afraid to touch him or anything in the house. I set the leftovers down on the counter.

"John, wake up!" I yelled and startled the man next to him. His eyes were wide and alert until he saw it was me and fell back against the cushion.

"You again?" he blew.

fall from grace

I kicked John's feet with my tennis shoes. "John!" His eyebrows twitched but otherwise, he didn't stir. I looked over the coffee table at the needles and pill bottles lying across it. "What did he take this time?" I asked the other man.

Looking at it all just pissed me off. This was the reason I lost Noah. I brought my foot up and kicked everything onto the floor. "What the fuck are you doing?" the man yelled. Gus barked at him.

I glared. "He lost his son and his wife because of this shit!" I hissed and he settled back down on the couch. "He should show a bit of remorse!"

I went back outside and grabbed the mop bucket then went to the sink. "What are you doing?" He knew exactly what I was doing. I carried the bucket full of water and smiled as I poured the ice-cold water over John.

He spluttered and coughed and jumped up. "What the fuck?" he roared, then he saw me and he cursed some more.

"Your son's girlfriend is here again and she's pissed as always," the man told John like he wasn't standing there glaring at me.

"I'm not Noah's girlfriend. I have a boyfriend now," I told them as I grabbed the leftovers and stuck it in the microwave. Only it wouldn't come on. I tried the plug. "John, your microwave is just about as useless as you are," I said, and the other guy laughed. John wasn't my dad. I didn't have to be nice to him. I could say exactly what I thought and hoped that one day, my words would make a difference. The same way I had told Noah his would.

John sighed and moved next to me. "Move," he barked and I did. After a lot of banging and cursing, it started up for him. A few minutes later, he was eating the food I brought.

"Have you tried to see if you can get the number to where Noah is staying?" I asked.

111

He snorted. "Yeah, like they are gonna let me have contact with him." Then they both started laughing like it was funny.

"If you tried to get help and get your shit together, they'd let him come home!"

"Yeah, it looks like I'm trying to get my shit together," John said, stretching his arms wide and they both chuckled again. "And ladies aren't supposed to cuss."

"Stop acting like you don't care!" I snapped, kicking his coffee table and it was a piece of crap so I ended up breaking one of its legs. "I saw you try the first few weeks after he left." I looked down at the broken table, feeling a little flushed with embarrassment.

"Aye, John, if we got an addiction problem then she's got an anger issue, right?"

They both started laughing again.

"John, please, if not for you then try to get his contact information for me," I said the same things every week and it never made a difference… yet. "I have to go, I'll see you next week."

"Don't come back," he said. "And stop letting that mutt in the house!"

"Come on, Gus," I called to him. "And we're coming back," I promised.

"If you got a boyfriend, why you still trying to get in touch with Noah?" he surprised me by asking.

"Because no one compares to your son," I told him the truth, and he surprised me with a genuine smile, one filled with pride. I walked out the door smiling because at least for a second, I could smile for Noah. Somewhere underneath his father's addiction might lay a man that loved his son.

fall from grace

18

Grace age 16

Noah age 17

I talk to Janet a lot about Grace. She wants to meet her, but I'm still waiting to reunite with her myself. I trust Grace's mom, Allison, but at the same time, I don't know how much longer I can wait.

The thought of someone stealing her away from me drives me mad.

What if someone already has? After all, I was only the trailer park boy that lived close by.

N.P.

"Grace, brake. Press the brake! The brake!" Mom screamed and I slammed on the brake.

"Mom!" I hissed, shaking like a leaf as I held the steering wheel with both hands. "Why are you yelling?"

"Because, the stop sign," she said dramatically, holding her chest.

I rolled my eyes and sighed. "I know, I was nowhere near being close to it!"

She looked at me all scared like. "I'm sorry. This just makes me nervous."

I groaned. "I know, Mom, but I'm more nervous than you are and your nerves are only rubbing mine *raw.*"

She laughed at my choice of words and I huffed. "You're right. I'm sorry. I'm sorry. Continue."

"I'd like to take my test by the end of this month," I told her and she nodded some more.

Thirty minutes later, we were parked at Stevie's—a small pickup burger stand beside the highway. We sat at a picnic table as we ate.

"So," Mom started, slurping on her drink. "You and Dustin?" she waggled her brows and I groaned loud enough for her to hear. "So, you're dating him but you don't like him?" she asked.

I shook my head. "I do like him. I just—"

She nodded like she already knew what I was going to say. "He's not Noah?" I gave her a tired smile and nodded.

"Do you think Noah still thinks about me like I think about him?" I asked lamely.

She smiled mischievously. "Of course, he does! You have my good looks and some long legs like your daddy, I know that boy ain't going to forget about you."

I placed my chin in my palm as I rested my elbow on the table. "Don't make it about looks, Mom… But, I can imagine what a few years would add to Noah… I bet he's even better looking now. I wonder if he grew any taller." My tummy felt like lava just thinking about Noah while every time I kissed Dustin, it was lukewarm.

"Your face is a little red, child, cool it down," Mom teased. "So, the boys play their first game this Friday, don't they?" Mom changed the subject and I nodded. "Who are they playing… Bulldogs, right? Jewel County?" Jewel County was right next to our county.

115

"I think so."

"You made the right choice by going back to the team."

I squinted my eyes. "You practically harassed me into getting back on the team."

She feigned ignorance. "I did no such thing."

"Anyway… I'm glad I got back on the team. It gives me something to do at least."

She smirked. "You won't regret it."

"I swear, if you plan on sneaking onto the bleachers and filming me cheering, I'll quit right now," I said. She giggled like a little girl. "I'm serious, your face has me worried."

She tossed her hand up. "Relax. I won't even get to go if I wanted to. I have to work one of the ball games for the middle school that night." She made a pouty face. "I really wanted to go." And the truth came out.

I pretended to be annoyed. "Why are you acting so childish?"

"You act like I'm old or something, I'm only thirty-eight."

"And you're onnneeee hottttt mammmaaaa," I started singing Trace Adkins, "One Hot Mama" and she pushed down her shades and bounced her head until I started laughing.

116

19

Grace age 16

Noah age 17

Please be there tomorrow. I need to see you. If I don't see you, I might have to go back on the words I said to your mom and come to you.

N.P.

Something had spurred Dustin's pushiness yesterday and today. Yesterday he had become more insistent about trying to come inside before Mom got home from school, and today he actually took his truck on the back of the mountain so that he could be alone with me. I had told him I hadn't wanted to come up here but he shrugged off my choice like it didn't matter.

I was slightly frustrated and even a little scared that he made this choice so he had to butter me up for a good ten minutes before I finally let him kiss me. Of course, he wanted more. That was the whole reason he brought me up here. I even tried to wrap my arms around him and I thought about the sexy way he smiled sometimes or the moments he actually knew how to be a gentleman and held the door open for people, but the moment he slipped his hand up my shirt, I tensed and started pushing him away. No matter what my reason was, I just couldn't do this with him. At least not until I was comfortable. It was okay to want comfortable. I wasn't going to feel bad the moment he leaned back and sighed. "What's wrong?" he asked, a little breathy. He did look good up close. His eyes were darker than his hair. He had perfect eyebrows too.

"I just want to take things slow. We've only been dating a few weeks."

"We can do slow," he said, pulling back and I blushed and looked away when he started adjusting his junk right in front of me. "You let Noah touch you. I figured you were ready to mess around."

I frowned. "Noah told you he touched me?"

He leaned his head back and smirked, the one he did when he was pissed off. "So, he did touch you? You let him touch you in middle school and won't let me in high school?"

I gaped at him. "You said it in a way that I would misunderstand." He had tricked me into getting an answer.

"Does it matter?" he asked. "We're dating now. What's wrong with wanting to know?"

"I don't ask you about all the girls you've fooled around with, let alone slept with." I crossed my arms and stared ahead. "Take me home."

"Grace," he said softly. "I didn't mean to upset you."

"Yes, you did. You wanted to guilt trip me into making me do more than I was ready for. Just take me home."

"I can't fucking help it. I'm so nervous that I'm never going to amount to him in your eyes. You won't even give me a chance."

"Because you're not wanting a chance, Dustin, you're wanting in my pants."

He placed his head on the steering wheel. "You're right, I'm sorry. I'm rushing you when I shouldn't, just because it's a little surreal that you are even giving me the chance and I'm already fucking up." I sighed and he added, "Forgive me, okay?" He took my hand.

118

"Take me home and start accepting my opinions like they matter if you ever want to get in my pants," then I pointed at him, "and, it wouldn't hurt for you to start treating me like I'm special to you."

"You are," he insisted with a crooked grin and I shook my head and smiled.

"Take me home, Dustin."

"Yes, ma'am." The dummy saluted me.

20

Grace age 16

Noah age 17

Shit. She's not here.

Never mind.

She storms in when I least expect her, my heart stops—the stars fucking align... then I see him go to her.

I'm going to kill him. I'm going to kill him. Those are the only words I can muster inside my head as I watch from a distance.

N.P.

Friday morning started out horribly. I awoke to a tiny bit of a cold and to make matters worse, Gus slept on my uniform and now his black hairs were all over it. I tossed it in the washer before going to school and prayed it didn't stink by the time I was able to get home from school and stick it in the dryer. *Only* to get home from school and remember that I couldn't stick it in the dryer. So, there I was, running around fanning my crinkled-up uniform all over the house, coughing every few seconds.

Sara would be here soon to pick me up and I was almost ready to give it up and call it a day. I didn't feel like I had it in me to cheer with a cough and damp uniform in late September weather where the nights were often chilly.

fall from grace

Dustin called and sounded all too eager that I should sit this game out, and when I called and told Coach, she told me it was fine. Sara didn't want me to miss the game and even threatened to still come get me but I acted pathetically worse than what I felt and she finally relented.

Great. I was missing the first game of the school year. So much for joining the team again.

Or so I thought until Mom burst through the door like a woman on a mission and eyed me and Gus viciously as we cozied up on the couch munching on popcorn. "Get dressed. You're not missing this game!" she yelled, running upstairs.

I looked at Gus and he looked at me... What was her deal? She came back down and tossed my uniform at me. "Mom, look, it's all crinkly and the game just started."

She huffed, crossing her arms. "I don't care. I got exactly ten minutes to get you to the football game before I'm needed back at the game I'm working," she said urgently.

"Mom," I groaned and smiled when Gus placed his entire head in the popcorn bag.

"Just get up, Grace. I told you, you're gonna regret these little chances to live and meet someone new at your age. Listen to your mom, she knows what she's talking about."

"Fine," I grumbled. "No more, Gus, your legs are too short. What if your belly starts hanging?"

She didn't even give me any time to fix my hair and face. I had just enough time to put on my uniform. So when she practically shoved me out the car door and left on the football field, I was still adjusting my uniform and putting my hair in a ponytail, trying my best to make myself presentable. I ran across the track and saw that we were booing while the other team was cheering. I saw why. One of the other team's player was running for a touchdown, our team way behind him.

121

And he just came to a complete stop, inches from landing his touchdown. Wait… was he looking at me—he was looking at me. Two, three—four of our school's players tackled him down at once. The whole crowd went into a panic and I brought my hands into fists and backed away. "Oh my God," I said aloud as I watched them climb off him. I saw Dustin was one of them. His #5 rested against our purple and gold school colors. He saw me and came running, removing his helmet as he scooped me up. "I thought you were staying home?" he asked and placed a quick kiss on my lips.

I covered my mouth and leaned away. "I have a cold," I told him and he placed me on my feet. "And Mom made me." I looked over at the other team's player. The other guy was #22 for the other team and their colors were black and blue. He was looking over this way… "Is that guy gonna be okay?" I asked Dustin and he pulled me forward.

"Yeah." He hurried me. "Go cheer for me," he urged me, smacking my butt and walking back on the field. I covered my butt and glared as he walked away before I caught #22 looking my way again. I tugged at my ponytail and looked away. This stranger was making me feel self-conscious. Maybe I looked worse than I thought I did. He had completely stopped running when he saw me.

I peeked at him again but he was gone from the spot he was before. It didn't take me long to see him getting into position. He was a tall dude. I couldn't tell exactly how wide he was with the shoulder pads on but he had a nice butt… Crap, I was getting curious. I scanned the field for my boyfriend and checked out his butt too so that I didn't feel so guilty about it.

"Yay!" Sara chirped. "What made you change your mind?" she asked as I got into position with the girls.

"Feeling okay?" Coach asked and I nodded.

"You're gonna be glad—"

Coach didn't let Tiffany finish. "We're offense now. We didn't come to chitchat. Let's get to cheering, ladies."

fall from grace

We cheered our butts off but after every play, I was making googly eyes with #22 instead of my boyfriend. I didn't know what was wrong with me. The flame that Noah left me without was stirring for the eyes that sought me out through #22's helmet—my faceless flame. I wanted to see what he looked like. Playing this eye game with him did more for me than kissing my boyfriend. I wanted to feel guilty, but this feeling was what I'd been searching for since Noah introduced me to it then stole it away when he left.

He ended up scoring a touchdown without me distracting him this time, and I hadn't even realized I had been clapping my hands and cheering for him until Sara laughed. "Um, Grace, are you cheering for the other team?"

"It's not the other team she's cheering for," Tiffany mentioned, waggling her brows.

I was still looking at #22. I sighed a little breathy. "I wonder what he looks like." I turned to see them give each other a suspicious smile. "What?" I said through a cough.

"You sure you don't know who that is?" Sara asked with a slanted grin.

Her words had me piecing together the static in my heart. I dropped my smile and turned to look at #22 again. The game was almost over. A few seconds left on the clock and it was our ball. Only #22 intercepted the ball but was tackled down by one of ours before he could get another touchdown.

They won. We lost.

While they were lining up to shake hands, I found my feet moving and then I was running onto the field. Dustin pulled his arm out in front of me. "Where ya going, babe?" I glared at him. He never called me that. I pulled away from him.

"You knew, didn't you?" I asked and looked ahead as the two teams were lined up to shake hands. I didn't see him anywhere.

123

michelle gross

"Wait, Grace," Dustin told me.

There he was. He still hadn't taken off his helmet like everyone else had. He was in the back of the line. I ran to him, ignoring Dustin as he hollered my name again. If I was wrong, this was going to be embarrassing. If I was right... Then the world would have finally righted itself again.

He saw me coming and lifted his head, my eyes took in his eyes before I raised to my tiptoes and yanked his helmet off.

I wanted to cry because, for the first time in three years, it felt like time began to move again. His hair was cut shorter now and at this length, it was a darker blond than when it was longer. Blue eyes so bright, crinkled in the corners as he tipped his chin up at me. "Finally figured out who it was you've been eyeballing all night?" he asked. So sweet... his voice, the sound deeper and older than when he had left me.

"Noah," I finally broke down. He wiped the tears that started up. "Noah," I said again, this time a little bit angry.

"You just had to show up when ya did, didn't ya, Priss?" I tilted my head at him. "I would have scored us some more points if you hadn't stolen my damn sight with your beauty." I wasn't sure what to say. I wanted to hug him. I also wanted to punch him for being so calm. "You and Dustin, huh?" he asked, sounding pissed. He was looking behind us. I turned to see if it was Dustin coming toward us. He looked back down at me. "You want me to give you a ride home?"

Give me a ride home?

He said it like he hadn't been gone over three years without so much as a hello. "So, you have a car?" I asked very soft and slowly. "And you have your license yet..." I kicked him in the knee then proceeded to throw my fists against his chest.

He started hissing and backing away. "Ow, Grace, will you stop?"

"You haven't tried to contact me at all! You've had a way to and you haven't?"

"Ow," he yelped, grabbing my hands and dodging my kicks. His teammates were starting to point and talk but I didn't care. "Grace, look at me!" I did. "I did try to get in touch with you, more than once. Let me take you home, and I'll explain."

"I'll be the one taking my girl home," Dustin interrupted. I was even angrier because it made even more sense that Dustin was calling me all those pet names all night, it was because Noah was here!

Noah let go of me and held his helmet against his side with a dark smile. "You didn't even tell her, did you?" Dustin tensed at Noah's question.

"Tell me what?" I asked.

"Can you give us a sec, Grace? Wait by the bleachers and I'll take you home if you'll let me."

"You're not taking her anywhere, Noah."

"I'm going to let him drive me home, Dustin," I told him quickly before walking off, childishly leaving Noah with my boyfriend to deal with. I heard Dustin mutter and swear under his breath as I stepped away.

Sara and Tiffany were standing off of the field waiting for me, I was sure. They were both smiling but I wasn't. "Did you guys know he played for them this entire time and never told me?"

They both looked guilty. "He wasn't playing until last year," Tiffany stated.

"That's an entire year."

"Why do you think I wanted you here tonight?" Sara asked.

I threw my hands up. "That doesn't even make sense when you could have just told me and I would have come."

"It was your mom, Grace… She asked us not to tell you," Tiffany finally admitted.

"What?" That caught me off guard. "But she's the one that wanted me here tonight… So, this was why?" I thought back to how insistent she had been about me joining the team again.

Sara shrugged her shoulders. "Maybe she changed her mind."

"Besides, Dustin also asked us to keep it a secret… I'm sorry, you know we have a soft spot for his mean ass."

"Unbelievable," I muttered, walking off.

"Grace, we're sorry." They both started whining the entire time I was walking away. "Besides, Noah could have gotten in touch himself…"

I stopped walking. They spoke of the devil and he ran up to me. "Are you going to let me take you home?" he asked again.

I crossed my arms and looked ahead. "Yeah, let's go," I mumbled like my stomach wasn't a big bowl of happiness to see him again. "I'll talk to you guys later," I told the girls while they gave me big wide cheesy smiles as they looked back and forth between us.

I turned my head back when he wasn't following. He smirked. "This way." He pointed his head in the opposite direction that I was walking. "I parked on the other side."

I turned around. "Well, why didn't you say so?" I was a bit nervous being this close to him as we walked. I slid my gaze up his body as he moved. He was tugging at his shoulder pads. His arms… His chest… His legs, everything was so much *more*. I took a deep breath and shook my head as if it would dispel the heat flash I was having. "You could have changed, ya know," I told him.

He dropped his hand from his shoulder and smiled. "And risk you leaving with someone else?" I felt his eyes on me as I stared at the ground. "You aren't going to ask about your boyfriend?"

fall from grace

I looked up. "I'm kinda ticked at everyone right now for not telling me that they saw you last year," I told him. "But most of all, I'm hurt that you are playing football and going on with life without a care that I've been waiting to hear from you."

"I called the school the week after I was put into my foster home and spoke to your mom," he said, and my mouth dropped. "All I could think about was getting your house number so that I could hear your voice and feel stable again, but your mom wouldn't give it to me."

My stomach sank. How could Mom do that? She watched me cry for him every night and I even asked her to find out what school he was switched to! "My mom did?"

"Don't look hurt," he said, poking my cheek. "I was hurt at first, too but after a while, her words made sense, and I knew I had my own self-worth that I wanted to prove, to her, and anyone else that wanted to decide the way I felt for me."

"What did she say?"

We passed the gate and he stopped at a black beat-up looking Jeep. "This is the one," he told me.

"Is this yours?" I asked, and he nodded.

"Yep," he said, tapping the top of it with his knuckles. "The couple I'm staying with gave it to me in return that I work at their garage a few days a week in between school and practice."

I couldn't help but smile. "That sounds like you." He smiled at me and I focused on the gravel instead. "Are they good people? Your foster parents?"

He nodded again, smiling. "They're great. They're an older couple that started fostering when both their sons joined the army."

I sighed in relief. "I'm glad."

He grabbed my wrist and pulled me in. He enveloped me within the confines of his arms. I didn't care that he was sweaty. It was the sweetest I'd felt in a long time. "Been wanting to wrap you up in my arms since the moment I saw you tonight." He released me and tugged me to the passenger side. "Here," he said, opening the door for me. I climbed in and he slammed it shut. It was a little messy but it smelled like Noah. All Noah. It felt a little too good to be surrounded by his scent again. He ran back over to the driver's side and opened the door. He opened his Nike bag up and pulled out a shirt then he stood outside his door taking off his jersey. My entire body flushed with heat as I looked away then looked right back.

Dear Lord, you did right with him.

I don't remember that happy trail being there last time...

He climbed in after putting on a white t-shirt and yanking out the pads in his pants. I looked ahead quickly and wiped my forehead. Shew, this was a little intense being around him again. "What did my mom say to you when you called?" I asked again.

He started the engine. "She said for me to let you go for now, and if a few years passed and I still couldn't forget you, then she'd let us hang out again."

"And you listened to her?"

He backed out of the driveway. "Of course, I did. Parents hold all the control when we're young, so I did the only thing I could do and followed her words. I *tried* to live without picturing you in it some way but you were everywhere. At the tables I ate, I pictured you there. In the way someone said my name, your voice would haunt me. When I laid my head down to sleep every night, you were there waiting for me behind my eyelids."

Noah had experienced the same things I did. "So, I called her back last year and she promised me that we'd cross paths again."

"And you just believed her?"

He pulled out onto the highway. "I did, I trusted her... Although, I was getting a little restless. I might have drove by your house one too many times after getting my license in hopes that I'd see you by chance. I didn't expect her to make me wait an entire year. I also told Dustin to tell you where I was and I even gave him my number to give you. Now I know why you never called."

"I've only been dating him a few weeks so I don't understand why he didn't tell me sooner." I sighed.

"Ah, I would have done the same in his shoes… Besides, I don't care that you're dating anyone, I'm just glad to have you back in my life."

Wait, whoa, hold up.

That was not the words I wanted to hear from him. Dustin knew what would happen if I saw Noah again and tried to prevent it because he knew I'd break it off with him, which I planned to do. Now I couldn't admit that to Noah without him thinking I expected us to go back to where we left off. I mean, I *did.* But maybe Noah's feelings for me had changed?

My hopes all but crashed and died.

Did he have a girlfriend? "Are you seeing anyone?" I looked at the road as I asked in hopes that it sounded casual.

"No."

"But you've dated?" I leaned over, not so subtly.

"No," he said again. I couldn't help but look surprised so he added, "Not that I haven't done things other than dating…" He flashed his teeth at me.

I was a goner. He clearly had no interest in me whatsoever now or he wouldn't have admitted to sleeping with other girls so easily.

And to think, I hadn't messed around with anyone besides letting Dustin have a bit of boob action.

"What about you?" he asked. He was looking ahead as he asked.

"What?" I played dumb.

"Got rid of the cherry yet?" I wanted to cover my face but I didn't. Why did he have to word it like that?

"Well," I started, "Dustin has umm, touched my boobs, and," I stopped when I saw the goofy grin on his face and swore. "No, I'm a virgin," I huffed, looking out the window so I didn't have to see his face, but I saw it anyway in the shadow of the window... My breath caught and my throat tightened when I saw the smile he was giving me while I wasn't looking... And how his gaze swept over my body intimately before he turned his attention back to the road and gripped the steering wheel tighter.

"You sound disappointed that you are still one," he said.

"I'm not having this conversation with you tonight," I told him.

"But we'll continue it soon?"

"Why?" I turned and asked.

He lifted his shoulders. "You're the one that said 'tonight' like you meant we'd get to another night." I blushed. Why had I said it that way?

"I can't believe that you've managed to out pretty yourself... Can't you just, I don't know, hide some of it?"

That was the stupidest thing I'd ever heard him say. "Huh?"

"You have more freckles now," he noticed.

"Yeah," I muttered, grabbing my nose. "It kinda happens when you're out in the sun every summer."

"You've gotten...," *so handsome that it's devastating to my heart,* "taller."

He arched his eyebrow at me then focused back on the road. "Nothing else?"

130

"You have muscles now?" I stuttered somewhat, and he smiled.

"Looks like we're here." *Already?*

Dad was standing out on the porch as he let Gus out. "Wait, stop!" I told him. "Just pull right here." He stopped in front of our neighbor's house. I exhaled when Dad went back inside, only Gus was outside and he seemed to be a dog on a mission. "He never watches Gus when he lets him out," I grumbled more to myself.

"Gus?"

It was like Gus knew I was in the strange Jeep 'cause he came over next to the Jeep and started barking at the door. "What the—" Noah rolled his window down to look at Gus. "Is this short-legged thing Gus?" he turned and asked.

I squinted my eyes at him. "Hey now, I'll have you know, he's very sensitive about his height. We told him when he was a pup that he'd grow big like a Husky, so imagine his disappointment when his legs had a stunted growth."

He burst into laughter as he opened his door and helped Gus in. He hopped in my lap and tried to lick me in the face. "So, they finally let you have a dog." He sounded amazed.

"It was all thanks to you," I said, but I didn't feel like bringing up the day his mom passed away, so I didn't tell him anymore even when his face told me to elaborate.

I tilted my head and just watched him pet Gus and smile… My heart was still adjusting to having him near me again while my mind couldn't believe it. "Noah." He looked up with a smile. "Are you truly okay? You're seriously in a good home and things—"

"I'm fine, Grace, you can start asking me anything you want to know and I'll answer." I believed him. He looked over to the trailers.

"Do you want to see him?" I knew he'd know who I was talking about.

"No," he said straight away. "He's not supposed to have any contact with me anyway, but the choice will be mine once I'm eighteen…"

"The trailer's falling apart." I scratched Gus's ears and peered out the window with a frown. "I kinda broke his coffee table Monday," I admitted.

"You've been going to see him?" He didn't sound happy, he sounded frustrated.

"Don't give me that attitude, Noah. Do you have any idea how much I cried when I knew they were taking you away and you weren't coming back? And week after week slipped by without any word from you. I knew you didn't know my number but what about a phonebook?"

"The number's not listed," he grumbled.

"I was so scared because I knew you were being thrown in a stranger's home and I didn't know where. My parents wouldn't try to help me. I knew Dad wouldn't, but I thought Mom would have but she just gave me speech after speech about things righting themselves in time."

He was the one to speak this time, "I was devastated. I lost my Mom and home all in the same night. I was terrified of saying goodbye to you that night because you were the one that mattered most to me. When I finally got in touch with your mom, I thought *finally*, I was going to hear your voice again soon and then she told me to live without speaking or seeing you, and in my head, I was thinking, 'how do I live without her when I need her just so I can breathe easier while I cope'… But you weren't lost to me, Grace, you never were. I knew I'd have you back in my life, it helped me remember that I was always going to prove I'm worth something and you're that pivotal person in my life that I want it to be around."

He was a little out of breath from all the words he spilled while I was speechless. Gus barked and we both jumped. Noah grabbed his mouth and looked ahead as if he was just realizing what he said.

fall from grace

I wanted to kiss, hug, and squeeze him after that speech. I still had a boyfriend though. I needed to properly end things with Dustin before... Before what? I couldn't tell if he meant I was his most important person as a friend or something else. It could be either, and considering he brought up the sex stuff so casually...

"I think your mom's calling for Gus," he said, pointing toward my porch.

I frowned. "I should go."

"Yeah," he added quietly.

"Thanks for the ride," I mentioned as I got out of his Jeep so very slowly. I walked around and he rolled down his window. "Bye," I told him.

"Bye, Grace," he whispered. *Say something else. Stop me or I'm gonna go upstairs and cry!*

Don't look back. Don't look back. Keep going. I placed Gus down and he started running circles around me. Wait a second, I turned back around but Noah was already out of the Jeep.

"Grace!" he called my name.

"Your number!" we said at the same time and started laughing.

Feeling a little flushed, I grabbed my phone out of my spandex underwear and skirt—I kept it on my hip. "Do you have a cell phone?" I asked.

"Yeah, give me your phone, I'll save my number." I did and watched as he punched it in. I heard his phone go off in his Jeep as he handed it back to me.

"That would have been so painful to leave you again without a way to contact you," he told me with a silly grin.

"It really would have," I admitted, feeling the pain all over again that he was leaving.

Noah started waving. "Hi, Mrs. Harper."

I turned around and saw Mom waving back with a know-it-all grin. "Hi, Noah," she whispered then pointed toward the house to let us know she was being quiet because she didn't want Dad to know.

He looked at me with a soulful expression. "Bye, Grace."

"Bye, Noah."

I didn't move from that spot as I watched him get in his Jeep. My phone beeped just as he started it up and left. It was a text from him.

I want that pic of u and Gus

He had to be talking about my home screen.

just send me every picture of you. I want them all.

I hugged the phone to my chest.

Seven-year-old Noah tried to claim my treehouse as his own…

Thirteen-year-old Noah stole my first kiss…

Seventeen-year-old Noah stole my air to breathe and his right to exist in this world anywhere without me.

"My, what a beautiful night we're having tonight," Mom chirped behind me.

I coughed as I twisted around. "Why would you keep us separated for so long?"

"Because was your night not full of surprises and new romance?" Mom waggled her brows and literally spun around on her toes. She looked at me and sighed. "Distance makes the heart grow fonder. With the two of you already pining over each other as kids, imagine what that could amount to when you get older."

I rolled my eyes and didn't smile—even though she looked goofy. "Mom stop making this a joke. You played with your daughter's feelings, how could you do that?"

134

fall from grace

From her expression, I knew she had become serious about it. "I wanted to see what Noah would do... I refused to give him our number and told him to adjust to his surroundings and not to disappoint me, and of course, I told him to do all this without having contact with you." Mom bunched up her shoulders as she walked across the porch and bent over the banister. "I told him to call me in a few years if he still wanted to get in touch with you, and of course, he called back. End of story."

"I don't get it. Why'd you do it?"

"Because, my darling daughter, you might not believe it but I've been rooting for Noah in my own way. I always will even though it doesn't look like it. I want Noah to succeed in whatever he plans to do with his life. I just know that you are a huge part of that goal." I frowned and she turned away with a smile. "I mean, you're the reason that boy doesn't know how to let anything get him down. He's got a lot to prove from the looks of it. I wonder who he wants to prove himself to and who it is he's doing it for?" She eyed the house then me before she started giggling like a kid. "I feel like I'm truly blessed to have gotten to see the two of you grow up together."

I shook my head and finally smiled. "I give up." I climbed the porch steps and hugged her. "Thanks for sending me back to Noah, and thanks for believing in him like I do."

"I believe in you too."

21

Grace age 16

Noah age 17

I'm giddy the whole drive home. I can't stop smiling. It doesn't matter that she's with Dustin. She's still the Grace I know. She's still my Grace. She'll come back to me.

N.P.

I called Dustin as I walked up the stairs but it went to voicemail. There was a good chance that he was ignoring my calls. I sent him a text.

Can you call me?

My phone beeped a few seconds later.

I'm not callin just 4 u 2 break up w me

I wasn't going to feel bad for ending things with him. He had kept Noah's whereabouts from me. He knew what Noah meant to me while he kept asking me out. Even though I said that, I still felt guilty. Maybe in his own way, Dustin really liked me or it could have just been because I never gave him attention like all the other girls… Maybe this was his way of being better than Noah. He had always been competitive with him.

No matter, it was my feelings that were never going to change. I couldn't keep seeing someone I wasn't attracted to, and not after Noah finally stepped back into my life.

Me: **It is over, Dustin, we both know it. I'm sorry.**

Dustin: **So that's it, ur getting with Noah just like that?**

Me: **Of course not! We didn't even talk about getting together. I didn't even tell him I was breaking up with you!!!**

Dustin: **If you say so.**

I stared at the screen as I shut my bedroom door behind me and plopped down on the bed. I tapped on Noah's text from earlier and started smiling. He saved his number under Noah, but I went in and added some heart and kissy faces next to it. *Ah, much better.*

I wondered how long it took him to drive home and if he was still on the road? I wanted to text him but I was afraid he was still driving. I wouldn't tell him I broke up with Dustin for now either. If I told him, I'd make it too obvious that I wanted to go back to what we were becoming to each other at thirteen. I understood his reason for listening to my mom more than anyone else that kept it from me. I knew Noah was someone that tried to respect and understand adults, especially my parents.

I sent him the picture of Gus and me then sent him a text.

If you're still driving, text me when you make it home.

After I hit send, I wondered if maybe I shouldn't have sent anything and just waited for him to contact me. I fell back and placed the phone on my head and sighed. I had no patience when it came to him. I'd waited almost four years to finally hear from him again.

I showered and blow dried my hair and came back to my room to see that I had a text from him. I hoped I didn't destroy my phone charger when I yanked it off charge.

I'm home.

This is a good pic of u.

I smiled as I climbed into bed.

Me: **You told me you'd tell me what I wanted to know.**

Noah: **I did. What do u want to know?**

Me: **I want to know about the couple that you're living with, and I want to know what you've been doing the past few years.**

Noah: **Their names are Dean and Janet. I already told u their boys are in the army... Dean owns a garage over here in Jewel CO. I've learned a lot of shit I didn't know about cars while working there. They're cool folk, Grace, stop worrying. They pay for my car insurance and everything, and wouldn't even ask me to help out at the garage if I didn't tell them I wanted to...for the Jeep, insurance, phone, and extra cash.**

Me: **So now that Mom set us up to meet again...**

Noah: **We can see each other whenever we want.**

He finished for me. My cheeks were hurting from smiling so much at the screen.

Noah: **Is Dustin upset w u?**

Me: **Yeah.**

I didn't text him what I really wanted to say: that I broke up with Dustin.

Noah: **Do u care if I call?**

Me: **Go ahead.**

I coughed a few times and straightened out my voice before it started ringing. I answered immediately. "Hey," I breathed.

"Hey." His voice sounded lively. "Seemed kinda pointless to text each other after going so long without hearing your voice."

"Yeah, I know."

"Don't let Dustin be an ass about me taking you home."

"I'm not," I told him.

fall from grace

"You looked beautiful tonight… You were always my favorite thing to look at though," his voice sounded like it had gotten deeper just now.

"Noah." I couldn't stop smiling as I covered my face for the billionth time because my face was so warm.

"I shouldn't be saying that to you when you're with Dustin, though," he added. Did he not want me thinking there were more to his words?

"Yeah, you shouldn't be."

He chuckled softly before he blew into the phone. "This feels so good, Priss," he admitted. "I've missed this so much, just being able to talk to you. I've missed you."

"I've missed you so much," I told him back.

"Finally, I feel like I'm finally getting somewhere. Life just makes sense to me when you're in it."

I knew exactly what he meant.

"I still can't believe I'm talking to you," I murmured.

"I know, I was beginning to think your mom had just told me to wait and was never actually going to give in … I'm glad she did though, I was at the end of my rope. I was about to come see you with or without her permission." I moved off the bed and turned off my light before crawling underneath my covers. Then I ended up having to bend down and help Gus up on the bed. "What are you doing?" he asked.

"I just turned off the lights and crawled underneath my covers," I said as I got comfortable.

"I was wondering why you got quiet on me." His voice was softer now.

"Keep talking," I ordered him as I closed my eyes and waited for his words.

He laughed. "Are you going to sleep?"

"It's just been so long since I've felt this comfortable," I mumbled.

"I feel like I can run a marathon after seeing you tonight, and I'm putting you to sleep? Just how boring am I?"

"You're not boring at all," I promised.

"Don't go to sleep on me, Grace, I don't want to let you go so soon."

"Mm."

He sighed. "Grace?"

"Keep talking," I whispered.

"At least I'm the last person that gets to hear your voice tonight... It's a start. Grace? You fell asleep for real, didn't you...? I'll never be able to sleep... and you're blowing in my ear. That's the best sound I've heard in a long time... Goodnight, Grace."

———

After falling asleep on Noah the night before, I was tempted to see if he wanted to hang out until I found out he was already at the garage working when I got up. I didn't know what time he'd get off.

I also had a bunch of text messages from Sara and Tiffany apologizing that they had done as my mom asked them to do. What was even more surprising was how the two were able to keep it from me since last football season. That was also why Sara tried to get me to come to the game. She knew he'd be there. I got it, I guess to them, me seeing Noah for the first time in that way would be a whole lot better than them telling me.

Around noon, Noah sent a text saying he had a few minutes to talk while he was eating.

fall from grace

"Hi, Noah," I basked in the glory of getting to speak to him again.

"What are you doing?" It was loud in the background where he was in the garage.

"Lying here with Gus," I told him. "How long are you going to be at the garage?"

"I normally leave around six," he said through bites of whatever he was eating. It would be too much trouble to ask him to come see me, especially when he lived in another county.

"How long did it take you to get home last night?"

"I think forty-five minutes? I don't know, I didn't pay attention." More banging in the background. "You got plans tonight?"

"Hold on," I told him as I looked to see who just texted me. It was Tiffany. "I don't have any plans but Tiffany just asked me to sleep over at her house today."

"You actually have sleepovers now." He laughed. "Well, besides the ones with me."

"Yes," I huffed. "You make me sound like a hermit or something."

"You never did any of those things when I lived there," he pointed out.

I bit my lip. *Because* I hadn't wanted to share him with anyone. And even before I became possessive over him, I never thought I needed anyone else besides him to play with. Now I wanted to do a different kind of *playing*. I rubbed my eyes, *listen to me.*

"I think it's great," he mentioned. "Tiffany and Sara are probably a lot more fun to hang out with than Dustin."

"Says the guy that was friends with him all through grade school," I couldn't help but say.

"And the girl that couldn't stand him in grade school is now dating him," he countered back.

I opened my mouth to say what I really, truly wanted to say, but I stopped. "You keep bringing up Dustin."

"He's your boyfriend."

"That doesn't mean you have to keep bringing him up."

"You're right."

"I want to hear everything you've done."

I thought I heard him choking on something. "What?" he finally said.

"I want to know everything you've done with another girl, and I want to know how many."

"Grace…" he said it like a swear. "I can't have this conversation here and now."

"So, tonight then?"

"That's not what I meant," he tripped over his words. "Isn't it a little inappropriate for you to be asking me this question when you have a boyfriend?"

I sighed. "You're gonna tell me… I'm curious Noah, you've gone and touched and *done it* with other girls…," *and not me,* "and I'm still stuck—" on *you.*

I heard another male in the background. "I gotta go, Grace, I'll call you tonight okay?"

I frowned. "Okay…"

The moment we hung up, I received a text message from him

I'll tell u whatever u want 2 know 2nite.

I sent him a happy face emoji.

fall from grace

Only I ended up staying the night at Tiffany's where her and Sara overloaded me on chocolate so that I would forgive them. I kept my phone close and sighed all night, disappointed that I was missing out on the conversation I wanted to have with Noah.

"After the show you gave everyone at the football game last night, everyone's going to believe Dustin," Tiffany bit into a piece of pizza as she spoke.

"Hello, earth to Grace, don't you care that Dustin's most likely going to make you sound like the wicked witch of the west?" Sara threw a chip at me. What was with my friends and them throwing stuff?

"Not really," I mumbled, glancing at my phone.

"Ugh!" Tiffany groaned.

"You two helped him keep it a secret from me," I mentioned and they both started smiling.

"Here, would you like another piece of cake, my Grace?" Sara bowed her head at me and I tried not to smile. "I've been rooting for Noah all this time, but I also wanted to stay chummy with Dustin, do you understand what I'm saying? Help a girl out! You can't have them both."

"I don't want Dustin," I told her.

She crossed her arms. "Then why did you say yes after all this time?"

My mouth fell open as I looked at her. "Because I wanted to…" They both started squealing and I rolled my eyes. "But I should have known I wouldn't have felt that bottomless feeling in my stomach with Dustin."

"I know I would," Sara said.

Tiffany shook her head at her. "So, you and Noah aren't together yet?"

I shook my head. "I want to see him again already but I don't know how to ask him. It's been so long, I'm afraid that this time apart has let him slip through my fingers."

"Nah," Tiffany and Sara both started saying the same thing. "He was looking for you on the field last year, and last night was the same way. Besides what boy is gonna contact your mom's work just to try and get in touch with you?"

"I don't want Noah as a friend though," I muttered. "I want all of him, in every way and it's making me want to breathe fire out of my mouth when I think of him being with another girl."

"It's not a big deal, Grace, most of the guys at our school aren't virgins. It was painful when I lost mine, I'm not gonna lie," Sara said, giving me a pained expression.

She didn't understand how I felt, though, neither of them could. Noah and I would have been each other's firsts. I could have shared that with him until life stripped it away from me.

"Just imagine, he's got the experience to make it feel better for you, for when you do finally," Tiffany winked, "ya know."

"You're so lame," Sara told her.

Noah already knew how to do those things before. I had already experienced a taste of what he could do to my body.

22

Grace age 16

Noah age 17

Every chance I get while I'm working at the garage, I pull out my phone and stare at the picture she sent me the night before of her and Gus. She's so damn beautiful I can't stand it. I need to see her again so bad that it hurts. I think it's worse now that I've finally seen her again. Now, I know what I've missed, how much she's grown like I have over the years and it's fucking depressing because I know without a doubt, Grace should have been my girl.

Somehow, Dustin got her.

Not for long.

My future hasn't changed. Grace is still the only thing I see.

N.P.

Sara said I looked a little too happy when she dropped me off at my house before going home herself. Noah left me alone last night so that I could hang out with the girls. After a fresh shower, Mom let me get some driving in today. I was going to call and make my appointment to take my test this week or next.

I sent Noah a text when we got home.

Me: **I'm home & I still remember the conversation we're supposed to have**

He texted back immediately.

Noah: **Like I could 4get how insistent and blunt you can be when it comes to... well, everything?**

I snorted and Dad looked up from his tablet. I moved from the couch and went to my room.

Me: **Good, as long as you know**

Noah: **No hot date with Dustin 2nite?**

Me: **Just me and Gus.**

I wondered how long I could keep from not telling him about me being boyfriend-less before I crawled onto his lap and let him figure it out on his own? Not that I had much to worry about. It didn't look like it was going to be easy to see him.

Noah: **Sounds like a wiener to me.**

LOL get it?

Winner.

I should just stop now.

I burst into giggles.

Shit. That didn't even make sense, did it?

Grace?

Dkjfkdfjgkfjkj

After all the texts, he called and I swiped my finger across the screen but couldn't answer because I was still laughing. "There you are," he said when he heard me. "Was it that funny? Breathe Grace. You need to get out more if you think my lame jokes are funny."

I finally calmed down somewhat. "That was just so random," I snorted and now he was the one laughing. "I don't know, I guess I haven't laughed like that in a while so it saw your lame text as a good outlet."

"I really want to see you Grace," he surprised me by saying.

"Me too," I said a bit too breathy for someone that was supposed to have a boyfriend.

"How about we… hang out next weekend?" he asked.

My heart leaped from my chest. "I'd really like that."

"Think your mom will let you?" he asked. She wasn't the one I worried about but I didn't plan on telling Dad as long as Mom didn't.

"Yeah." I curled my feet up as I sat on the bed. "So…"

"I know where you're going, and we are not having this conversation at two o'clock in the afternoon," he paused. "I'll call you tonight then you can ask me whatever until you're satisfied."

"I feel like you're trying to prolong this conversation as long as you can."

He sighed into the phone. "I don't want to tell you what I've done with another girl."

"Too bad," I said.

"Why are you so curious?" he asked suddenly. "I feel like this will only make the distance between us seem bigger than I want it to be."

Because I was a glutton for punishment, apparently. "We've always been close, even more than Sara and Tiffany, you've always been my best friend… What's wrong with telling each other these things? I would tell you if I had…"

"All right, Priss," he muttered. "I'll tell you everything in *detail* tonight so that you're pretty little head is satisfied."

I wasted the day away waiting for night to fall just so I could hear Noah's dirty details. My brain wasn't wired right when it came to him. I was sad that he had been with other girls but at the same time, I couldn't wait to hear what all he'd done. Maybe if I hadn't seen Noah this Friday, I would have eventually gone further with Dustin and would've had a story to share with Noah. But more than a story, I wanted Noah to be in mine.

Now that I knew where to look on Facebook, I found myself on several people's profiles that went to the same school as Noah and regretted it as soon as I had. A lot of the girls had pictures of him in class, on the field, just doing all sorts of things. I saw several of him from two years ago and my stomach dropped that I had missed little things that all these other people got to see. If only Noah had an account, I would have been able to find him sooner... He never cared for things like that though... I stumbled across a picture of him with some pretty blonde hugging him and he was smiling in a different direction from the camera...

Yep, I thought that was enough of torturing myself for the evening.

Dustin had also switched his status back to single and posted obvious quotes aimed at me... I rolled my eyes and tossed my phone on the bed.

Ugh... *Call me Noah.*

Gus was at my feet biting my toes to get my attention. I scooped him up in my arms when my phone started going off. I squeaked and jumped on the bed with Gus. His ears flattened as he momentarily looked at me like I had lost my mind.

"Hey," I said nice and easy despite my excitement.

"What are you doing?" he asked. I heard rustling in the background.

"What are you doing?" I asked.

"Nothing, just got out of the shower. Heading to my room now," he said.

"Well, now, shall we begin?" I got straight to the point.

He laughed lightly. "You don't waste no time."

I helped Gus with the cover after he struggled to get himself underneath it before I climbed underneath it myself and lay on my side.

"Well, what do you want to know?"

"Everything," I told him. He groaned so I asked, "How many?"

"Just one."

"Just one?" I repeated, incredulous. "I've not even gotten to the one."

"Is this what this is about?" I could hear the smile in his voice. "You hate that you're still a virgin? Dustin that lacking when it comes to kissing?" he couldn't help but ask.

"Don't change the subject," I griped. "Did you like her...?"

He laughed at me. "Well, I sure didn't hate her."

"You know what I mean," I groaned. "Was it l—love or just—"

"I just wanted to have sex, Priss, I wanted to explore the female body inside and out so I did. So that I can please that special someone when I finally..."

He let his words fade and I blushed. "So... What did you do with her?"

"Everything."

"Everything?" I covered my mouth and repeated. My face was so warm.

"I guess not everything... I haven't tried anal."

"Noah," I gasped and he laughed. This was painfully embarrassing for some reason. "I don't think I'd ever want to do *that*," I told him honestly.

"I was waiting for you to say that."

"Well." I smiled and gripped my phone. "Did you make her feel good?"

"You should know better than anyone that I'm all about making her feel good... don't ya, Grace? After all, you were the first girl I ever gave an orgasm to." I felt his words between my thighs. I pressed them together. This was the first time we were bringing up the events that happened before he was taken by social services. At the same time, my heart hurt because I wanted those things with Noah. "What's wrong? You've gone all quiet on me," he whispered, his words almost seemed sad.

"I hate it, Noah," I couldn't stop myself. "I thought I'd be—that you'd be—"

"I know," his faint voice soothed and broke me all at once. "When I contacted your mom the second time, I didn't know what we'd go back to, I made the choice to do things. I thought that you would make the same choices. Hell, I was terrified that you would forget about the trashy boy that was your best friend."

"I could never forget you, Noah."

Silence.

He finally said, "Even after all this time, nothing's changed, has it? To me, you're my best friend." He paused. "You're still everything."

I sunk my head into my pillows to stifle the tears. "You're my best friend too, Noah. Always."

23

Grace age 16

Noah age 17

I want her to come to me. I want to wrap my arms around her and strip her bare, just being able to hold her will be enough, but I can't do those things because of the fear that I'd only push her away since she's with Dustin. I'm in her life as a friend, but that's definitely not where I want to stay.

How do I seduce my best friend into leaving her boyfriend without hurting my relationship with her?

N.P.

Dustin ignored me all week and there were rumors circulating around Monday that I cheated on him, which probably came from his mouth. Not that I cared as long as it didn't give me trouble with the other girls on the cheer squad, I couldn't be too sure about some of them. I also checked our schedule to see if the boys would be playing against Noah's team again, and we were, next month.

I didn't visit Noah's dad this week. I didn't get to talk to Noah much either between school, practice, and two ball games we cheered this week. It was the same for him plus he worked at the garage and had weightlifting.

I scheduled my driver's test for the next week and got Mom's okay to go out with Noah this weekend, neither of us told Dad about it either.

I left Gus in the house when I slipped outside to wait on Noah to pick me up. Mom and Dad were in the kitchen cooking and I didn't know where Mom told him I was going. I just wasn't ready to let him know that Noah was back in my life.

I put on a bit of makeup despite telling myself not to. I couldn't help it, I'd been looking forward to seeing him again all week. I was wearing a pair of jeans and a lowcut shirt that revealed what my mama gave me. I had on a thin gray jacket and boots. My brown hair was down and straightened.

And when I saw his Jeep coming, I ran through the yard and out in front of him before he could even stop. So much for playing it cool. He looked like he was laughing as I darted around his Jeep and climbed in. "You don't even give a person time to stop," he told me, his eyes roving over me. "You look good, Priss, real good."

I raked my eyes over him the same way he had me. He had on a pair of light colored jeans with a plain black t-shirt that hugged his wide frame. He smelled good too, like *really* good. Whatever cologne he was wearing had me wanting to crawl over onto his lap. His smile, though, that was my favorite. He had a dimple when he smiled but only on one side. "You look good and smell good too," I told him and looked ahead to keep from feeling put on the spot.

He started driving and I found myself staring at his arms, and chest, and well, *everything*. I looked up, feeling sneaky for checking him out for so long. "So, what are we doing?" He never told me over the phone, he just said he'd think of something.

He tilted his head back and smirked at me. "I seem to recall a promise I made, to always take you on an adventure." I smiled at the memory and he turned his attention back to the road.

fall from grace

"Just what kind of adventure are we talking about here?" I asked him.

He gave me a devious grin before moving his hand to the back seat. When he brought his hand back up front, he held a flashlight that he shined in my face before turning it back off. "A spooky one." He laughed mechanically.

I stared ahead and leaned back into my seat and said, "Oh, dear God."

"We'll grab some burgers on the way," he added.

"We're seriously going somewhere creepy, ain't we?" I asked, feeling my stomach knot up.

"Yea, I'm glad you wore boots and jeans. It'll be dark in another hour or so." His eyes lit up with mischief.

After going through the drive-thru at Wendy's, we ended up at the end of some random hollow. He parked off the small one-lane road on the grass. I hoped whoever's yard this was didn't mind. I noticed a small foot trail heading into the trees. We weren't going through that, were we? It was almost completely dark outside; another ten minutes and it would be. The burger I ate rested in my stomach uncomfortably.

"Here, wear this over your jacket. It might get a little too chilly for that thin one you have." He handed me a hoodie from the back seat. I put it on before getting out. I took another look at the trees, so eerie and way creepier than what I remembered the woods being as a kid. Maybe it was because it was dark. "I feel like… I'm not as brave as I was when we were kids," I whispered.

He walked up next to me and laughed. "No kidding. You're a lot different than what you were when we were kids. I can remember you hated the idea of kissing and things." I rolled my eye. "Now look at ya, you're frustrated that you're still a virgin."

I glared at him. "That's because you scarred me for life with that porn video."

He shook his head. "Come on," he said with a smile on his lips and when his hand came out for mine, I didn't know how to react. I just stood there. "I figured you'd rather me hold your hand as I walked us to where we're going... I was gonna fill you in on the story of Burt's wife and how she still roams these woods after Burt tied a noose around her neck and left her hanging in the tree to go find her secret lover... But I suppose Dustin wouldn't like that. Does he even know you came here with me?"

I grabbed his arm and held on tight. "It's probably better this way, right?" He kept turning the light on and off. "Will you keep it on! We can't even see anything." I paused a moment. "What about wolves or bobcats?" We started moving and I looked around but couldn't see anything beyond what the flashlight showed me. "What about bears?"

"Don't worry, your loud mouth will scare anything around away," he teased, letting me lean into him as we walked. "Watch out for that log," he told me as we stepped over it.

"Where are we going?" I said in a hushed tone. Something other than us made a sound in the trees. "Did you hear that?" I asked.

"No," he leaned in, "what was it?"

I strained my ears. "I hear something, Noah, it's like something's walking besides us."

"I don't hear anything." How could he not hear that? "Is it a female voice crying out, '*Burt, I'm coming for you... Burt*'." He was messing with me.

I smacked his arm but still held onto him. "Seriously, Noah, I hear something." There was a scratching noise. "I'm scared," I panicked. He wrapped his arm around my shoulders and I instinctively wrapped my arms around him.

His light went out. "Shit," he muttered.

"What's wrong?"

fall from grace

"I think the batteries need to be changed."

A male voice shrieked somewhere in the trees around us and I screamed as soon as I heard the painful wail. I clawed at Noah, forcing my way into his hands. I fumbled around in the pitch black. "Grace," he whispered, sounding panicked himself. His hands came over my butt and hauled me up but I was too wild for that to happen smoothly. He held me upright as he fell to the ground, keeping me tucked above him.

I was still screaming when the flashlight came on between us. His evil grin played with my heart as he shined the light in his face and started laughing like a hyena. Now that I wasn't screaming anymore, I could hear two other voices laughing behind us. "Noah," I hissed, jabbing my elbow into his chest until he hissed. "This is not the kind of adventures I was talking about."

"Ow," he said while laughing. "You never were specific."

"Damn," a male muttered behind us. I moved off Noah and stood. "I bet my parents could hear her back at the house."

"What the hell are you two doing here?" Noah asked as he stood.

"Here's the keys," the other guy tossed them to Noah.

"We couldn't help it," said the black-headed guy. "When we heard y'all coming up the road, we ran up here to wait to scare you both."

"Like I wouldn't know it was you guys," Noah told them.

"You didn't plan it then?" I squinted my eyes at Noah.

"Finally, it's nice to put a face to the one he talks about all the time since his ass moved over here in the seventh grade."

"Jack," Noah warned. "These two idiots are Jack and Lance." He pointed to each of them.

I pushed my hair back and tried to smile. My heart was still racing from being terrified. "I'm Grace."

"Oh, we know who you are," Lance informed me and I couldn't help but smile.

"Okay, you had your fun," Noah told them. "We're heading up to the cabin. Tell your dad I said thanks for letting me bring her up here."

"We picked up what you asked for," Lance said then winked at me. I gave Noah a strange look and he just shook his head.

"What was he talking about?" I asked once we started the opposite direction of them.

"You'll see." It only took a couple of minutes to get to the cabin. It was small and simple. I saw power lines so it had electric. "It's not your treehouse but it's close enough," he told me as he unlocked the door and turned on the lights. Everything was all in one small room. A small gas stove and table with a bed at the far end on the left. There was also a small TV. The bathroom had to be the door on the right.

"This place is cute, I like it."

He turned back and smiled. "I knew you'd like it." He walked over to the TV. "I've spent a lot of weekends here with Lance and Jack."

"They seem like decent guys despite giving me a heart attack earlier," I told him.

"They are," he agreed.

"I'm glad you were able to make friends… It seems like life has been good to you the last few years…"

"It has, but nothing was worth losing you for that time."

I placed my hands together before he tossed something at me and I had to jump to catch it. I smiled when I saw what it was. "*The Neverending Story.*" We watched both one and two religiously during the winter months when we were stuck inside.

"That's what I had them pick up for me."

fall from grace

I blushed because I had thought they had been talking about something very different. "Oh."

He smirked. "Yeah, *oh.*" He took off his jacket. "I don't know what you're thinking but I'm sure you shouldn't with a boyfriend."

"You don't know anything," I muttered and he turned around, *don't make eye contact Grace.* "So, they're okay with you staying overnight with friends and things?" I changed the subject.

He nodded. "Yeah, they trust me." I took off my jacket and sat down on the small yellowish sofa. "What time do you have to be home?" he asked.

"Eleven."

"So, we should probably leave around ten," he thought about it. "That gives us a few hours."

"Put in the movie," I shooed him up when he was about to sit down next to me.

"Always the Priss." But he put it in. "Popcorn?"

I shook my head. "No, just come sit down and let me see if you're still as comfortable as you use to be." I patted the spot next to me.

He plopped down and my shoes were already off when I put my feet on him. I leaned back. "Ah, yep. Nothing like the comfort of having you next to me."

"Yeah," his voice sounded weird.

Only as the movie played, we were oddly quiet and what was once comfortable was quickly becoming an outlet of energy that flowed between us. I found myself eyeing him instead of the movie, then he'd do the same to me. I couldn't find any words to say that wouldn't end with me admitting that I haven't moved on from where we left off at thirteen. Noah was quiet too, but I didn't know his reason like I did mine. He rubbed his fingers against the bottom of my feet through my sock and I'd snicker then get quiet again. Our eyes kept meeting across the glow of the low-lit room. Sparks were freaking flying was what it felt like to me, but I also tasted the fear as it rested at the end of my tongue, telling me that Noah might treasure me in a different way than I wanted him to—the way he used to.

By the end of the movie, I felt like I'd combust from all the sexual tension I created inside my head just being around him. I couldn't even think of a conversation to have with him, I was so disrupted by it. This was what I wanted, what Noah so easily gave me, but I was afraid to act on them. I was afraid to tell him the truth about breaking it off with Dustin last weekend because being with Dustin when I had been pining over him had been futile from the very beginning.

And just like that, my night with Noah came to an end. The silence absorbed us even on the way home. Noah's brows were pinched together and he kept gazing at me from the corner of his eyes but he wasn't smiling. It made me anxious. I didn't get his smile until I was stepping out of his Jeep.

"I had fun Noah," I told him. "I'm a little sad that it's over so quickly."

That was when he smiled. "I know what you mean."

He argued with me to go inside, but I protested and watched him go because I wanted him to *stay*.

I tiptoed into the house but Mom still stepped out to check on me before going back to watch whatever she had their TV on. Once I was in my room, I slid out of my jeans and left Noah's hoodie on that he hadn't asked to have back and climbed underneath my covers where I slipped my hand inside my panties to relieve what Noah had caused. I didn't even have to work for it, it came so easily. Gus eyed me afterward and I placed the cover over my head and turned on my side to ignore his judgmental stare.

24

Grace age 16

Noah age 17

Two weeks of nothing but phone calls. Nothing but her voice. I'm on edge. I can't be around her like I want. It's too dangerous because if I act on what I feel, I might ruin everything. I can hold out until Dustin's out of the picture. It doesn't even feel like he's even in the picture. It feels like I get all her time on the phone at night, but maybe I'm only thinking what I'm wishing for.

I flirt, I tease just enough that she has to notice because I get her to blush and sometimes the way she talks, it's like we are on the same page, yet she's still with Dustin and I'm still tiptoeing around her when all I want to do is bulldoze into her.

I can hold out... Who am I kidding? I'm fucking miserable. She's right there, yet... I still can't have her like I want.

N.P.

I passed my driver's test Thursday morning. Noah was the first person I told other than Mom who had been with me. She dropped me off at school and went back to work herself, her sub was only there for one class period.

I spent the next two weeks talking to Noah constantly on the phone or through text. It was often after one before we got off the phone. There was just one problem.

He was avoiding me.

He had no problem with us talking all the time… He just always had something else to do every time I asked him if he wanted to hang out. I knew he worked at the garage and had weightlifting and practice to deal with, but he still had his Saturday evenings and Sunday's. Now I was beginning to overthink and worry that something had gone wrong when we hung out. I had been quiet that night because I wanted to kiss and touch him, but I was starting to think that Noah's silence had been the exact opposite. What if he didn't even want me as a friend anymore? What if… after hanging out with me for a few hours, he realized how boring I was?

That Saturday morning, I decided I was going to ask him about it… in person with Gus as my companion. He had told me the name of Dean's garage last week while we were on the phone. It was called "Dean's Auto Repair". I wasn't familiar with Jewel County and the fact that I was a new driver was worse, but I didn't let that stop me. I borrowed Mom's car and turned on the GSP lady and punched in the address I had found on the Internet for the garage.

What was about an hour drive, took two hours for me. The GPS lady had pulled me directly into someone's driveway which was so *scary* because a man had come out. I had no choice but to ask for directions while Gus barked like a crazy dog when he was coming but shook like a leaf when the man was standing next to the window. Needless to say, a computer was giving me trust issues but thankfully the man had given me better directions. Turned out, I was just a couple of turnoffs away from it. I looked for the red sign he had told me about and squealed when I saw it in the distance.

"We're here, Gus," I said as I put the car into park. "Thank the heavens." My mouth fell open when I saw how big the garage was. It was a lot bigger and cleaner than I had imagined with an ordinary name like *Dean's Auto Repair*. "Wow, this place is nice," I muttered to myself.

I rolled the window down at first, not sure if I should take Gus out with me. The huge garage door was wide open and the machine

160

noises filtered out. An elderly man stepped out and approached me. "Can I help ya, Miss?" he asked. He was greased up and oily but he looked like a kind person—sometimes you could just tell that about a person.

I stepped out of the car. "Um, is Noah here?" I asked.

He took another long look at me before smiling and taking off his hat to reveal his gray hair. He offered his hand to me and said, "You must be Grace." I nodded and shook his hand, feeling a little pleased that he knew about me, which meant Noah talked about me, which also meant that this must be—

"Dean?" I asked.

He nodded, adjusting the ballcap back on his head. "Yes, I reckon I'm the one." He looked into the car where Gus was giving me puppy dog eyes. "He won't hurt nothin' if ya wanna let him out." I opened the door and Gus jumped out. "Aye, Noah, you got a pretty little visitor," Dean shouted and I blushed as he turned back. "That's what you came here for, ain't it?" He winked and disappeared back in the garage. I peeked inside and saw Noah sliding out from underneath one of the vehicles. His eyes met mine immediately and his stunned reaction to me being here had me second guessing my decision. I smiled painfully bright and he finally smiled back.

"Gus!" I yelled because he was sniffing around the garage where others were working.

"He's fine," Noah said, standing up. I could hear someone talking to Gus and there was laughing but I couldn't take my eyes off greasy Noah. There was something appealing about the look of a hardworking man that wasn't afraid to get his hands dirty. He had on a pair of jeans and a black shirt with grease smearing his face and arms. His jeans were ruined already with old stains.

He strolled over to me. "What are you doing here, Grace?"

"I wanted to see you," I admitted.

161

He looked at Mom's car. "You drove?" he asked and I nodded. "How did you not get lost?"

"I did get lost," I mumbled. "I ended up in someone's driveway. He helped me with directions though."

He ran his hand through his hair, making it stick straight up. "That's dangerous, Grace. I can't believe your mom allowed you to drive this far when you just got your license a couple of weeks ago."

I sighed. "I'm not a bad driver, I'm just a nervous one," I defended myself. "Besides, if you would see me instead of blowing me off, I wouldn't have come over."

"You think I don't want to see you?" he asked, dumbfounded.

"You've dodged hanging out with me for two weekends in a row!"

"It's not as simple as I had wanted it to be." I held my breath, waiting for what he was about to say. "I thought I could see you as we are now, *friends*, but I can't. I don't. I *won't*." He brought his arms up.

"Do you mean…"

"Are you happy with Dustin? You don't even talk about him and it doesn't even seem like you hang out with him considering how much we talk to each other."

"About that," I started then my words got lost when I saw three men wandering around the front of the garage, watching and leaning in awfully close like they were being nosy. Noah turned around and they all busied themselves. One of them had been Dean.

Noah slowly exhaled before he turned back to me. "We can hang out this weekend."

"What about the game? We play you guys this Friday."

"Good," he nodded. "Catch a ride on the bus or with Tiffany or Sara instead of driving. I'll take you home after the game."

162

"Wouldn't that be too much trouble? Last time it was a home game for us and you were already close by. You'd be making a long trip to take me home this time."

"I didn't plan on taking you home straight away, you came all this way to make plans, didn't you? I'm giving you what you want."

I frowned. "Come on, Gus," I started hollering. His head popped out from Dean's arms.

"Oh no, what did I do now?" Noah asked.

"Nothing," I muttered. "I just feel a little foolish for coming so far to see you then even when you make plans with me, it feels like you don't want to. It makes sense, really, we're older now. I don't know why I expect you to want to still spend time with me like you used to."

Crap. I said too much. I was acting so immature and whiny. I was acting like... a spoiled girlfriend, when I had no right. I just wanted some of Noah's time, instead, I showed up at his workplace acting like a crazy person.

"Woah," Noah said, lifting his arms to grab my shoulders. "Where the hell is this coming from? I'm so damn confused, Priss, did I do something wrong?"

I dropped my head, embarrassed. "No," I mumbled. "I'm just being weird." Gus finally made his way back to me and Noah released my shoulders so I could pick him up. "I'm going to go. I'm sorry I came and acted like such a brat." I lifted my eyes to meet his and waited a second before I asked, "Are you mad?"

He smirked. "Why would I be? I got to see something interesting."

"Interesting?"

"I feel like I'm more important than Dustin, and it feels really fucking good."

163

I felt the heat rising in my cheeks and turned my face away. I was being so obvious that he was starting to notice. If I told him about Dustin now... What would he say? Why couldn't I say it? It felt like I was going to break out in hives to tell him the truth. What if I told him and he disappeared again?

Was that what I was truly worried about? Him leaving once we got close again?

"Are you going to be able to make it home?" he asked when I didn't say anything.

"I think so."

"Text me when you're home so that I know you made it back safely," he said before he flicked my nose. I grabbed it and finally looked at him again. "I'll talk to you tonight?"

The drive home consisted of me going through all the emotions: to embarrassment, giddiness, mortified, then back to feeling happy, followed by my other pal, ashamed that I came over and acted the way I did.

My feelings for Noah were changing me into this person I didn't recognize.

I kept regretting my decision to go see him, then I'd think it over and decide it was worth it because I made plans with him.

I was a hot mess.

Thank you, Noah.

Sincerely, my sanity.

25

Grace age 16

Noah age 17

I should have known. I should have trusted what I felt. The splash of red across her freckled cheeks always told me the truth, just like it is telling me now. Grace is my girl, not Dustin's.

She's never been anyone else's but mine.

N.P.

I stepped off the bus with Tiffany and Sara, pulling my spankies out of my butt crack. I was giddy with excitement that I'd get to see Noah play tonight. Talking on the phone with him every night only made me miss him more. I hated that we lived in different counties.

I decided I'd tell him I broke up with Dustin recently and say it casually, ya know, like I wasn't hoping he'd realize my body and *I* were waiting to get back in touch with him.

It was cold today so we wore our purple long sleeves underneath our uniforms which were also purple and gold. GO PIRATES!

"Someone's excited," Tiffany said, nudging my shoulder.

Sara leaned in and waggled her brows. "I wonder why?"

I shoved them both away and started scanning the football field. We were too far away to make out anyone.

"Let's beat these little shits tonight," Dustin yelled, stepping off the bus and looking my way like he hoped I heard him. The others shared his enthusiasm.

"Make us proud, boys," Sara yelled.

"What?" Dustin pinned his dark eyes on me. "No good luck kiss or are you saving it for the other team?"

"Like Noah needs luck," I couldn't help but say as I turned and headed for the field. "But good luck, boys!"

"Grace?" Noah's voice spooked me enough that I jumped. He wasn't even on the field. Lance and Jack were with him. I looked back at everyone staring at us… How much had he heard? He shook his head at me. "You're so jumpy." My eyes slid over him. "It's a shame you have to cheer for the losing team." He smirked at me.

"Ready to lose tonight, Noah?" Dustin yelled.

Noah lifted his head and smiled. "Ready to lose the best thing you got?"

Lance and Jack started singing, "*Ooohhh.*"

The blood had rushed to my face because while those two were laughing about it, Dustin and everyone looked slightly confused. Dustin turned to me, taking in my expression before he smirked. "Ah, does he still—Does that mean I'm still in the running, Grace?"

I caught Noah's expression when I turned, now he was confused.

Tiffany and Sara looked stunned before they both started laughing. "You're not referring to Grace, are you?" Sara asked me. "They're not even together anymore."

Noah's eyes zeroed in on me. "I've been meaning to tell you," I stammered.

Tiffany laughed. "Grace broke up with him the night we played you guys last month."

166

fall from grace

"Tiffany!" I hissed.

"What?" She winked. "He should know." She turned to Sara who also looked pleased.

"Maybe she didn't want to," Dustin jumped in. He grinned at me before he stepped onto the field with a few of our other boys.

"Come on, boys!" Noah's coach, I assumed, yelled at them.

I looked at Noah. "Um, Noah?"

He turned away and headed to the field without so much as a glance my way. My heart sunk. "I can't believe you haven't told him yet," Sara said as we started walking towards the bleachers where some of our squad already was.

"I was going to tell him tonight," I muttered. "Now he's upset."

Tiffany snorted. "More like he's probably on cloud nine."

"I can't believe you two," I said.

They wrapped their arms around me. "Ah, come on, that's what best friends are for," Tiffany added with pep in her voice.

I kept my eyes on Noah the entire game, and my stomach fluttered at how awesome he was on the field. Dustin and Noah seemed to bait each other the entire game but every time one was tackled, they'd be the first to help each other up. It was nostalgic to see them together on the field, only this time they were on opposite teams. I hadn't realized it had been Noah I had been ogling until the end of the game last time, so I had missed this feeling before.

Noah didn't speak to me during halftime when he stepped back out of the locker rooms. He didn't do anything but make eye contact with me the entire game. We lost again and by the end of the game, I was so spent with worry that I was tempted to crawl onto the bus instead of seeing if he still planned to take me home.

I followed Sara and Tiffany to the bus when they both turned around and stopped me. "Woah, where do you think you're going? I thought you were hanging out with Noah after the game?" Sara asked.

I tried to step between them. "I'm too afraid. He's going to wonder why I didn't tell him, and then he's going to realize my feelings. Besides, he hasn't even spoken to me since you guys told him"

Tiffany pointed behind me. "Here he comes for you." With a smirk from my two horrible friends, they turned around and walked off.

I turned around. Noah slowed to walking once he was several feet in front of me. He already had his jersey and pads off. He had a white t-shirt on that was heavy with sweat. "I thought I was going to have to chase you outta the bus when I saw you walking off with the rest of the girls," he said at ease despite the sweat glistening his body.

"You guys won again," I stated quietly.

His brows rose. "Like they stood a chance."

"See ya, man," Jack said to Noah before heading toward a black truck with Lance. "Bye Grace."

I waved bye to both of them while we walked to the parking lot. "Noah, I was going to tell you," I started.

"Next year?" he asked.

"Are you upset?"

I saw his Jeep. "Almost a whole month, Grace, you could have told me," he sounded upset.

"I know, it was dumb of me but it would have been embarrassing to admit that I broke up with him the same day you came back in my life."

The next thing I knew, he had me pressed against his dirty Jeep, gripping my shoulders roughly. "How so?" he asked, his eyes searching mine. "So much time has been wasted with us being apart, to think that another whole month, lost…"

"Lost?" I glared at him. "How is that? This has been the closest thing I've had to perfection in almost four years."

"I know." He hissed. "But it's still such a damn waste because this whole time I've been biding my time and waiting when I didn't have to…" His eyes singed mine before they fell to my lips. "To think that this whole time, I could have already done this." He kissed me. His lips bruised mine, it felt so rough. A fire burned inside me.

He pulled away. "Noah," I breathed right before I pulled his head back down and swept my tongue in his mouth. He groaned and I felt weightless.

His breath, his taste, was what I needed and I welcomed his tongue with greedy kisses and suction. Someone beeped and car lights moved around us. He pulled away from me again. "Slow down, Priss," he croaked. "Let's get out of here."

I nodded and stumbled around to the passenger side and got in. He started the Jeep and gave me a smoldering look that set me aflame. I didn't want to go anywhere. I didn't want to have to wait to touch him again. After buckling up, I sat quietly and never took my eyes off of him while he pulled out onto the road. He didn't make it a mile up the road before he pulled off the two-lane road onto a patchy spot of grass. I tore out of my seatbelt and was climbing across the gear shift before he even had it in park. He didn't complain at all though. He leaned back and welcomed me in his lap as he cut off the engine. He moved the seat back as far as it could go and helped me place my legs over each of his sides while I pressed my nose and mouth into his neck.

His hand tangled itself in my hair. "You feel so fucking good in my arms," he spoke into my ear, sending shockwaves of heat to my core before biting into it with his teeth and gripping my butt. I gasped and lifted his face to kiss him. I was moving against him, loving what I felt pressing against my inner thigh. I pulled and clung to his shirt. "You can slow down. I'm not letting go of you anytime soon," he murmured in between kisses. "We can stop if the sweat bothers you."

I met his eyes. "Are you kidding? I feel like watching you play is some kind of foreplay with how hot and bothered I get watching you on the field." He nibbled at my collarbone and I moaned.

I grabbed one of his hands and placed it between us and leaned back. "Touch me, Noah, please."

"Like I could ever say no to you," he blew across my neck as his hand slid underneath my skirt. "These panties are too tight. How the hell are you even wearing them?" he muttered and I lifted my butt and started pushing them down. "Jesus, Grace," he swore, "you're killing me."

It was hard to get out of the spankies with what little room I had, but I made it work with the heat coursing through my veins. When his hand grazed across my flesh, I bucked and collapsed back onto him. "That's more like it," he muttered as he worked circles over my needy flesh. I reached down and gripped his length through his pants and he groaned. His hand slid further down to my opening. "You're wet."

"You have no idea how much I've needed your touch," I whispered while kissing him.

"Believe me, I *do*," he told me while meeting my eyes. "Grace… have you had your fingers inside of you before?"

I shook my head. "No, I get off with the way you showed me before," I admitted softly.

"I'm going to use my fingers. It might be a little uncomfortable at first," he was still meeting my eyes, waiting for approval before he did.

I nodded. "Please."

He didn't waste any time. I felt his middle finger press against my entrance. The twinge of pain was there, unused to the foreign feel but with his kisses across my neck, it eased the discomfort into a tickling of warmth. He moved it in and out before applying his thumb against my swollen flesh and making circles that made the pleasure bubble to the surface. It felt new. It felt amazing. I laid my head against his shoulder and just let him make me feel, and I felt everything.

The orgasm took me under quickly, bursting out of my skin so much that I was twitching all over. Noah claimed my mouth. "I feel you coming on my finger, that's so fucking sexy," he groaned as he finally relented with his finger and let me calm against him.

I lifted my head and gazed into his eyes with my own heavy lids before smiling. "Your turn," I told him and starting with his pants.

"I'm good, it was enough to see you get off."

"I don't think so," I told him. "I want to make you feel good too. Help me with your pants."

His head fell back with a groan before he pulled down his pants. My stomach grew tight with need as it sprang free. It was veiny and long. I wrapped my fingers around it and he hissed. I took pleasure in seeing the beautiful expression marring his features. "How do you want me to—" His lips crashed into mine, pulling me close. We both went still when his hard-on rubbed against my soaked flesh. I opened my eyes and waited, before giving in and sliding over him.

He groaned but stopped me. "That's a little too dangerous, Priss, you're breaking my willpower."

I nibbled his ear. "We won't put it in, just let me…" I started rocking against him, creating a mesmerizing friction that was pulling me into another orgasm.

"Grace," he murmured then his hands were on my butt, pressing me against him even harder as he tried to control my rhythm. "My Grace, my fucking Prissy Pants, I can't believe your sliding across my dick right now. Do you have any idea how many years I've been fantasizing about doing this kind of stuff to you?"

His words were pulling me over the edge. "You don't think you didn't leave me with all these unresolved feelings that only you can satisfy?" I asked him. "You turned me into this."

He grabbed the back of my neck and kissed me. "I plan to keep you that way." We became more frantic, clumsier, and rough with each other. "Shit," he grunted before he separated us right as he started coming. I took in the way his face pinched together as the pleasure took control of him. His shirt was ruined but when he opened his eyes and smiled at me, I didn't think he cared too much either.

He kissed my nose before he took off his t-shirt, wiped himself off, and grabbed a different one from his bag in the back seat. I watched him with a satisfied smirk. "I'm hungry," I said, randomly.

He grinned. "I'm famished, and it looks like it's going to take several lifetimes of you to have my fill." I started looking for my spankies. "Looking for these?" he asked, lifting them up in his hands. I grabbed them and started moving across the middle console. I saw him peeking between my legs with a smirk. "You can't expect me not to look when you're raising it up in the air."

"I'm trying to get in the other seat," I protested.

"What do you want to eat?"

"Taco Bell?" I offered. He nodded and drove us to the nearest one. We stopped inside and ate. I picked a booth and was even happier about my choice when he slid in beside me, resting his hand on my leg.

"You're my special someone, Grace," he blurted out as we ate. I tilted my head. "You're always going to feel like air to me. I need you, no matter what anyone says. I know when high school's over, or if it's ten years from now, you're gonna be it for me." I covered my mouth as I tried to swallow the bite of taco in my mouth. "I've wanted to tell you that since the moment I saw you again, that my heart just knew all over again. But you were with Dustin."

"With the way you acted, I thought you didn't care at all that I was with someone."

"Are you kidding? It drove me fucking insane that you entered my life at a time when you were with someone else."

"I wanted to tell you that I was going to break up with him that night but when you brought up the fact that you weren't a virgin anymore and didn't seem to care that I was dating, I chickened out."

This was so much better, getting to tell Noah everything.

"That was me doing the same thing," he scratched his chin and said. "Are you... upset with me for having sex in the time that we've been apart?"

"I can't say I wasn't hurt," I told him honestly. "Right before you left, our relationship was changing but with your mom's passing and my own mom's meddling, it was destroyed. I get it. I do. You wanted to try things without me." I took his hand. "But I'm glad you called her back."

He squeezed it in return. "I wish you would have done the same."

That wasn't exactly what I wanted to hear. "Why?"

"Don't give me that look," he said, pulling me into his arms. "I meant so that you would know that no one's ever going to work but me."

"Cocky much?"

He squeezed me tightly. "It's not me being cocky, it's me trusting us."

"Now that we... there will be no others?"

"I'll never touch another woman," he swore.

I laughed. "You don't know that. We don't know what our future holds."

"Then do you want me to be with another one besides you?" he asked.

"NO."

"Then I won't. It's that simple. We never defined our relationship before, we never put a name on it but we will now. I'm going to make you happy, Grace."

"You already do."

"I'm your boyfriend," he told me then he stood up in the empty restaurant and yelled at the workers. "I'm her boyfriend. That means I get to do the dirty with her." The workers shook their heads and laughed in the back.

I covered my face. "Noah!"

He sat back down. "I'm gonna make you happy, Grace," he said again.

I shook my head and smiled. That was Noah. He'd try his hardest to please me now or he wouldn't have uttered the words so easily.

This with Noah, felt like it was only the beginning.

All things started beautifully, did that mean that they all had to end ugly?

26

Grace age 16

Noah age 17

I finally have what I've always wanted. I know not to take it for granted.

I'll savor her, treat her like the jewel that she is in my eyes.

She's everything and more… So much more.

I might still be young, but I know what I want.

N.P.

I wasn't the only one in a good mood Saturday morning. Dad twirled Mom around in the living room, saying a bunch of gooey crap that had me shaking my head and smiling. "Okay, what's going on?" I asked as I maneuvered around them to flop down on the sofa. Gus was wagging his tail and attacking their feet.

Mom was laughing and swatting at Dad. "Your father remembered that our anniversary is today, it seems," she told me.

"Nineteen years. Doesn't seem like it's been that long," Dad muttered with a kiss to her lips. "Still feels like the first time."

I covered my ears. "Y'all are being too ooey-gooey this morning."

They both sniggered. "Your dad's going to take me out later, you'll have to cook for yourself today," Mom informed me.

"I'm going out later anyway."

"Who with?" Dad made sure to ask. "Are you still dating the Dustin kid?"

"I'm not," I said, hoping he wouldn't ask who I was going out with again.

"What happened? He seemed like a good kid."

I glared. "You met him one time when he came to the door." Noah was ten times better than all the guys I went to school with but Dad was so judgmental when it came to him.

"All right," Mom intervened. "Which one of you want to help me with breakfast?" Dad pointed at me the same time I pointed at him, then our eyes locked in a glare again.

Mom swore and walked away. "You're such a bad husband," I told him.

"You're such a bad daughter," he countered back.

Then we smiled and went to go help Mom in the kitchen.

———

An hour after Mom and Dad left, Noah pulled into the driveway. I petted Gus before locking the house and rushing to the Jeep. Once inside, Noah pulled me into a kiss. "I don't know how I'm going to manage through the weeks now without seeing you," he said as he pulled out.

"You just saw me last night," was what I said, when in reality I felt the same way. I hated that we lived in different counties and went to different schools.

"I want to be with you, always," he told me.

"Ah," I mumbled, pleased, "you have a way with words, don't you? Better not be whispering sweet nothings to nobody else but me."

176

fall from grace

He grabbed my hand and kissed it with a smirk. "Never."

I monkeyed with the radio as he drove. "Are you sure they don't care that I'm coming over to eat?"

"Are you kidding?" he asked. "Janet is so excited to finally meet you. She'll probably cook everything in the kitchen."

I leaned my head back and admired the way he smiled. "You really seem to like them. I can tell by the way you talk about them."

"Of course, I do," he said without hesitation. "I could have been placed in a shitty home with someone who only fostered kids for the check every month, but for once, luck was on my side and I got Dean and Janet. They're amazing people, Grace, and I can't wait for you to get know them." He *wanted* me to know these people, and to me, that was what made it important. I wanted to see the couple Noah wasn't embarrassed to talk about. This was so unlike the boy I grew up with. That boy didn't have parents he wanted me to meet. From what little I spoke to Dean the other day, I had a good feeling about them too.

Their house was like any other two-story, it was their yard that I knew I'd love in the summertime. It wasn't much land but they had all kinds of apple trees, and just picturing what it looked like in the summer had me smiling. Two other vehicles were in their driveway and a boat was covered underneath their shed.

Noah walked around the Jeep as I got out and took my hand as we walked to the door. Dean opened it and stepped out before we made it to the steps. I smiled because he was grinning at me, and I just wasn't one to refuse a smile. "It's good to see you again, Grace. Come on in," he took me away from Noah and pushed me inside the house. "I'll introduce you to my darling wife. Janet," he called for her, but all I could focus on was the delicious aroma coming from their kitchen.

"Something smells good," I mumbled, taking in the homey feel of the place. It reminded me of my grandparents' house growing up before they passed away.

"She baked some BBQ ribs, taters, and all kinds of other foods that we hope you like," he said as Janet stepped out into the hallway.

She was short with brown hair and highlights of gray peeking through. Her face was red from cooking but she welcomed me with a smile and before I knew it, she wrapped me up in a hug. "It feels like I already know you, child, with the way Noah talks about you," she said, and I stole a peek at Noah who was a little red himself.

"Let's get out of this small hallway and into the kitchen," Dean told everyone.

My stomach got a hunger pang just looking at all of the food on the table. "Everything looks and smells so good," I told Janet.

She beamed and ushered us to sit down. "Come on, let's eat."

"We haven't had a girl over since our boys were in school," Dean added with a smile.

"Noah told me they were in the army."

Dean nodded. "Yeah, one's in Iraq and the other is stationed in Arizona living with his family, so we don't get to see them much."

"Good thing we found Noah when we did, things were a little boring around here with just Dean," Janet winked and I laughed.

"I'm glad you found him too," I said and everyone looked up from their food. "Honestly, it feels like the weight has been lifted to know he's been living here in this kind of warm environment… Was it hard?" I asked them all.

Janet set down her fork. "Yeah, you made it hard on all of us, dear."

"Me?" I blinked.

"Janet," Noah groaned, covering his face.

"All we heard from him was about how much he needed to get back to you. He tried his hardest at first to make himself look like a bad kid." She paused to laugh. "And we'd catch him crying and at first, we thought it was because of his situation and the fact that he was living with strangers… but it was because he was missing you."

I smiled over at Noah who was still covering his face up. "Did you cry over me, Noah?" I asked him playfully but I was trying to keep the tears at bay as well. "I cried for you every day, for a long time too." I grabbed his hand and he finally moved his other hand to reveal his reddened cheeks.

"That Mom of yours, I felt like calling her up myself when Noah told me what she said," Janet muttered.

"Janet," Noah said again.

"I know," I found myself agreeing.

Janet nodded as if she knew I understood. "But, Noah talked good of her and if he was willing to do as she said, then I wasn't going to stop him. Calling her did help, though. It was then when he allowed us to get to know him."

"Yeah," Dean agreed. "He's a good boy, he is."

I lifted my face and smirked. "That's something I've always known." They both smiled at me.

"Do you have Facebook?" Janet asked and I nodded. "I would like to add you so we can keep in touch."

I couldn't help but turn and glare at Noah. "Really? Everyone has Facebook and you don't?" He shrugged his shoulders sheepishly and Janet laughed.

"I don't know anything about the Internet, but Janet likes to have that ole' Facebook so that we can keep up with the boys… We have a granddaughter on the way."

"Congratulations," I told them. "Well, she's gonna be very lucky to have grandparents like y'all."

michelle gross

"Yes, hear that, Noah, we'll make really good grandparents in the future as well," Janet said it like she was hinting around. Now I was blushing like Noah. Elderly people were so different than the rest of the world. They didn't care to pair you up when you were just a teen.

After we finished eating, Noah showed me to his room upstairs. Once the door was closed, I grinned and said, "I feel like they're the type of people that end up with a lot of grandkids for letting the opposite gender share a room."

He laughed. "They're very laid back."

"I like them, they're very easy to be around."

I looked around the room and saw some of his woodworks in the corner. He turned around and grabbed a bag off the TV stand. "Come here," he said as sat down on the bed. I joined him on the bed and he placed the bag in my lap.

"What is it?"

"Just open it," he urged me. I stuck my hand in the bag and immediately recognized what was inside. I pulled out the one top. A sticker was placed on it that said: 16.

"Happy late birthdays," he smiled and it made my stomach clench up. "Next month, I want to be with you on your birthday."

It was an owl, and it was so beautiful. "You still made them every year?" I asked a bit emotionally.

He nodded. "Look at the rest." I pulled out an Indian head that had 15 on it, then an eagle with 14. "When I brought you over that first crappy piece of work and handed it over to you for your seventh birthday and saw the way you looked at it like it was the best thing ever, and the way your mom praised me for it, I don't know… I guess it just made me feel like I could do anything if it meant getting to see you smile."

"Where's the one for my birthday coming up?"

fall from grace

He arched a brow. "I don't think so. I'll give it to you on your birthday. Besides, I'm still working on it."

I studied the rims of his blue eyes. "How is it you are so good all the time?"

"I'm not good," he muttered. "Even as a kid, I've had this thing for you that's run so deep and for so long that I'm afraid of what I might become now that I have you."

I pressed my thighs together and cupped his face with my palms. "You're never going to be one of the bad boys but when it comes to me, I hope you want to do *bad* things. Dirty things."

His eyes took on a whole new meaning as he scooped me up and placed me in the middle of the bed before pushing me down. "Oh, you have no idea." He leaned over me, his hand crawling underneath my t-shirt as he bit into my neck.

I gasped. "No, Noah, *you* have no idea what you've made me into. You don't know the thoughts that keep me up at night, all the ways I've imagined while waiting to find you."

He pushed my bra up and gripped one of my breasts. His rough touch was just what I wanted. He placed my nipple between his fingers before pinching and pulling it up to his mouth where he bit into it through my shirt. I exhaled and moved my legs. The ache was already there, pressing between my thighs. "I'm pretty sure it's nothing compared to what I've pictured doing to you." He tortured my nipple then did the same to the other, and he wasn't even lifting up my shirt.

This conversation was burning me from the inside.

"Show me," I begged and he kissed me. *No*, he breathed fire into me because that was what his touches felt like to me.

He moved down, yanking up my shirt and revealing my breasts. He dropped his face between them. "I'm so weak when it comes to these. They look even bigger, how is that possible for someone as tiny as you?"

181

"You're a boob guy."

"No, I'm a sucker for everything-that-is-*Grace* guy." His hot mouth came down over one of my nipples and I moaned, pulling at his hair. I rocked my hips into him and his fingers crawled down my body and unbuttoned my pants before they disappeared into my panties. I arched into his touch immediately.

"Noah, can you come help with the truck for a second?" Dean hollered from downstairs. I deflated against the bed, the heat of the moment leaving me as I remembered where we were. "You can get underneath it easier than what I can," he added.

Noah eyed my breasts before dropping his head between them. I giggled. "What were we thinking? They're right downstairs!" I asked him.

"We weren't thinking," he said, climbing off me. He leaned back down as I pulled down my shirt and tucked my hair behind my ear. "And I want to think. I don't want to rush, and I feel like that's what we're doing. The last thing I want to do is ruin this with you."

I cupped his hand that played with my hair. "Maybe we are moving quickly but these are all things that we would have done if you hadn't been taken from your dad."

"My pace will be your pace," he whispered softly.

"Then I want you to take my virginity on my birthday."

The expression on his face said it all.

27

Grace age 16

Noah age 17

It's a little surreal knowing that I'll finally be eighteen come May next year. Finally, after all this time spent waiting, I'll be in charge of my own life. Not that I'm not already. I always have been, but I'll be in control of every aspect of my life. The mistakes and choices I make will be mine to bear.

I wonder what Grace will say when she finds out my plans. She hasn't asked yet but I know she will.

She should know. She's every bit of my future.

N.P.

Noah stole my laughter during the nights as we talked for hours over the phone. He made me smile even when he wasn't around. It was worth stubbing my toe every morning on the dresser from being so tired when I woke just to hear his voice as the nights turned to mornings.

October quickly flew by before I realized, time with Noah seemed to pass by so easily. I didn't see him anymore other than an hour on a Sunday two weeks ago inside his Jeep where we kissed and groped until he was gone again. It was miserable not seeing him, but gas wasn't cheap and he worked every hour Dean would give him. I wouldn't beg for his time, I'd wait for him to give it to me. Besides, Noah, in my eyes, was the boy that worked for the things he wanted. The fact that he managed school, football, a job, friends, and a girlfriend effortlessly

183

without making me feel like I was less than anything else in his life was amazing.

Or maybe Noah just couldn't be dimmed in my eyes; he was too bright and I felt lucky to even have someone like that wanting me.

"Grace, stop staring at your phone," Sara muttered.

Sara and Tiffany were spending the night at my house. Janet posted a picture of her meal online. I drooled and clicked the like button. Lance and Jack had also added me on Facebook and placed a bunch of hearts underneath my relationship status. Even though it didn't show that it was Noah, they knew who I was talking about and couldn't help but act childish. I felt like I was slowly getting to know them over the weeks because they were always yelling through the phone when Noah was around them while we were on the phone.

"Let me see," she yanked the phone from my hand and gasped, "Oh, my God, he's so hot."

"That's Noah's friend, Jack," I said with a smile. "Jack's dad offered to pay Noah to change his oil and tires. That's what he's doing this evening."

"From the sound of it, Noah picks up a lot of odd jobs," Tiffany mumbled while scrolling through her phone. "Is he saving up for something?" I had truthfully wondered the same thing. Noah did do a lot besides working at the garage.

"I'm not sure," I admitted. "We haven't talked about those things… It could be possible though. I don't think he ever spends any money unless it's gas." Now I was curious.

"Noah seems so responsible for his age," Sara said with a laugh. "Hell, if I had a job, my checks would go to food."

I smiled at the compliment she had given him. "He is." Of course, they didn't see life the same way Noah had, and neither had I but I had watched his life from the outside and it still got to me some nights.

fall from grace

I would go visit John tomorrow. I hadn't since meeting Noah. It wouldn't hurt to go check on him and bring him some food. He didn't deserve it, and even though Noah didn't talk about him, I knew he would have still been trying to keep his dad alive if he hadn't gotten taken… Or did he truly give up on his dad the night he lost his mom?

My phone dinged.

Noah: **I miss you… it's been too long since I've seen ur pretty face**

I smiled at the screen.

Me: **I miss you. Only 2 more weeks until my bday!**

Noah: **I don't think it's ur birthday that's got you so excited…**

I sniggered and felt the rush of tingles between my thighs from just a text.

Me: **I hate waiting! Come take me now**

I was half being serious, half just teasing to see what he'd say.

"What are you over there giggling about?" Sara asked.

Noah dinged me again: **I'm almost done with the tires, say the word and I'll come get you.**

"Your face is red," Sara kept talking, "hmm, what is Noah over there saying to you?"

Me: **Sara and Tiffany are here, remember?**

Noah: **I'll have u soon.**

Sara almost took my phone away from me again. "Will you stop?" I groaned.

She laughed. "I want to know too."

Tiffany finally set her phone down and said, "I'm just hungry and wanting to know when we are going down to the fridge to raid it."

———

"What's with you lately?" Dad asked as I replied to Noah's text saying that he couldn't wait to see me this weekend. "Are you dating someone?" Tiffany and Sara had just left after spending the night.

I panicked. "Why?"

"You're always smiling at your phone and giggling."

"I can't smile?" I deflected.

"Do you know?" he turned to Mom.

She kept her eyes on the TV. "Who knows."

He studied her. "Hmm."

She finally turned to him. "What?"

He grabbed a strand of her hair. "You got a little gray… right here."

She smacked his hand and focused back on the TV before practically growling and facing him again. "You ruined the movie for me!"

He smiled. "You know you're beautiful." She tried not to smile. I smiled and disappeared into the living room where I grabbed some leftovers from last night and slipped the plastic containers in my bag before tiptoeing by them.

"Where are you going?" Dad asked.

"I'm going to take a walk."

"A walk?" Dad repeated. "It's cold out."

fall from grace

I shrugged my shoulders. "I'm wearing my jacket. It's stuffy in here."

He shook his head and turned back to the TV. I exhaled slowly and hurried outside. I darted down the road and across the street to the trailers to John's house. I didn't even knock, I just stepped in. He wasn't in the living room. "John?" I called out.

He stepped out of the hallway with a snort. "And here I thought you finally left me alone."

I rolled my eyes and took him in. He was the same. Scrawny but no skinnier than what he already was. Noah got his height and looks from him but John hadn't taken care of himself and it showed. Noah, on the other hand, was bulging with muscles.

"I brought you some food." I waited for him to say something. "Do you want it?"

"Hand it over," he told me and I did. "So, any reason as to why you ain't been here in a while then suddenly show up again?"

I sighed. "I'm dating Noah."

I surprised him. "You got in touch with him?" he asked, stunned.

I nodded. "Yep. No thanks to you."

"Ah, I guess that's good," he said, still clearly surprised. "So, you have his number?"

"I'm not giving it to you if that's what you're getting at."

"He'll be eighteen in May," he sounded more like he was saying it to himself than me. He sat down on the couch and looked at me. "What is he gonna do then?" His question caught me off guard. What was Noah going to do? He leaned back and sighed, "He's probably got it all figured out, no doubt."

"I'm leaving."

"Grace." I stopped and waited at the door for him to continue. "Has he been in a good home?"

I looked up to the ceiling. "Not that you should be allowed to ask that question since you never tried to get your son back but... yeah, they seem like genuinely good people and Noah really likes them."

He was quiet before he finally laughed. "Well, that's good. That's good."

"I can't tell if you care about him or not. One minute it seems like you do then the next, I'm reminded that you let him go and kept your drugs."

"It's not easy, you wouldn't understand."

"I don't ever want to understand." I walked out without another word.

————

"Please stop going over there, Grace," Noah told me over the phone. He sighed for the twentieth time. "People change after they take something, believe me I know. You can't predict how they're gonna act. Why do you think I slept on your floor some nights?"

I blew into the phone. "I know, Noah." I rolled onto my stomach and almost squashed Gus in the process. "Honestly though, I wasn't there for you after you lost your mom, I couldn't be so I want to know how you really feel about everything now?"

He paused. "What do you mean?"

"Are you going to have anything to do with him when you turn eighteen?"

"I haven't thought about it," he answered.

"What will you do when you turn eighteen? What happens? Do you get to live with them until you graduate at least?"

He laughed. "They'd never make me leave if I didn't want to." That made me smile. "But they already know I'm planning on moving out when I turn eighteen."

"What?" I raised in the bed. "How come you haven't told me?"

"Because I was going to surprise you with it."

"Surprise me...?"

"Yeah, I'm going to transfer senior year. Truthfully, I've already applied for the apartments in Lee County. I'm on the waiting list but since it takes a while, Janet told me I should go ahead and apply since she knew my plans on wanting to transfer schools to see you again."

"Wait, you had this planned before you even met me again?" My heart raced.

He chuckled. "Yeah, Priss, I have." I grabbed my chest and thought I might get all weepy. "It's nothing to brag about right now. The apartments are in a shitty environment but it's a start, and I'll gladly move into a dump if it means being closer to you. I'm still going to work at the garage, Dean already promised me a job for as long as I wanted it. I won't play football our last year and I might pick up another part-time job... So, what will it be, Grace, are you okay dating a guy with little time on his hands to please you right?"

I wiped my eyes. "You've got it all figured out, don't you?"

"Are you crying?"

"Mmm." Then I cried harder. "You keep stealing every part of me, I'm not going to have anything left... Noah, without me ever saying it, you know, right?"

"Don't say it over the phone," he stopped me. "I already know, Grace. I'll tell you what you already know too, this weekend."

"Then I'll be waiting."

michelle gross

28

Grace age 16

Noah age 17

Grace is so sexy and sensual with the little everyday things she says and does that I don't even think she realizes what she does to me. Or maybe it's just me and everything that I feel for her. It bleeds through every part of my life. I met her too young. What I've felt for her kept growing with us to the point that it's all-consuming.

And it's the best fucking feeling.

She's mine, and I'm hers.

I wonder if she knows the hold she's got on me? Surely, she does.

N.P.

Mom let me drive her car to meet Noah in the parking lot at Walmart Saturday. I wanted to make it easier for him so that he didn't have to drive so far to see me then take me home. When his Jeep pulled in next to me, I jumped out of the car. He hurried out when he saw me standing in the rain. "Grace, what are you doing?" he asked right before I attacked him with a hug, wrapping my arms and legs around him. He held me up and laughed as I peppered his face with kisses. "It's fucking cold, Grace."

"I missed you, it's been three weeks since I last saw you," I told him.

"I'm well aware of that," he walked to his passenger side, carrying me. "It's not easy being with me, is it?" he asked.

I grabbed his face and whispered. "It's super easy." I dropped my legs and got into the Jeep as he shut the door and ran around to the other side and got in. I climbed over on top of him when he did.

"What are you doing?" His voice didn't sound too upset with me even though he tried to play it off that he was. "I thought we were going out to eat?" he groaned. "I can't do anything when you nibble on my ear like that." He finally grabbed my hips and pulled me onto his lap the rest of the way. "I give up," he murmured, stealing my lips. I sighed happily into his mouth.

When our kiss broke, I looked over in the seat. "Whoops, I forgot that my boots were wet." I sniggered as he wiped off the seat with his hand before I sat back in it and buckled up.

"How about we order some takeout and eat in the Jeep so that we don't have to deal with the public?" he asked me as he pulled out of Walmart's parking lot.

I grinned. "Sounds like a wiener to me." He shook his head in laughter.

Thirty minutes later, we were sharing a full rack of BBQ ribs and other messy foods that you shouldn't try to eat in a vehicle. We set the food between us as if his console and gear shift were a table. I had my boots off with one leg underneath me as I sucked the BBQ off my fingers. I watched the rain beat down on the fogged windows before smiling toward Noah. "This is strangely romantic," I whispered.

He looked to the window then back at me with a smirk. "Kind of puts one in the mood, you mean?" He waggled his brows.

I snorted. "So that's why you brought us somewhere secluded to eat."

He grinned. "Like I even had to. It's already dark outside, nobody is going see anything we're doing with this rain either."

fall from grace

It suddenly felt a little too stuffy in here. I blinked my eyes and took a deep breath. "Are you sure buying this kind of food was okay?" I asked him. "I want you to be able to save up so that we can spend our senior year together."

"I've been saving for a while so buying you a meal when we're together isn't going to change anything," he informed me before letting out a heavy sigh. "I'm stuffed." We just stared at each other for a long time before he said, "Finished?"

I started closing all the boxes. "Yeah."

"Good." He started helping me. "Get in the back," he murmured unexpectedly.

My stomach heated as I raised up and slipped between the seats and waited. After he placed the food back in the bag, he jumped out in the rain and opened the back door and climbed inside with me. Once he shut the door, I studied the droplets of water on his face and hair as he turned on the interior light so that we could see better. He then grabbed my legs and pulled them toward him. I fell back against the seat and watched as he tore at my zipper. I grabbed my stomach. "I have a food belly," I said out of embarrassment, regretting all that food I just ate.

He never lifted his eyes up to meet mine. His focus was solely on what he was doing. "You're perfect," was the only thing he said before he yanked my jeans and panties down. I squealed and went to cover myself. It was hard not to feel embarrassment when he was coming on so strong. "Are you getting embarrassed now? If you are then you're really going to feel it when my face is pressed against your pussy." I was at a loss for words as he pulled the jeans off my legs. I didn't know why but hearing him call my vagina that was so unexpected and even a turn-on that he wasn't afraid to talk dirty with me.

His eyes took me in as he lifted my butt off the seats, *literally*. He folded me up and held my legs and butt in the air. It started out awkward. "Noah, this is embarrassing," I screamed but then his mouth came down over me and everything else was forgotten. I bucked but he held me in place as he swiped his tongue over me leisurely at first. "That...," I started, "feels good."

He wrapped his arms around my legs and gripped them tighter before letting one of his hands slide next to his mouth. "I'm going to use my fingers too," he let me know before placing one inside me. Like the first time he did it, it felt foreign at first but quickly became something amazing. He relentlessly hit something inside me that built and with the feel of his tongue against me, I scattered into a million different pieces in what felt like a hundred different ways until I started jerking when the sensation quickly became ticklish now that it was over.

My entire body felt like Jell-O as he gently placed my lower half back down on the seat and came down over top of me. He kissed me with the taste of me on his tongue and when I opened my eyes to see him again, his eyes were heavy and so droopy looking that it was downright sexy.

He played me with his fingers once again. I gasped when one slipped inside and he took the opportunity to conquer my mouth with his tongue. It was wild, *terrifying* even, the way he could unravel me so easily. I wasn't Grace Harper when he touched me, I was just *his* and whatever he wanted me to be.

"Noah," I cried.

"What is it?" he dared to ask.

"Just take me right now," I whispered and his finger stilled inside me.

He lifted his head. "You don't want me to take your virginity in the back of this rusted down Jeep," he said it like he really believed himself.

"Those things don't matter to me. You could toss me into the rain and do what you wanted to me and I'd let you because it's *you* that matters." He continued to look at me in silence. "Don't you want to?" I asked.

fall from grace

"Are you kidding me? Do you really have to ask?" he asked. "Your pace is my pace," he whispered before he pulled his finger out and immediately replaced it with two. I jumped from the discomfort and pain. "You're perfect, Grace, it's not going to be the most amazing feeling the first time because you're a virgin."

"Let's get rid of the pain," I whispered. "So that I can enjoy the pleasure with you in the future."

He smiled softly as he moved his fingers inside me. It still hurt and a bit of unease crept through me at how much more I might feel. I wanted him so much more than my fear of how painful it was going to be though. "Let's see how much I can work you with my fingers," he murmured as he wiggled and spread out his fingers inside me. I gasped as he watched me with hooded eyes. He pulled his fingers out before raising up and getting something from his back pocket. He pulled out a condom and scooted me down further. My nerves were a web of excitement and fear as I watched him unzip his jeans and reveal his erection. I still found it strange to look at but at the same time, my mouth felt heavy with the need to do the same to him as he had done to me earlier.

He tore open the condom and wrapped himself before bending down over me. "We'll stop if it's too much," he promised, and all I could do was nod as I wrapped my arms around him. He spread my legs further apart as he sank closer. My stomach was a quivering mess. Then I felt him at my entrance, and it was like there was no entrance for him at all because my body automatically resisted him. He sighed, "You have no idea how much I want this. Let me try to get you there with my fingers." When he started to pull away, I held him tight.

"I know it's gonna hurt," I mumbled in his ear. "But I want it to be this way. It might sound silly to you but I want it to be your… not your fingers." His eyes devoured me whole.

He started making out with me slowly but heavily. It pulled me from my worries until I felt him nudging my entrance again. I tensed, but this time Noah ignored it and spread my legs further apart and pressed harder. I hissed and gripped underneath his shoulders as the pain grew worse. I couldn't even tell if he was even making any progress but I had already been wet from the orgasm and when he finally forced his way past my entrance, I felt it. I cried into his shoulder as my legs automatically fought to keep him from going any further. "Let me get it all the way in, and I'll pull it out," he whispered hoarsely. I felt his arms tremble around me and I wanted more than anything to tell him not to stop but the sad truth of it was, I wanted the pain to stop. I felt no heat anymore, just the tearing and burning of discomfort.

He raised up and looked down at me, placing a hand against my face as he caught the tears that fell. And just like he said, Noah pulled himself out and scooted me over and cradled me in his arms. "Don't cry," he murmured as he kissed my cheek.

"I'm sorry," I sniffled. "Are you mad? This was my idea and I couldn't even handle the pain."

"This is me, Grace. I want you always. I'm not lying in this back seat to hurt you. The only thing I want to give you is pleasure and that's not what you were feeling. It'll go a little easier next time."

"It doesn't bother you that you didn't get off?" I asked.

He smirked. "What? Having you wrapped around me, even if only for a minute felt like heaven. I'll have my way with you in time and I promise it'll be good for you."

"See? This is why I always want you. Your words turn me into liquid but no sooner you used that," I pointed toward his erection pressing against me, "it hurt like hell!"

He laughed. "It'll make you scream from pleasure soon enough." He pulled off the condom and tossed it on the floor.

"I hope," I mumbled. He started attacking my neck and face with kisses until I was giggling.

"Grace."

"What?"

"I'm still waiting."

I was mesmerized by his blue eyes peering down at me. "I love you, Noah Phillips."

"I've always loved you, Grace Harper."

The rain stopped but Noah and I stayed in the back seat of his Jeep talking and taking pictures together. I laughed with him until I had to leave him for another long week.

———

November 11th

I awoke Thursday morning to another text from Noah that read: *Happy Birthday. Can't wait to see you this weekend.* He had stayed on the phone with me until midnight just so that he could tell me first. I was smiling about it until I stubbed my dang toe as I tried to walk out of my room that morning. This time, I really did it. I bent my toenail back. I cursed and hopped before falling on my butt until the pain dulled enough that I could remember how to walk.

"Happy Birthday, Happy Birthday to you," I heard Mom's singing as she walked up the stairs and groaned. I fell backward onto the carpet. She stepped into the doorway with a pile of pancakes. "Did you stub your toe again?" she asked before she scrunched up her nose. "Ew, that looks terrible."

"It feels worse," I grumbled.

"Is Noah coming over to eat cake with us today?" she asked, placing her hand on her hip.

"No." I finally stood back up. "I'm going out with him Sunday."

She shook her head. "Nonsense. Ask him to come over."

"Mom." I looked at her like she was crazy. "You understand why the thought of bringing him back home is terrifying, right?"

197

"You can't keep hiding it from your dad." I knew that Noah also wanted to tell him. He was more obedient towards adults than I was. "It'll be worse if you keep hiding it and he finds out." She turned around. "Tell him, okay?"

"Yeah, okay." I was so not telling him.

————

My eyes must be playing tricks on me. School ended a couple of hours ago, I had just gotten off the phone with Noah who said he had practice today... I was standing at the front door with only one possible explanation. MOM.

"Noah?" I gave him a startled look as he stepped aside and revealed a carved bear made from a log. It went up to his waist. I momentarily forgot that I was ambushed as I covered my mouth. "Noah, it's so beautiful." He had painted the bear black and in the bear's paws was a sign that said, "I love you."

"Thanks for coming, Noah," Mom said to him, stepping next to me with the same reaction I had just given him to his newest wooden creation. "Oh, Noah, this is perfect." She stepped out onto the porch and examined it. "This shouldn't go inside your room, Grace, it's better to display it outside for people to see its beauty."

I squinted my eyes at her and stepped next to her. "I don't think so. This is my birthday present, not yours... but you're right, it'll look best outside." I started pushing it next to the door.

"I think it will look better in the yard," she mumbled.

"I'll put it out there this summer. For now, the bear stays here," I grunted and moved back to admire it again. I pulled out my phone from my back pocket and took a picture of it.

"Do you like it?"

"I love it!" Mom answered for me and he smiled at her compliment.

fall from grace

"What are you guys doing with the door open when it's this cold…" Dad's words died out as he stopped and looked at Noah from the doorway. "Noah?"

"Hi, Steven," Noah said casually. "It's been a while."

Dad's eyes hardened on him as if he was remembering that night he hit Noah like I was. "What are you doing here?" he asked.

"Dad…" I started.

"I'm dating Grace," he replied smoothly. "And it's her birthday so I didn't want to miss it."

He stepped into the doorway and eyed the trailers with disgust. My heart sunk. "You living around here again?"

"No, I'm living in Jewel County."

Dad's eyes hardened. "Oh, so that's where you've been? And you just came back into Grace's life after all these years now… because?"

"Because of me," Mom intervened. Dad looked genuinely confused. "I asked him not to contact Grace for a while."

"If you were gonna do that, then you should have told him to stay gone."

"Dad!" I flushed with anger and embarrassment.

"It's fine, Grace," Noah told me but it wasn't. Noah was used to certain adults treating him like dirt but that was something I could never get used to.

"Hush, Steven. I was the one that invited him over for cake," Mom said, disappearing into the door.

"Well, come on," Dad muttered. "We're running up the electric bill with the door wide open like this."

Noah and I stepped in with Dad still giving him a bad look. When we passed him, Noah whispered, "It's fine, Grace. He'll come around."

"I hate anyone treating you like that, even my dad," I muttered.

"Look at it from his point of view. You're his daughter and he walked in on me in your room in the middle of the night when we were only thirteen," he tried to tell me, and I sighed and dropped my shoulders because I did understand. That one small decision we made only worsened the way Dad looked at Noah. He took my hand and walked into the kitchen with me. "I can handle it. One day, I'll make him see that what we have isn't puppy love."

"Birthday girl gets the first piece," Mom chirped as she cut into the cake. "Didn't you see if Tiffany and Sara wanted to come and have some cake with us?"

We sat down at the table. Dad didn't even bother coming in the kitchen. "Mom, I'm too old for that kind of thing. Besides, I think they are taking me out to the movies tomorrow night."

"Which means they are using your birthday as an excuse to get you to go with them." Noah nodded with a smile.

"Exactly." I agreed.

"Taking her out somewhere yourself Noah?" Mom asked, lifting her eyebrows mischievously.

Noah dropped his head with a smile. "I am. I'm going to take her somewhere Sunday."

"Oooh?" Mom hummed, and I felt the heat across my cheeks. Were our plans still the same? Was I going to let him try again?

29

Grace age 17

Noah age 17

She puts the fire in my veins. In a way, I fear that I am like my parents. Like them, I'm an addict. My drug's name is Grace, and she's feeding my addiction with every word she speaks, every touch I place on her skin, every night and day she gives to me, even if it's only by a phone call.

Yeah… I've been in love for a very long time.

She's not a drug, but she's the sweetest addiction.

N.P.

"Where is he taking you?" Dad asked for the tenth time as I peeked out the blinds and waited on Noah to pick me up.

I tossed my head back and groaned. "I don't know, Dad. He never told me. I just know he's gonna get me good food." And since Noah grew up with me, he knew everything I liked and disliked already. Actually, he probably knew everything about me.

"I'd like it if you weren't going out with Noah," Dad muttered next to me. "What happened to the other boy?"

I scowled at him. "He's ten times the gentleman than Dustin was."

Dad looked surprised. "Wait, that Dustin tried something on you?" Now, he looked upset. "You better not let any boy push you into doing anything you don't want to do. I raised you better than that."

"Exactly," I told him. "You raised me. I know I make mistakes but Noah will never be one of them."

He paused. "Even if he breaks your heart?" Dad raked his hands through his hair. "Gracie, what happens when he becomes his father?"

"That's not even fair. Noah is not his parents. You know him! He practically lived here growing up."

He dropped his head. "I know he's a good kid, but I've seen plenty of good people turn into bad ones who I never thought in a million years would."

"Those chances apply to all of us, Dad!" I hissed, staring at him before finally looking through the blinds again. "Noah's here. I'm leaving.'"

"Did you bring another girl besides me here?" I asked Noah as we walked the trail to Jack's dad's cabin.

"No, but I can't be sure as to how many Jack and Lance has brought here," he told me and I snorted.

"So... bringing me up here to seduce me?" I teased.

He teased back, "Like I even have to seduce you."

I opened my mouth wide and pushed him. "That is so... true." I looked up at the darkening sky. "This is what I miss about summer... the sun always leaves us too soon in the cold months." I started blowing out air to watch it fog.

"Tell me about it," he said, placing his hand on a tree. I watched him step ahead of me and a wicked idea came to me.

fall from grace

I stopped and started creating distance between us. "Noah, I want an adventure," I told him randomly.

He turned his head and squinted. "What are you up to?" He eyed me suspiciously.

I was still backing away from him. "I'm a damsel running in the woods trying to make it to my prince's castle." He tossed his head back and groaned and I went on with a smile, "There's a beast-boy in the woods out to get me, a complete savage he is."

"Let me guess…" He tipped his head forward. "I'm the savage?"

I nodded before placing the back of my hand against my forehead dramatically. "Oh, what he'll do if he catches me. Oh, how he might ravish me and make me his."

"Just what kind of books have you been reading lately?" he asked with a smirk.

"Catch me if you can," I told him before I took off running toward my left. I wasn't a rookie when it came to running in the woods but this was something I wouldn't have done if it had already been completely dark outside. Hopefully, he caught me before it got any darker though. I couldn't hear anything over the noises I was making on my own and my heavy laughter. I peeked back to see if I saw him and screamed when he grabbed me. I started laughing again when I saw that he had even put his hood over his head. I tried to get away from him with real effort but he tossed me over his shoulder easily.

"I probably should have gotten further away before I had told you the plan," I said into his back as his fingers slid between my thighs and gripped my leg fat possessively. The only thing he did was grunt in response as he placed his fingers over my sex, and I reacted to his touch even with my jeans between us. I knew I was supposed to be kicking and screaming, but the only thing I could manage to do was slide my hands around him to admire the ridges on his stomach before feeling the bulge in his jeans. I continued touching him everywhere as he carried me in silence. My body was lit like a candle, too much longer and I feared I'd turn to liquid.

When I saw the cabin in the distance, I decided to get back into the idea of fighting him to get free again. I started squirming and pinching his back but his grip was made of iron and soon my stomach dipped into my toes as he tried unlocking the door to the cabin. "I don't think so," I mumbled as I pressed my leg onto the cabin wall and pushed. I didn't expect Noah to lose his balance like he did, but he started pulling me up as he fell backward so that I would land on him. I was breathing heavily as I smiled and hurried to get away. His hands slipped around my waist and jerked me back onto him.

"Damn, Priss, you're feisty" he grunted. "Too bad you're mine now." He held me tightly against his chest as he stood back up and carried me into the cabin where I continued to fight him every step of the way as he kicked the door shut. He didn't even take the time to carry me to the bed. He threw me onto the small table. It skidded with my weight and we both paused a moment until it stopped.

"What do you think you're doing?" I asked him, continuing to fight off what he planned to do.

He yanked my boots off before he pulled my feet and legs back and started tugging at my jeans. My core tightened as his azure eyes devoured me while he stripped me of my jeans and panties. I clamped my legs shut and placed my hands between my legs. His eyes met mine. "Think that's going to stop me?" he made the words sound like a growl. My breaths were coming out heavy and my heart pounded against my ribcage until I heard it in my ears. I was so turned on, I wasn't sure how to react. He forced my legs apart and pressed himself between them so that I couldn't squeeze them back together while he pried my hands off my opening. My strength was nothing compared to his though, and the moment he got what he wanted, he went down on me.

I gasped, his tongue ended with me thrusting myself into his face. He gripped my hips as he teased and molded me with his mouth. He pulled away only to add his fingers. His eyes watched my body as I whimpered and came undone. He raised up and leaned over me while adding another finger. He increased how hard and fast he moved his fingers. He'd never been so rough before. I lifted my legs up and spread them further apart in hopes that he'd continue. He bit into my neck and the orgasm that burned into me was as violent as his fingers were. He didn't give me time to recover before yanking me off the table and carrying me to the bed.

He tugged at my shirt until I lifted my arms. He tossed it to the floor and tore out of his as he came down over me. Everything was happening so fast, yet I couldn't imagine ever wanting it to stop. This was it. I knew it was. Noah had a look I'd never seen on him before. He was so careful with me, always giving into what I wanted, yet never showing me what he wanted.

He kissed my collarbone before kissing my lips. I arched my back when I felt him trying to take off my bra. Soon, it too was on the floor. He grabbed and squeezed them before he was pulling away again. I reached for him until I saw what he was doing and waited with anticipation and nervousness rolling into me. He unzipped his jeans then pulled out a condom... And it was happening all over again.

He was back above me, pinning my legs back as he claimed my lips and pressed inside. The pain was immediate, but Noah pinned me down harder when I cried out and tried to push him away. He smothered me out with his tongue and didn't even give pause when he was completely rooted inside of me. He pulled back then slammed back in. "Noah," I cried against his mouth. It hurt so much but it was the strangest thing, the pain started to bring on a new sensation.

"Just let me have you," his words almost sounded like a plea.

He pulled out, slammed in. Something sparked, wanting to change because a slither of something amazing hit my insides and I slowly relaxed and welcomed the next thrust. I whimpered when the pleasure slowly tried to burn through the pain. Noah's body was completely rigid as he grunted with his next movement. "I think it's coming," I sobbed as I wrapped my arms around him and he kissed me and increased his tempo. "Oh, God!" I moaned as I shattered and pulsed around him.

"God, Grace," he hissed. I felt his release inside me and gazed up at him as he collapsed on me. He lifted his head and kissed me like a man that hadn't just had me. "You're perfect, and now you're feeding my addiction of you."

———

I sat on the couch with Noah's shirt on and a blanket as he put on a movie. I admired his shirtless physique while he was turned away. Sex wasn't just about having sex with Noah. To me, it was wanting to share every moment with him, to know him in every way.

I had bled a little more again this time like I had in Noah's Jeep last weekend, but he had cleaned me up afterward and offered me his shirt to wear until we had to leave. That was the problem. I didn't want to part with him after what we just did together. I was so hopelessly attached to Noah in every way.

"Are you sure Jack or his dad won't just barge in?" I asked, gazing down at my bare feet peeking out of the blanket.

"No, his dad knows we're up here and Jack's out with his girlfriend."

He turned around and smiled at me. "Come here," I mumbled, opening my blanket to welcome him. He sat down next to me, pulling me onto his lap. "What are we watching?"

"Thirteen Ghosts." He grinned. We had loved that movie when we were younger. It had seriously freaked me out.

"You ever want to watch something we haven't seen?" I asked him.

"I'd rather watch something we've seen so that I get more of your focus."

I laughed. "Jealous of the TV, are we?"

206

fall from grace

"We got many years to watch new movies together. Nothing wrong with appreciating the fact that I shared all these memories with you as a kid and get to feel nostalgic about all the times I was planning to make you mine." He squeezed me tightly. "And, look now. You're mine."

"I'm seriously curious about the way you saw me as a kid."

"I never saw you as a kid," he whispered. "I saw you as a girl I loved."

"You were always my favorite person," I told him. "Still are."

"Let me be always."

30

Grace age 17

Noah age 17

I'm not my father. I'm nothing like him. All that I have left to feel when I think of him is anger and hollow pain. I say hollow because it feels so void and pointless. I shouldn't give him any emotion. He shouldn't even exist to me, but I still wonder, I still worry, I still hope that he'll let go of his cravings and set himself free. Not in the way Mom did.

I'm set free of him. Only I'm not.

And I want to be free of the pain my parents brought me.

I'd rather immerse myself in Grace and stay in her prissy confines and drown in happiness.

N.P.

Football season was over and our first snow fell. School was canceled and it left me with little to do Tuesday morning. Noah had gone to the garage since he didn't have school either. I was tossing some miniature marshmallows into my hot chocolate and waiting by the microwave for the popcorn to finish when someone knocked on the door.

Gus took off running and I followed after him. When I opened the door, I hadn't expected it to be Noah's dad. "John?" I asked, alarmed and quickly slipped on the closest shoes by the door and stepped out into the freezing cold. "What are you doing here?" My parents wouldn't like him being here. Dad wasn't home but Mom was in the shower. She had nowhere to go with school being canceled.

John's skin color was a sickly brown with the snow reflecting off it. He held his small jacket around him and shivered. "About Noah… I need you to give me his number."

"Why?" My hackles rose. "You know you're not allowed to have contact with him."

"Do you know if he's working or anything… or if the people he's with give him money?" My shoulders dropped. This was about money?

"Don't come back over here," I told him, turning around then stopped. "I can't believe you want me to contact your son just to get money!" I yelled.

"He's my son. He should want to help his dad," he had the nerve to say.

"He's seventeen! You were supposed to take care of him!"

I opened the door and was about to shut it when he muttered, "My power is about to be cut off in a couple of days… if I don't come up with the money to pay it. Please," he paused, "it's November and snowing!"

I walked inside, slammed the door, then closed my eyes and took a deep breath. I didn't want to tell Noah. I didn't want to burden him with his dad's problems. I didn't want him to feel more tossed aside and hurt than I could imagine he already felt when it was about his dad… But how could I ignore someone going without electric in the winter? My chest felt like it had been dipped in acid because I knew I was going to let him know even though John wasn't worth it.

I'd let Noah make the choice once I told him.

I sent him a text telling him to call me when he got the chance. No sooner than I sent it, he called within a minute. I answered as I walked into the kitchen and grabbed my hot chocolate that I didn't even feel like drinking now. "Hey."

"What's wrong?" he asked immediately. "Don't say nothing when I can tell by the sound of your voice." I heard the machinery at the garage in the background.

"You could have waited to call me when you got home," I told him.

"I was just changing someone's oil, no big deal. What's wrong?"

"It's your dad, he just came to the door."

He sighed. "I told you to stop going over there, Grace."

"He came over here!"

He paused. "What did your parents do?"

"Dad's working and Mom's in the bathroom so she didn't hear him knock, don't worry about that," I told him. I took a deep breath. "Your dad was wanting your number. I didn't give it to him, though."

"Good... What did he want?"

"His electric is about to get cut off... is what he told me."

I could imagine the frustration and disappointment reflected in Noah's eyes and closed mine as if that would make his sadness fade from my mind. "And let me guess, he wants money from me," he swore. "After all this time, he wants to use my connection with you to get in touch with me... just to get money."

"I'm sorry, Noah," I whispered. "This is my fault. I shouldn't have told him I was dating you."

He laughed sadly. "You're never to blame, Grace. I just can't stand him coming to you... Can I ask you to do me a favor?"

"Tell me what you want me to tell him and I will," I replied right away.

fall from grace

"You're not getting off the phone with me, but I need you to get my dad's electric bill from him."

"Noah… you're really going to help him, aren't you?" I wanted to drive all the way to him just so that I could hug him, if only the roads weren't terrible.

"If it's really a bill that needs to be paid… then yeah, I'm going to. He's not worth a damn to anyone else but he's still my dad."

"Stop, Noah… I understand you, I always have. I just hate…"

"Don't start crying," he ordered me, and I looked up to keep the tears from spilling as I ran to the door and slipped on some boots. "Are you going?"

"Yes," I mumbled as I opened the door. "Come on, Gus." He darted out into the snow and disappeared. I ran and fell on my butt in the process. I got right back up until I was knocking on John's door.

When he opened it, I held out my hand. "The bill. Where is it?"

He saw the phone in my hand and started stepping back. "Give me a second." He hurried to the table and knocked a pop can over in the process. "Shit," he muttered as he grabbed the bill and came back to me.

"I got it," I told Noah.

"Pass the phone to him." I did as he asked and handed my cell to John. He took it.

"Hey Son," John went on, "how have you been?" John paused and was nodding nervously and looking over at me. "I'm sorry I had to ask. There's been a lot going on and I've gotten a little behind on the bills…" He looked at me again. "Ah, it's no big deal for me to talk to Grace now, is it? She's going to be family one day, right? Fine, I'll leave her be," he said into the phone. "So, you're going to pay it for me? You're a good boy, Noah, always have been. It was good to hear your voice… Do you plan to come home soon when you turn eighteen?"

There was another pause and nodding from John. "I'll talk to you later. Yep."

He handed the phone back to me. I wiped the screen over my pajama pants before holding it away from my ear. "Noah?"

"You can leave now," he whispered then paused a moment while I turned around and stepped off the porch carefully. "Sorry about that Grace."

"Are you okay?"

He sighed. "Just freezing my balls off outside... I didn't want to have that conversation with everyone in the garage, ya know?"

I peeked inside the bill and gasped. "Six hundred dollars? Noah, you can't pay this!"

He blew into the phone. "Figures. He's probably just been paying enough every month to keep it turned on. It's fine, I told him I'd pay it this once and that was it."

"When are you coming to get the bill?"

"I'll come get it this evening when I leave the garage."

"The roads are already terrible and it's still snowing."

"Grace, I *need* to see you after hearing that man's voice. I want to wrap you in my arms and recharge." I smiled and tripped over Gus in the snow at the same time. "Are you okay?" he asked immediately when I gasped as I tried to catch myself from falling.

"Dang it, Gus, that's twice I've fallen in the snow today!"

Noah started laughing in my ear and it made me smile again. "Shit, I can't wait to hold you," he told me again.

"Grace, what are you and Gus doing in the road?" Mom yelled from the porch with a towel over her wet hair.

"He wanted to play in the snow," I told her and she shook her head.

"At least put on some more clothes," she said before walking back in and shutting the door.

"I'm gonna get back to work. I'll see you later, all right?"

"Can't wait."

———

"Hi, Noah," Mom yelled from the couch as I tried to sneak him up the stairs.

"Hi, Allison," Noah said with a smirk as he leaned his head down to peer into the living room from the stairs.

"You came over in this snow?" Mom asked him. "Grace never said you were coming over."

"It's not too bad. School's already been canceled for tomorrow too."

Mom nodded. "You know your dad will be home soon, don't you?" She was talking to me now.

"He doesn't plan to stay long," I mumbled, tugging at the bottom of his shirt as I continued up the stairs.

"If that's all right with you?" Noah asked her.

She smiled and shooed us upstairs. I let go his shirt once we entered my room and he shut the door behind us. He was quick to pull me into his arms and scoop my feet off the ground as he dropped onto the bed with me. "All I need is you every day, in my arms like this. I couldn't ask for anything more."

I smiled and kissed his cheek. "Let's grow together, not apart."

"I've been apart from you far too long already," he agreed before kissing me. He pulled away too soon. "I don't want a repeat of what happened the last time we were alone in your room."

"You're right," I agreed but that didn't mean I liked it. "Too bad," I whispered and bit his ear.

He groaned, pulling me as close as close could get. "Just wait... I'll get you this weekend," he cautioned before sitting up with me in his lap.

"Too far away," I whined.

"Grace!" Dad yelled downstairs.

I looked at Noah and groaned. "You probably should head back before it gets worse."

"Or... we can go downstairs and watch a movie so that I can spend a couple more hours with you."

I kissed him quickly. "That sounds like a wiener."

He tossed his head back and laughed. "You've got to stop with that already."

"Never," I promised.

He stood up. "Where's his bill?" I pointed toward the nightstand. "Come on, before your dad comes up here and drags me out." He stopped me at the door. "I told him to leave you alone, just leave him be. I can put up with him myself, but the one thing I'll never be able to tolerate is him coming to aggravate you."

"I'm fine."

"Seriously, Grace... I'll tell your parents if I have to so I know he'll leave you alone."

I grabbed his hand. "Come on, let's go watch a movie."

I understood Noah's words a few days later when his dad approached me as I got off the bus Friday evening. I didn't have anything to drive yet so I was stuck with a bus for now. I watched him nervously as he stepped up next to me as the bus left. "Have you talked to Noah today?" was the first thing he asked. I simply nodded. "Do you think you could call him up for me?"

"No, John," I muttered as I headed for the house.

"You wouldn't happen to have ten or twenty dollars on you, would ya?"

"Are you already trying to bum more money?" I turned and scowled at him. "You took six hundred dollars from Noah that he's gonna need once he hits eighteen!"

"Just ten dollars, that's all I need," he went on, completely ignorant or he just didn't care that I wanted to punch him in the face or cry for Noah.

I went into my purse and yanked out a five-dollar bill from my wallet before I slapped it into his palm. "Don't come asking for money again."

Only once you gave someone the chance to take advantage of you, they would.

———

"Thanks for having me this Thanksgiving," Noah said to Mom as he helped her carry the food to the table.

"Blame her if it tastes bad," Mom mentioned, tilting her head at me. I blushed and looked over at Noah who was grinning at me. "Grace said you guys were going over to eat at…" She looked to Noah for their names.

215

"Dean and Janet," he finished for her.

Dad grunted at the other end of the table. I gave him a dark look as he quietly sat and displayed his dislike of Noah being there. He was such a sour patch.

"So," Dad finally started and I inwardly sighed. "What's your plans after you leave high school?"

Noah sat down next to me. "Well, I've been working at a garage and I like the work so I figured I'd probably stick to mechanics." Dad said nothing, only nodded as he took a bite of his mashed potatoes.

"What about you, Grace?" Mom asked.

"I don't know," I replied honestly. "I haven't thought about it."

"You only have a year left before you hit college and have to decide from there," Dad added.

"I know," I muttered.

"You can always become a teacher... Then we can be the mother-daughter duo," Mom voiced, batting her eyes like a child.

I grinned. She was still young at heart when it came to certain things. "Next, you'll be wanting to dress us the same," I told her.

Her eyes twinkled. "Want to?"

Noah laughed. "You two already favor each other, I think it could work."

I groaned. "Let's not give her any ideas."

After leaving my house, we went to Dean's and ate where I got Janet to give me her potato casserole recipe. It had been delicious. My favorite part of the day was when I finally got to be alone with Noah. He brought me up to his room.

fall from grace

"All this food has made me so tired," I grumbled as I flopped down on his bed.

He joined me. "No kidding."

I rolled over against him and nuzzled his neck then oh, so slowly slid my hand down and grabbed his erection. He rolled over atop of me and we made out for the longest time, rolling all over the bed. We ended up napping with me lying completely on top of him. Janet came upstairs and woke us up to play some UNO with them. Noah laughed and pointed to the huge drool spot I had left on his shirt while I admired the cute sleepiness in his eyes.

Everything was going great. A little too perfect. I should have known life would rain on our parade.

31

Grace age 17

Noah age 17

Through the week, my mind is all about Grace… I move through classes, talk to friends, work at the garage, effortlessly, but she's always there, even when she's not here, she's inside me. That's why I know she's my one. She's my always.

Everyone's catching affections in high school, back and forth, new and old, they all move together but none of them are looking for everlasting.

I think I'm an old soul, or I think that's what people might call me. Or I'm just a guy that gets fixated on one girl and that's it. There's no going back, no changing it because I don't want to and I'm never going to try. I did once when I was asked, only because it was Grace's mom, but never again.

I'm connected, completely whole with Grace. We fit. We mesh. We go together.

N.P.

"Are you sure you don't want to go with us?" Sara asked me as she pulled into my driveway. She offered to drop me off from cheer practice—football season was over but basketball was just around the corner. I needed a vehicle but at the same time, I didn't want to ask my parents for one. Maybe, like Noah, I should think about getting a part-time job.

fall from grace

"Who's that?" Tiffany asked in the passenger side seat. I scooted up in the back seat and looked back and wished I hadn't when I saw who was waiting by our mailbox. I didn't know his name, it was the young guy that hung out at John's all the time.

"I don't know," I lied and slid across the seat to open the door and get out. "I'll see you guys later."

Sara looked back at him again. "Are you sure? Are your parents' home yet?"

"Mom's car is here," I told her. "Bye."

He waited until she backed out of the driveway before approaching me. I turned around and headed for the porch even though I saw him coming. "Grace!" he yelled and I was tempted to ignore him.

I turned around. "My dad would skin you if he saw someone like you standing by our yard," I told him as I crossed my arms. "He's about to come home too," I made sure to add.

He smiled and threw his hand up. "Aw, now, come on. Don't treat me like that. You're dating John's boy now."

"And?"

"And, that makes us cool."

"Let me make this clear, we are not cool. I only ever came over there to get John to straighten up and get Noah back, which NEVER happened. I'm done trying, so leave."

"Think you could give me Noah's number?" he asked me.

"Do you even know him?"

"I'm just trying to help John out. He has a son that can help him. That's what family does."

Now I was getting pissed. "Maybe—sometimes I might have thought I saw a flicker of a father in John when I was younger. A glimpse here and there that he cared for Noah but I was wrong."

He smiled, completely blowing my words aside as he said, "Think you could give us a twenty? John can pay you back on the first when he gets his check."

"Hello, I don't have a job!" I hissed at him.

"Then, can you call up Noah and see—"

"I'm not calling up Noah so you guys can have money for your pills or whatever," I muttered as I turned around and stormed inside.

What was even more chilling was when Dad came home and said, "There's a man that was hanging around the house, but he walked off when he saw me pull up." He asked me if I had known him and even told me to be careful because of it.

The next day, they must have been waiting for me to get home from school because the moment Mom took off to the grocery store there was a knock on the door. I mean, not minutes, it only took seconds. I had stayed home to catch up on a show I watched while I waited for Noah to get home from the garage to call.

I'd never been afraid of John until I peeked out and saw him and that guy at my door. I waited several seconds actually considering the idea of just not answering. "Grace, we see you at the door," said the other guy.

I calmed myself and opened the door. "What are you two doing here?" I asked.

"I really need Noah's number," John stated.

"I wouldn't have let him pay your bill if I had known you'd keep this up. He's only in high school and if you haven't forgotten, he's in foster care. He'll be on his own in a few months." I didn't tell them that they had already offered to let him stay longer because it was Noah's choice to leave.

"He's my boy. He can come home. Hell, that is his home."

fall from grace

That rage I felt just listening to this man… I squeezed my fists and took a deep breath. "Just go."

"I have nothing to eat. I just need a little to go out and get something," he told me.

"You don't even have a ride," I muttered. John hasn't had a vehicle in over a year or longer.

"I do," the other guy said with a smile.

"If you don't want to bother Noah, could you give me about twenty dollars? I'll pay you back on the first."

I rubbed my head and sighed. "I swear this is the last time, don't come back or I'll get my dad involved."

He shook his head. "No need to be like that. You're my family while you're dating my son."

I didn't even know what to say. I just slammed the door in their faces and went into the kitchen to grab my wallet from my purse. Mom and Dad both gave me money through the week… I sighed and walked back and opened the door.

"Here," I muttered, handing him a twenty.

"Thank ya, you're a lifesaver." I nodded and shut the door. I found my way back to the couch where I no longer felt like watching TV. Instead, I placed my head in my hands and took a deep, shaky breath. I knew it wasn't going to stop. I already knew John was taking advantage of the situation and it was all my fault for telling him I had gotten in touch with Noah again. If I told Noah about it, I knew he would keep helping his Dad so that he'd leave me alone or worse, he'd tell *my* dad and that'd be one more thing he'd hound Noah about.

My phone started ringing. I felt relieved just seeing his name pop up on the screen. "Hey," I chirped as I answered.

"Hey, Priss," he mumbled. "What are you doing?"

"Sitting here on the couch."

"… Okay, what's wrong?" he muttered. "Your voice doesn't sound right."

I smiled. "You've got to stop doing that, or I'll never be able to hide anything from you."

"I don't want you to hide your feelings from me, ever. That's not us."

"I know," I whispered. "Just one of those days, I guess, and I think I have a migraine coming on." I stood up. "Most of all, I just miss you and I hate this only seeing you once a week or worse, longer!" It wasn't a lie, I just left out the worst part, his dad.

"I know," he agreed. "It won't be like this forever."

Mom stepped into the house carrying bags of groceries. "Grace, help me carry in the groceries."

Noah must have heard her. "I'll call you back in a bit."

I knew that was for that best. The longer I was on the phone with him, the easier he'd find out something was wrong.

———

Sara took me home from practice again the next day and guess who was waiting for me? Mom wasn't home this time and an awful amount of dread hit me at the thought of dealing with him again. I had just given him twenty yesterday. I thought I might have fifteen left in my wallet…

"Who's this guy?" Sara asked as she pulled into the driveway. "Seriously, it's starting to get creepy, these dudes hanging around your house… it looks like he's waiting on you."

They didn't know he was Noah's dad. "It's one of our neighbors."

"I didn't realize this was a bad neighborhood," she mumbled.

"It's not bad," I told her, trying to dismiss the dread I felt. "Thanks for taking me home again."

"Ask your parents for a car." She had been saying that since I got my license.

"Bye."

When she pulled out, John approached me. "No," I said right away.

"Hear me out," he started.

"John, please," I blinked and muttered. "All I have is fifteen dollars!"

"Look at this house." He pointed toward it. "You guys have money."

"No, my parents have money."

"Will you give me Noah's number?"

"I've been coming over with food for the last few years. I begged and pleaded with you to try and get your son back but you never would. You never once asked me for money then but since I told you I'm with Noah, you've changed! You'd be freezing right now if it wasn't for your son having a heart."

"I would have gotten by just fine without his help, I always manage to make it through."

I sneered. "Then stop asking me for money."

"This and that are different. Kids should want to help their parents out."

"You need help, just not with money," I argued.

"I know, I know." He nodded. "Will you loan me some money until I get my check?"

223

Talking wasn't working with him. I stormed away from him but he grabbed my bag to stop me and in the process, half of what was inside spilled to the ground. I sighed and bent down to pick it up while John did the same. He reached for my wallet and handed it to me. "I won't help you destroy yourself with your addiction," were the words I said as Dad's truck pulled into the driveway.

I hurried to put my things in my bag and stood as Dad jumped out of the truck looking furious. "You better not have been doing what I think you're doing," he yelled at me as he looked to John.

"Dad," I started.

"Are you taking money from my daughter?"

"She was only loaning me some until I got my check in a few days," said John as he backed away. At least he was smart, but Dad came at him.

"You worthless piece of shit!" he yelled at him right before he punched him in the face. Dad was a big guy, especially compared to John who was so underweight. John fell into the cold, wet grass. "If I ever catch you on my property or around my daughter again, I'll kill you!" Dad threatened. "In the house, Grace." He grabbed my arm and led me into the house, tears sprang from my eyes.

Once we were inside, he slammed the door shut. "Why would you enable his drug problem? You do realize by giving him money that's the only thing you were doing?" He looked genuinely disappointed with me and it hurt.

I dropped my head. "I know. I wasn't going to give him money. I was heading inside."

"How many times have you given him money?"

"He only started asking this past week."

"Jesus, Grace," he swore, rubbing his eyes before meeting mine with another disappointing stare. "Did Noah know about this?"

fall from grace

"No!" I yelled immediately. "He would have been just as upset as you."

He shook his head. "I can't... I just can't allow this."

I already knew where this was going and felt sick in my stomach. "Dad, this has nothing to do with him! Noah doesn't even live with his dad anymore."

He grabbed my shoulders. "This is life for Noah. This will always be the way it is for him. It's not just Noah, it's his family. Being with him won't be easy. You're young and haven't even gotten out of this town, there's so much out there. I want that for you. I don't want this—if you stay with Noah, you're taking his dad in too. I know you don't think it's that way, but it is. His dad coming to aggravate you for money, that's only the beginning... He'll always leech off his son, and Noah will never be able to cast him aside because it's his dad and that's just how Noah is. He's a good kid, Grace, I know. I've watched him grow up but he's not going anywhere in life."

I pulled away from him and couldn't look up because I knew some of his words were right. Noah had already paid his electric bill and he hadn't even spoken to his dad in years... Noah was one of the good guys and I would always love him, no matter what.

"I love him, Dad."

"And I love you. That's why I can't let you stay with him."

"You can't make me stay away from him."

He turned away. "Yes, I can and I will. You're not eighteen yet and Noah lives in a different county. This won't work out, no matter what you believe."

That was the way it was for Noah and me. There was always so many obstacles in the way of us being together, and the worst one had yet to come.

But when it came, I would fall to pieces… pieces even Noah might not be able to pick up.

32

Grace age 17

Noah age 17

Is it May yet? The need to be independent. The need to be closer to Grace is so strong. I'm already thinking of ways to convince her parents to let her spend nights with me once I have my apartment. The possibility of getting nights with my priss makes me so damn giddy, I got a pep in my walk.

N.P.

Dad hadn't been kidding. When the weekend rolled around, he hovered around me mercilessly. He wasn't going to let me hang out with Noah this weekend, or at all if this kept up. Mom didn't agree with him, but she had been upset that I had given money to John. She wanted to tell Noah about it but I begged her not to. He also didn't know the reason Dad was suddenly even more against me being with him and I wanted to keep it that way.

Luckily for me, Mom helped me out so that I could still see him Sunday. She convinced Dad that she was taking me to Sara's—driving me herself so that I wasn't going to sneak off and see Noah when she was actually taking me to meet Noah in the parking lot of Walmart. It was raining the last time I met Noah here too.

"Your dad's going to be mad when he finds out. I'm going to tell him that I took you to see him when I get back," she told me as she parked.

"Why?" I unbuckled as we waited for Noah to arrive.

She turned and smiled. "Because he's my husband and I love him and he's your father. I don't agree with him wanting to keep you from Noah so I did this but I do plan on telling him… So, expect him to be mad when you come home."

"I know. Thanks, Mom."

She smiled. "I wouldn't do this if it were any other boy, but I kept him away from you long enough and I know you two… I trust that you guys are going to think about your futures in between this passionate love you two have for each other, right?"

I nodded. "Noah seems to have it all figured out while I… Is it bad that I still don't know what I want other than Noah?" I found myself asking.

She laughed. "There's nothing wrong with wanting someone, it's only sad when it doesn't work out… You and Noah have grown and matured this long together, I don't see why you can't keep doing so." She shook her head. "Listen to me trying to sound like I know a thing or two."

"I like the way you say things, Mom, you don't treat our relationship like we are going to grow out of it."

"I'm a hopeless romantic. I can't help it." She pointed behind me. "I think it's Noah."

It was. He hopped out of the Jeep and ran to Mom's door where she rolled down the window. "You're getting wet," she told him.

"Nah, it's just sprinkling right now," he said with an easy grin. "Thanks for bringing her out here."

"He'll come around." We knew she was referring to Dad. "Grace is his baby."

"Mom," I groaned.

fall from grace

"She's my everything," Noah didn't hesitate to say.

I smiled as Mom wiggled her finger at him. "See that, I like how you aren't afraid to say what you're thinking, even the mushy stuff." He laughed and wiped his eyes. He was getting soaked standing in the rain. "Go on, you two. Bring her home by ten. Her dad's already going to blow once he finds out I didn't take her to Sara's."

He nodded. "Will do."

I opened the door. "See ya tonight, love you!" I told her.

"Be careful on these roads, Noah!" she yelled through the opened door. "It's supposed to turn into snow later. Bring her home sooner if it starts getting too bad, okay?"

"Will do," he told her. "You be careful too."

"Love you," she told me as I shut the door.

Once we were inside his Jeep, he started it up. "Shit, I'm cold," he hissed.

I grinned at him. "You're the one that stood in the rain and got soaked."

"It'll be okay," he muttered when his phone dinged. He picked it up then started grinning. "Look." He leaned over and showed me the screen.

I'm rooting for you.

So, don't disappoint me.

It was a text from Mom. We both start laughing and watched as she pulled out. I buckled up. "Where to?" I asked him.

"To Dean's to watch a movie and cuddle."

I leaned over closer to him. "I love the way you say cuddle, as big as you are. So *sexy*."

He looked over and smirked. "You love me. Period."

229

"I do," I didn't waste a breath.

Only when we got to Dean and Janet's house, he did something that gave my heart even bigger wings. He cranked up his stereo with something country instead of turning the Jeep off. I gave him a strange look and he just grinned and ran out into the soft but frigid rain. I shook my head and watched as he made his way to my door and opened it. "What are you doing?" I asked.

"Giving you another adventure," he answered with his hand stretched out for mine. "Come on, this one will be in the rain."

"Are you crazy? It's the first of December and it's freaking cold out!" I screamed as he took my hand and pulled me out into the rain. I hunched my shoulders up and laughed as he pulled me into his wet clothes and spun me around before lifting me over his head.

"You make a good umbrella," he teased.

"It's freakin' cold!" I shivered as he placed my boots on his and started moving us to the music.

"You're not shaking from the cold, you're shaking because you love me so much."

I threw my head back and giggled. "You say the stupidest things." When I met his eyes, I whispered, "How do I fall for everything you say?"

"Because... I've been working on me since we were kids so that I could have you and keep you when we got older." I wrapped my arms around him. "I've also been working you over too since we were kids."

"Good Lord, what are you two doing out here in this freezing rain?" Janet yelled from the porch. I turned back to see her smiling at us like we were crazy.

We ran for the porch where Noah childishly pushed me back over and over to keep me in the rain. "Noah, I'm gonna kick your butt," I huffed.

He snorted while Dean chuckled in the doorway. "I don't think it'd be wise to pick a fight with someone his size," Janet informed me.

"Mind telling us what you guys were doing dancing in the rain?" Dean said, stepping aside so that we could all come inside.

"Someone made me promise her adventures in exchange for being her friend." Noah looked at me after he spoke.

"Sounds like a smart girl," Janet said with a wink.

I wrapped my arms around myself. "I'm freezing!"

"Have Noah give you a change of clothes and I'll dry those before you leave."

Noah took my hand and led me upstairs after pulling off our boots. I peeled my wet jacket off as he shut the door and tore out of his hoodie. "I'm freezing thanks to you," I nagged. "Give me something to wear."

"How about I warm you up?" He turned me around to face him and started lifting my shirt.

"What about Dean and Janet?" I whispered, already sounding breathy.

"The door's locked." He bent down and kissed my neck as he unhooked my bra next. Once it fell to the floor, he stood back and stared before he bent down and started tearing me out of my pants. The next thing I knew, I was naked and being thrown on the bed as he towered over me.

There was a knock on the door. "If you hand me the clothes, I'll dry them," Janet called through the door.

I smiled up at him. "I knew this would happen."

He sighed and climbed off me as I grabbed a blanket and covered it around me as I walked to his dresser to grab something to put on. I chose some jogging pants and a black t-shirt. It was so obvious I didn't have a bra on but my bra was wet too. I put my panties back on though and handed the rest to her to dry.

Once she headed back downstairs, Noah wrestled me back down on the bed where we ended up talking. "So, you want to be a mechanic?" I asked him.

He placed his head in his palm as he lay on his side and made circles with his fingers across my stomach. "I like to be hands-on with my work so yeah, I wouldn't mind opening my own place later on down the road. I've never seen myself at a desk or behind a computer, that's just not me… Does that bother you?" he asked.

"Why would it? I'm just a little envious that you know what you want and I don't have a clue."

"You used to go around yelling that you'd be a teacher like your mom, what happened?"

"Um… I realized how crappy students were?" I offered, and he laughed. "Mom does have a way of making it seem fun though," I drifted off as I stared at the ceiling.

We ended up napping again. I felt like we were already one of those old couples that fell asleep any and everywhere together. It was hard not to when I always felt the most at peace with Noah.

Maybe that should be our slogan… *Couples that nap together, stays together.*

I hadn't realized I had left my cell phone in the Jeep until he was taking me home. When I grabbed it, I panicked at all the missed calls from Dad's cell. I had a text from Mom two hours ago that read:

Might need to come home. Your dad's not happy at all. I'm afraid he's gonna come get you himself at this rate.

"Dad's called a billion times," I told Noah as he started the Jeep and pulled out of the driveway. "I'm gonna call Mom." Only she didn't answer her cell phone and I was a little nervous of the idea of Dad answering the house phone if I called.

My phone lit up with Dad's cell phone. "It's my dad," I said nervously.

"Answer it," he told me. "Don't worry, I'll be with you. We can get chewed out together."

I smiled and answered. "Hello?"

"Grace." Something was very wrong with his voice. "I've been trying to get a hold of you… You need to come to the hospital," his voice was choked up and my stomach felt every bit of it. "It's your mom."

———

I felt like I would throw up the entire drive to the hospital. Noah kept a hold of my hand as we drove in silence. We didn't walk, we ran into the hospital and didn't stop until we were in the ER and Dad was there with his hands on his lap looking down at the tiled floor.

He looked up when he heard us. His gaze landed on Noah. "Where's Mom? What happened?" I asked.

"She wrecked her car… Apparently, she lost control and hit a tree."

My chest was killing me. "Have you seen her? How is she?"

"She's in surgery. They took her back right away. I haven't heard anything else."

"Why was she out?" I asked him.

His eyes darkened toward Noah. "She was going to get you."

I shuddered. "That doesn't make sense, she knew Noah was taking me home. She didn't even know where he lived."

"You weren't supposed to even see him! I told you no! And you weren't answering your phone!" he yelled and I stepped back.

"I left it in the Jeep." When Noah had pulled me out into the rain, I had forgotten about it. That was the truth.

"Leave," he said to Noah.

"At least let me wait to know how Allison is," Noah told him.

Someone stepped out of the door. The doctor wiped his face with his sleeve as if to hide his exhaustion as he approached. Dad got up…

Only to fall right to his knees.

I didn't hear what the doctor was saying. It was like a shield had gone up to prevent my ears from hearing his words. I stumbled back, hands caught me and held me up.

More words. More words. I didn't want to hear them.

There was no escaping the ugly that came and stole everyone's happiness.

———

Everyone came. So many. Mom was loved. She didn't look right lying in that casket. Nothing about any of this was. It didn't even look like her. I was convinced this person wasn't her… But apparently, this was as pretty as they could make her after the wreck… destroyed her.

The numbness that had passed over me since the hospital was frightening, even to me. My insides were screaming. I was drowning in my thoughts and these feelings, but none of it would make its way to the surface. Noah was there, always, never wanting to leave my side until I made him… Even then, he looked as if he wanted to deny my cold, hard stare and stay.

I kept my phone in my hand and I'd stare at her last text, telling me to come home. Then I felt the piercing in my chest and wondered if she was truly coming to get me when she had no idea where I was… Or did she?

Dad was a mess, and I wondered if maybe he was the reason why I didn't do the same. It was scary the way he wouldn't look at me or how he didn't ask when I was coming home or offer me a ride home from the funeral home. He completely ignored me when I wanted nothing more than to cry with him.

Noah tried to comfort me during those nights but I couldn't stand to be touched. I just wanted to be alone. I could feel it… Noah's fear. It was in the way he held onto me stronger when I pulled away, in the way he kissed my forehead once more after I had just shoved him away, in the way I pushed him out of the house every night during the funeral when he wanted to be there for me.

I would step into the living room where Dad would sit on the couch in silence then he'd cry. I'd sit down with him because I knew I needed this just as much as him… I wanted to cry too. All of these bottled up emotions were slowly consuming me, but he got up and walked upstairs when I tried to be next to him.

If Mom was here, she'd know how to fix us but she wasn't. She was gone, and she was never coming back. She'd never be able to stitch Dad and me together.

I pulled out my phone again and stared at her text in the darkness of the living room all alone… Still, I didn't feel like I was worthy to cry for the woman I loved most in this world. The ones that fell down my cheeks that night didn't count. I didn't make a peep, no matter how much I wanted to scream. I thought I was holding it all in.

The day she was buried, I followed Dad out the door and climbed into his truck with him. He didn't speak to me. He continued to ignore me as we drove to the cemetery. Still, as the silent tears slid down my cheeks, I held it in.

Noah was there trying to hold me and I distanced myself from him again. And I knew he was starting to sense it because the fear in his eyes became terror.

I let him drive me home afterward but instead of taking me home, he pulled off beside the road. "You've done nothing but cry the last few days. Please, Grace, talk to me," he begged.

I thought I was holding it in? I made sure not to cry… Only Noah was right, it wasn't my tears I was holding in, it was my words, my voice. I hadn't spoken since the hospital.

I pulled my phone out again and stared at Mom's text. "Grace, whatever dark thoughts you're having, let me take them from you… Please don't," his words convinced me that he knew exactly what had been plaguing my mind since she passed away.

"Noah," I croaked, "did Mom know where you lived?"

"Grace," he was begging me again, and my stomach was churning. "Stop. Our love didn't kill her."

More tears. "Did she?" I asked again.

Noah looked like he was crying too. "Yes," he finally said.

I sucked in air before screaming as I broke into tears. "Mom," I found myself saying, and screaming all the things I wish I didn't have to say.

"Stop apologizing, you did nothing wrong," he broke down with me as he grabbed me and pulled me into him. I pushed his chest but he held tighter. "It was an accident, accidents happen every day."

"She was coming to get me. Dad hadn't wanted me to see you but I convinced her anyway."

"Grace!" I knew he wanted me to open my eyes but I couldn't.

"My dad won't even look at me!"

fall from grace

"Just a few more months, Grace, and I'll be on my own. Come live with me then." I opened my eyes and met his beautiful blues. That sounded beautiful, wasting away on Noah in a small apartment... But I no longer saw that future. It wasn't fair for me to love Noah when I lost Mom, and Dad lost what I wanted to have.

"You'll be eighteen, I won't..." I yanked my arms from his grips. "I can't leave my dad, we just lost Mom. I just lost her." Saying it made me start crying again.

"Grace, I won't let you push me away," he whispered inside his Jeep, but I wouldn't look his way again.

"I'm not pushing you away, I'm leaving you."

"You're not serious."

"Yes, I am! Take me home."

He started driving again and with the wheels turning, the heaviness in my heart grew. I hardly gave him time to park before I jumped out of the Jeep. I heard him get out and run to catch up to me. He jerked me around to face him. "I can't leave you alone when I know you're hurting, please, just let me hold you. Let me take care of you!" he pleaded with me. "I cared for her too, and I know how painful it is to lose your mom."

"You don't know! My mom centered her world around me while yours didn't even know she was in this world half the time," I said the words before I could think of what it was I said. He looked taken aback and I stepped back. "Just, please, Noah, let's end this... before I become this ugly person that you're gonna hate." I met his eyes and hoped it would make him understand as I rubbed my hands over my hair. "There's this ugliness I feel growing inside of me. I feel like it's going to get worse, not better."

"Yeah, it's going to get worse... before it gets better." He stepped forward, cupping my cheeks. "I don't care. Be ugly. Show me how damn ugly you can be. I want all of it, just don't leave my arms.

237

You know it's where you belong." The way he said things stirred my craving of him so easily... so easily that I found myself moving into his arms instead of away.

I placed a peck on his lips, but Noah placed his hand into my hair and tried to consume me with a real one. I pulled our lips apart. "I'm going to be okay without you, and you're going to go on without me like we did before we met for the second time."

I stepped back and he reached for me. "Stop... I feel like I'm really losing you," he croaked.

"Don't get the apartment. Don't come to my high school. Stay at Dean's until you finish high school so you can save up money and go from there."

He looked at me like I had lost my mind... or broken his heart. "You know I can't do that."

"You will," I told him. "I don't want to see you. I don't want to pass you in the halls. I don't want to see you, period," I repeated.

There was a hint of malice in the way he smirked at me. "Because you know this is stupid! You can't bear the idea of seeing me without *being* with me." That was exactly it. I turned around and headed in. "We're far from over Grace. We're just getting started."

Only I wished I hadn't looked outside the window and saw him trying to pull himself together in his Jeep before he took off.

Mom was gone, Dad was lost, and I was broken, and I couldn't let myself be healed by Noah. Not when we were to blame for Mom's death.

33

Grace age 17

Noah age 18

My love hurts. She's truly gone ugly. I pull and she pushes.

I reach out with phone calls, I drive forty-five minutes to her house almost every day where she doesn't come to the door, and then another forty-five to get back. I'm anxious and afraid, yes, she has me terrified, and it's truly the worst when it's her that's making me feel this way because she's the one I want, the one I need when I feel lost and confused.

I stare at her mom's text and convince myself a dozen times that she supported us. She believed in me, but I can't say those things to Grace because she's letting the guilt she feels swallow her whole. I want to save her, save us, but she won't let me. If I push her on it, I'm afraid of pushing her away from me completely.

When I'm afraid that the guilt is threatening to swallow me whole along with her, I turn to Janet and let her listen because I need someone to listen and tell me that the one thing I've had that's beautiful and exceptional hasn't led to this. My feelings for Grace are powerful, they're real and strong. That's why it hurts so much more to think that we kept making mistakes when it came to her parents.

I know my priss loves me, it's plain to see... that's why she's trying so hard, but I know her efforts are in vain. She won't stop loving me, just

like I let her make me suffer, and suffer even more because I love her,
and I still think my future's worth the pain she's bringing me.

Because she's the only future I've ever seen.

N.P.

Our house was no longer a home. It was a place where two people ate, slept, and lived without interaction. Not that I was the one making it that way. The first few weeks after Mom passed away, Dad went to work and came home and slept... I didn't know if he was eating, I wasn't...

I finally built up the nerve one day to tell him we needed food at the house, so he simply gave me money and I started going to the grocery store once a week in his truck. I'd make food, sometimes I thought my food tasted good, but most of the time it couldn't compare to Mom's cooking. I'd wait for him to get home before I'd eat in hopes that one day he'd sit down and eat with me. Instead, he chose to eat before coming home or eating when I was finished.

I thought I might understand Noah a little more in the past few months... The more Dad ignored me, the more I needed him to smile at me again. The less we talked, the more I missed him even though he was hurting me. If Noah craved his parents' affection the way that I needed Dad's right now, I don't understand how he could smile and go on like he did growing up.

Dad stopped asking about Noah. He stopped asking about my life or caring since Mom faded from this world. Not that I had a life now. I rode the bus to and from school every day and that was it. I quit cheerleading. I stayed home on the weekends. I cleaned this empty house and washed our clothes while Dad stumbled around the house in a stupor. I wanted to be mad at him, but when I caught him with that look in his eyes sometimes or the way he cried while holding a picture of the three of us together, I'd run to another room and cry for Mom and wish she was here to make us better.

fall from grace

Noah tried to reach out to me every day. He came to the house every other day and on Christmas but I didn't answer the door and Dad never came out of his room. He left me a present, a small necklace with my name written in cursive. I told myself not to wear it, but I never took it off once I tried it on that night. Every night he called and texted me knowing I'd never respond back. Dean and Janet tried reaching out to me many times.

Noah finally stopped coming in May and that set my world into another crisis. Even though I wouldn't let myself have him, the thought of him giving up on me was hard to swallow. For six months I've ignored him, I didn't plan to change it now. Even on the fifth, I never called and wished him a happy birthday when I should have. Noah deserved so much love, yet I only knew how to be this ugly creature right now. He might meet someone soon. What if she set his world aflame much better than what I could? My flame had dulled into a rotten apple.

I hated this future girl with a burning passion. I hated this pathetic person I'd become. Her friends were slowly giving up on her. Her father already had, and one day, Noah was going to wake up and see how dim she'd become. Or maybe he already had because he no longer tried to get in touch with me...

Until the day he sent me a friend request on Facebook. In my mind, I was already panicking because by doing this, I felt like he was invading on what I hid from him. The online world was always safe from his eyes. I never took our pictures off my page, I never changed my relationship status to single.

But I couldn't for the life of me be angry because his profile picture was one of me and him. It was taken the first night we tried to have sex and we were lying in the back seat of his Jeep holding each other with smiles that I thought would never leave our faces. I covered my face and cried because the relief I felt was instant and it made me sick and happy all at once.

He hadn't given up on me, even when I was trying my hardest to push him out.

———

Noah never transferred senior year. He still wasn't calling or texting me, but I wondered if he kept up with me through Facebook the same way I saw when he was hanging out with Lance and Jack when they'd tag him at places. I'd randomly post pictures just for him to see. Noah never posted anything, but he followed everything I posted.

I knew it was wrong of me to keep him this way, wrong of me to cling to him when I needed to cut ties completely.

I wish I could say John changed, but it took him months of occasionally asking for Noah's number or money before he found out my mom had passed away. You'd think he'd see the empty spot where her car used to be and at least wonder, but it wasn't until I finally broke down and told him that she was gone and that I was no longer with his son that he had the sense to look sorry. It kept him away for a bit but he eventually came back and it was after Noah turned eighteen that I handed over Noah's number.

I never saw Noah's Jeep at his trailer, not that I looked for it every day, and John finally stopped coming around completely. It made me wonder if Noah was letting him take advantage of him, not that I had a right to care or even think about him every day like I did.

The nights I was tempted to break down and call him, I'd pull out my phone and stare at Mom's text and remind myself that my feelings for Noah led to her death even if the wreck was an accident that could have happened to anyone, these feelings of guilt were never going to go away.

And neither would my feelings for Noah. I grew into him, and I loved him for too long and so deeply that his presence was never going to leave its place in my heart or mind.

fall from grace

That was maddening itself when you were trying to push him out while desperately seeking your father's forgiveness.

Some nights I cried for Mom, other nights I cried for Noah, and the nights I cried for them both were the worst.

––––––––

Noah had quit the football team senior year, I had only found out when Jack posted about missing him out on the field. Sara and Tiffany's magic was slowly working on me again because it was easier to want to get out of the house as time passed. I ended up going to the movies with them or escaping to one of their houses on the weekend to take my mind off everything else. Instead of dwelling on the things I wish I could change, I started avoiding my thoughts with my actions.

I stayed busy. I smiled too much and laughed at things that weren't funny. I flirted with Dustin at school and I'd feed him the illusion that I wanted him. I dyed my brown hair completely blonde. I actually liked it and thought Mom would have too. She was always into fashion and all the cool things, unlike me who was only ever into Noah.

My eighteenth birthday came that next November and I was left with another gift from Noah on the porch that he placed on the other side of the doorway. I knew Noah loved me and that was the reason he did it, but my knees hit the cold wood as I fell and cried as I stared at his creations. Mom's voice drifted through my head like a ghost and I swear I could hear her saying how much she loved this one too.

When I thought I was doing better, it all came rushing back.

––––––––

Graduation was near and everything was changing for everyone. We decided to stay or leave this town. I told Mom I'd think of my future and I hadn't.

Only I couldn't think of the future when I got on Facebook to see a picture of Noah that he was tagged in. It was a group picture but he was smiling and talking to some girl that wasn't me. She was cute and I knew that look well, she liked Noah.

I felt like throwing up. The picture made me restless and I couldn't stop wondering if Noah smiled and laughed like I did or if he was truly happy without me now. I hated the twisted way my mind thought. I started wondering if he touched another girl the same way he touched me and when I did, I started shaking because the thought killed me. Once again, I wasn't moving on and *he* was.

When Sara asked me to go to the bonfire Mark was throwing for our graduation, I said yes because I felt like it was time for me to change. I needed to fully commit to letting Noah go, but first I needed the ability to stop thinking about him to do it.

In my head, I heard Sara and Tiffany rambling on about how I needed to experience more than Noah. They always said how could I know Noah's the one when I hadn't tried any others? The words were calling to me tonight and I began to wonder if maybe I could find someone that could make me forget the way Noah made me feel. Maybe there was someone better, someone that I was allowed to love and touch and keep without feeling the guilt.

Sara handed me a drink, then it became *drinks*, and soon I felt freer than I'd felt in a long time. Everything felt and looked so loopy. Tiffany steered me away from the fire as I laughed. And when a guy from my class named James approached me, I didn't stop him when he kissed me. Even with the alcohol giving me that freeing feeling, it wasn't enough to make James a better kisser. It wasn't enough to send me free-falling. I let him kiss me, still hoping for a miracle until someone jerked my shoulder back. I looked up to see Dustin lifting me to my feet.

"Okay, pretty sure you don't want to be kissing James," he told me as he seated me on a different log.

"I did," I corrected him as I almost fell backward. I would have if it weren't for him catching me.

He frowned at me. "You make me sad, Grace."

fall from grace

I smiled, leaning into him. "Why? Do you want me to kiss you instead?" I slurred, leaning in to kiss him.

He held me away from his face with a sigh. "No, I mean. You acting this way, it's not you. It's like you're begging someone to ruin you."

I pulled away from him to stand but he planted my butt back down. "I didn't come here to get lectured."

"I know," he muttered. "You came here to feel numb. Too bad it's not what you're gonna get."

Sara came to my rescue. "Leave her alone, Dustin. She needs to let go and live a little." She pulled me up and he let her. "But even I know it's just not you to go kissing someone to forget Noah," she told me once we were away from him.

I swallowed and looked down at our feet. When I looked back up, my eyes widened. Tiffany was kissing another girl. Sara saw my expression and smiled. "She's been meaning to tell you, but you've been… ya know, weird about Noah and losing your mom."

"How long?" I asked.

"She's been dating Brittany for a few weeks. It's not a phase, Grace, she's bi." I looked back at Tiffany and smiled as I watched her laugh and kiss the other girl. She looked happy. Just what kind of friend have I been not to have noticed? "No need to look guilty. She understands you've been dealing with a lot… Let's just pretend you didn't see so she can tell you herself, okay?" I smiled and nodded. Sara stopped abruptly and I looked at her. She pointed ahead, and my chest seized.

Noah stood a couple of feet in front of us, only his eyes weren't smiling as he took me in. I shrank back in my skin as I turned to step away from Sara and stumbled in front of her. "Grace!" Sara screamed because I was too close to the bonfire.

I didn't have to see who it was that yanked me back, but I did and was met with his hard glare as he picked me up in his arms and carried me away from the fire despite my protest. "Let me go! What are you even doing here?" I growled.

"Dustin sent me a pic I couldn't ignore so I came here to take your ass home."

"I'm not going home," I slurred and pushed at his chest.

"Home or you're stuck with me."

I stared at his lips then turned my entire head the opposite direction. "Home."

He pulled me into his arms tighter willing me to look at him once again. "You little asshole, if I didn't love you, I'd—"

"You'd what?" I poked back, even pinching his arm to provoke him into making him say something that would give me a reason to hate him.

He snarled and jerked his arm away from my fingers as he searched my face for something. "How much have you been drinking?" he asked.

"Not enough," I muttered. I still felt entirely too much being in his arms. When I remembered that it had been over a year since the last time, I felt like attacking him again.

"Drunk enough to have some guy's tongue down your throat?" he asked darkly. "Dustin sent me a picture. It's crawling through me right now, I'm so fucking pissed that I had to see something I didn't want to!"

"Then why'd you come?"

"To stop you from doing something stupid. I gave you space so you could find acceptance, not to bring us further apart."

Tears stung my eyes and I looked away. "Put me down. I can do what I want with who I want. You have!"

"What?" he growled. We were at his Jeep now. He placed me on my feet. "What are fucking talking about?"

"You've probably already slept with someone else since we broke up, why can't I?"

He pinned me to the Jeep. My insides were burning, I was so angry. I wish I was only angry. Livid Noah was doing something to my ovaries, my entire body was tingling with him near. His angry blue eyes glared into mine as he got up in my face. "Why the hell would you think that?"

"I saw the picture of you guys with all those girls," I yelled. "I saw the way you were laughing with that girl!"

His eyes softened as his smiled dipped into victory. "That's it." He beamed as he pressed into me with a renewed look, one that flooded my panties. "You think I've been with someone else so you're kissing some guy."

"Have you?"

"Fuck, no," he answered. "Are you drunk?" he asked again.

"I don't know!" Our faces were so close, I could feel his breath across my cheek.

"Are you drunk enough to let me fuck you?" His eyes were smothering me. I could do nothing but swallow and look down. He leaned away only to grab my arms and flip me around so that my breasts were pressing over the hood of his Jeep.

"What are you doing?" I stuttered and shook from pleasure passing through me for what was to come.

"Showing you… and me that we still belong together," he whispered into my ear as he yanked my shorts down.

"Someone will see," I said right before I gasped as he pressed into me violently. It hurt because he never prepared me for him, and the rude awakening felt too good. He grabbed my hips and bit my shoulder as he pushed himself in deeper until I relaxed against the hood and took what he gave me. It was beautifully disgusting how perfect this felt to have him inside me again. It was nice to feel something other than self-hate. He fit so perfectly that I whimpered and cried out as he slammed into me like we were two deer rutting. Something felt different, more intense than every other time before, like I was feeling him so much more. It had my stomach basking in fire and his ongoing thrusts.

"Fuck, Grace," Noah grunted as he pressed his face into my hair. "How can you keep me from this? What we have?"

His words provoked a violent tremble through me that exploded into an orgasm. "Noah," I moaned and his rhythm increased to the point that I could hear him slapping against my butt. I couldn't recall hearing him open a condom though, and the way it felt was too delicious. I lifted up and turned my head. "Noah, I'm not on any birth control."

He grabbed my neck and tilted my face back to kiss him. "Shit," he groaned as he thrust one last time before he pulled out and came on my butt. I watched every second as he did with a heated look. He stepped away and grabbed some napkins from his Jeep to clean me up.

I had a terrible thought, an awful pang of disappointment that he pulled out. In a way, I had wished he had taken the chance and tried to keep me. It was a horrible thought... but my twisty mind wondered if he had thought of it too.

"Still want to go home?" he asked, hopeful.

I nodded and he dropped his head. We rode in silence to the point that it was killing me. The closer we got to the house, the more I didn't want to waste having him so close without expecting anything. I straightened up in the seat and sighed, grabbed my hands and squeezed before I finally turned to Noah. "Pull off beside the road," I said harshly, moments away from breaking into tears. He didn't even ask any questions, he just did as I said even making sure that we were well hidden from the road if any cars were to drive by like he knew what I planned to do.

fall from grace

He was already opening his arms and waiting as I yanked off my seatbelt and shorts once more and climbed onto his lap. "Unzip your jeans," I whispered as a tear slid down my cheek. The moment he did, I sank down onto him and we both cried out. I rocked onto him slowly, touching and kissing the places I'd missed as his hands traveled over me leisurely. He kissed the tears that fell, slowly rubbed my body, and gazed at his necklace I wore around my neck like it was a treasure itself that I wore it for him. I fell apart in his arms so slowly that the orgasm that passed over me this time felt like it lasted a lifetime. "Oh, God," I whimpered and sagged into his arms only to have him lift me up off him as he came on one of my legs and shirt.

I let him kiss me for a long time once we were finished, neither of us said a word so that I didn't have to face the reality I created inside my head of what I thought was right and wrong.

Then it came to an end and I moved out of his lap and he drove me home.

I thought our night together would end like that, without us talking but of course, Noah jumped out of the Jeep and followed after me. "I don't suppose to you want to come back to me now?" His voice was raw and unmasked.

I blinked my tears away as I turned to face him. "I'm leaving this town." It was only when I said those words that I realized I had made a decision for my future.

He nodded, placing his hands in his pockets as he looked down then back up at me once more. "I'm going to wait for you," he promised.

I covered my eyes and whispered, "Don't wait."

"You're it for me. You're always going to be it." He stepped closer. "So, go find your yourself. Find that peace you need and while you do, I'll be building our future until you come back to me."

My lips quivered as I cried, but I didn't uncover my eyes. "What if I don't come back?"

"Then I'll still be waiting." I couldn't see the blue in his eyes, it was so dark… they were truly haunting me though, his earnest gaze and rugged beauty. I wanted to forever push him to see how much he stayed. I was twisted because I wanted him to while I continued to make myself suffer… that's what I was doing, wasn't it? Making myself miserable to accept the guilt. "I can't have you right now. I see what you're doing to yourself and us. I can't walk away, I can't stand to see you this way but you won't let me be next to you. You've got me stuck in a pause. You know it, I know it, and I can't *not* wait for you… so yes, Grace, I'll still be right here waiting for you to realize how wrong you are about what you should feel."

I dropped my hand and met his eyes. He was so beautiful standing underneath the moon with his heart on his sleeve and his soul bared for me to see within the words he spoke.

"You won't wait. You'll move on," I cried childishly, knowing I wasn't supposed to want him to wait but I still did.

He wrapped me in his arms one last time. "I promised, didn't I? I don't want anyone else. I don't want to touch another woman and I won't. Just like I said."

"Don't wait," I denied my feelings once again as I walked away from him. I pushed his reassurance right back in his face.

Dad was sitting on the bottom step when I opened the door and it spooked me enough that I jumped, grabbing my chest. "Was that Noah?" he asked.

I was too stunned to answer at first, I couldn't believe Dad was still up waiting for me to get home like he cared. I slipped off my shoes and looked at him. His red hair was unkempt and he was wearing his sleeping clothes. He had lost weight in the last year. "Don't worry, we aren't together," I muttered. "I went to a bonfire and drank a few, so Noah thought he had to show up and bring me home." He nodded and it made me angry. "What? You're not gonna get angry that I was out drinking?" I laughed sadly. "You really don't care at all anymore, do you?"

I didn't wait for him to reply.

———

The next morning, Dad stepped into my bedroom and sat down on my bed. I gave him a wide-eyed look as I peeled my hair from my face. He placed a bank book in front of me. "It's your savings account that your mom and I made for you when you were little. I should have told you about it once you turned eighteen," he mumbled as he got back off the bed quickly.

"I didn't know I had one," I told him.

"Your mom didn't want you to know. It was meant to be a graduation present." He placed his hands in his pockets and looked at the picture of me and her on my nightstand next to another one of me and Noah when we were kids. "I'll buy you a vehicle for graduation, something I'll be comfortable with you driving all year round."

I raised up and frowned. "I don't understand…"

"You're planning on going to college somewhere other than here, ain't you?" he asked. "I heard bits and pieces last night… your conversation with Noah."

"That's not what I mean." I sighed. "I mean, why are you suddenly doing this? That eager to get rid of me?" It hurt even more to say the words.

He walked toward the door. "I don't know how to be, Grace. Your mom took care of you and me both. I miss her so bad I can't stand it." He hurried back out the door no sooner than he said what he wanted to say.

He brought me home a white Ford Escape the following week and handed over the keys. The money Mom and Dad had saved up for me since birth was enough to do me for years, but I had already decided that I would search for a job once I moved to Kentucky. I decided on an out-of-state college. It wasn't about the school as much as it was just wanting to get away from Dad and all these memories. It also hadn't

251

been easy to find an apartment that allowed dogs. I couldn't leave Gus behind.

I spent my summer hanging out with Tiffany and Sara before we all went our separate ways. I didn't talk to Noah anymore, but I kept up with him on Facebook.

Then fall arrived, and Gus and I were gone.

Only a few days after we settled into our apartment, there was a knock on the door. When I opened it, I was surprised to see a familiar face.

"Dustin?"

And, so college life began.

Life without Noah and Mom was...

34

She leaves, taking my hopes and dreams, my very future with her. I let her go because I think she'll come back. I trust that I'm somehow embedded into her so deeply that she can't stay gone too long, even with her ugly thoughts. The ones that are making her run from me.

I don't let it eat at me like she does. If I did, then there would be no one to fight for us, and what we have, what I feel, and what I know she feels, is worth fighting for.

I'll keep my promises.

Even when I know that she's going to try to erase me with another guy's touch. The very thought rips my chests open and I feel like murdering something. I still believe, no I fucking pray, that no one can ever do her like I can because I cherish every damn part of her, inside and out.

———

My dad finally gave me the push I needed to leave him behind, let him go, and set myself free of my childhood. The day I found out what Grace kept from me, the fact that he had harassed her for money when we were together... I clocked him in the jaw and said the same words to him that I said to him when I was thirteen. The night Mom passed away. Only this time I meant them.

I'm furious but that small bit I didn't know, renews my faith in Grace coming back to me. She waited for me once, she looked for me, and she put up with John with no plans of telling me because she loves me.

michelle gross

That's what people that love each other do. That's not what my parents taught me, that's what Grace shows me.

————

I live and breathe for what Grace shows me through Facebook. With every post, every picture or status update with hidden meanings, I feel like she's secretly reaching out and communicating. My necklace is right where it's always been, around her neck in every picture she posts.

————

She keeps showing and giving over the Internet. I only smile because I know what she's doing. She wants me to see, so she shows me in a way that makes it look like she's not. It keeps her safe without having to admit it to me or herself.

She keeps me updated, yet I give her nothing online in hopes that curiosity will bring her back.

————

I'm one step closer to our future. Another few steps and she'll force me to come get her if she doesn't give in soon.

Life without Grace was… planning all the ways to get her back.

N.P.

Finale:

Catching Grace

35

Grace age 22

Noah age 23

Grace is graduating this week. I won't go see her, even though I want to. I'm almost ready to go get her. Just a few more things and I'll be completely prepared. She's not faded from my thoughts at all, and I'm willing to throw my heart and soul out there once again in hopes that it reaches her this time. I'm coming... soon, whether she likes it or not.

I've let her run, now it's time to catch her. Days aren't guaranteed, we should both know that given everything with her mom and mine. I don't want to waste another year letting her hideaway in guilt.

I want her in my arms.

N.P.

"Here you go, Ms. Harper," Jimmy said, handing me a piece of paper. I looked down and saw that he was giving me a goodbye note. Within the next few classes, I would receive even more papers or hugs from the students I had been with the past semester. Today was the last day of the school year.

A girl named Sarah almost tackled me with a hug last period. "Are you going to be back next year?" she asked me.

I smiled. "I don't know," I told her honestly.

"You're really cool," she told me and I beamed from the compliments all these fourth and fifth graders were giving me.

fall from grace

After the last class ended, Mr. Collins walked up to me with a smile. "So, you're not going to take the job they've offered you?" He went straight for the kill.

I picked up my purse from the desk. "I don't know..."

"Sounds like you do know," he said with a grin. He offered his hand out to me and I took it. "It was a pleasure having you with us this semester if I don't see you back in the fall."

"I'm glad I was able to student-teach under you," I replied. "You made it easy for me."

He chuckled and walked out of the school building with me. "You're a natural," he told me. "You said your mom was a teacher, didn't you?"

I nodded. "She was."

There was a thumping sound coming from someone's speakers as we stepped into the heat, and my eyes scanned the parking lot and hardened on my Escape. I waited until Mr. Collins said goodbye and left before I headed down the steps to my vehicle that wasn't going to have any speakers left in it if Dustin didn't stop headbanging in the driver's seat. He saw me coming and grinned as he turned it down.

"Well, hello, Ms. Harper," he chirped as I climbed in the passenger. "Any love notes on the last day?" he asked.

"Could you be any more embarrassing?" I huffed as I buckled up. "Even though this was my last day student-teaching, I still don't want to leave a bad impression." He laughed as he pulled out of the parking lot. "Do you work today too?" He nodded. We both worked at Applebee's together. "Rachel drive your truck to work today?" Another nod from him.

Rachel was Dustin's girlfriend and our third roommate but I guess she wasn't really a roommate since she slept in the same room as Dustin. Yes, Dustin moved in with me a few days after showing up at my door. Turned out, he was going to this college as well and only found out that I was here too by Tiffany. We built an unlikely friendship over the last few years. It was just me and him until last year when he met Rachel. I'd never seen him so smitten and it made me happy to see the growth in his character since him and I dated.

After work, I let Dustin drive us home because my feet were killing me from waiting tables but the hundred and fifty dollars in tips had been worth it. I normally didn't get this much unless it was the weekend. "How much did you make?" I asked him.

"Eighty-seven," he told me.

"One-fifty for me," I bragged, sticking my tongue out.

"Must be nice to have tits," he muttered and I laughed. "Grace." I looked over at him when he spoke. "Are you going back home now?" My stomach knotted at his words.

"Why are you asking?" I tucked my hair behind my ear.

"When is the last time you've talked to your dad? How about Noah?" I looked ahead to ignore him. "And no, stalking his Facebook is not talking to him." I felt the red splash my cheeks. "You're finished with college now, it's over for you. What are you going to do now? You look happy again. Why aren't you going back?" He kept bombarding me with questions I didn't know how to answer.

"What about you? When are you going back?" I dodged the questions.

He shook his head as he stared at the road. "I'm different... But if you want to know, I'm thinking about asking Rachel if she'd come back home with me after she finishes up school."

Wow, that was huge. "She'd faint if she heard you talking about your future with her in it."

He smiled like a person in love. "Yeah, I know."

"You're stupidly good at making her think that you don't care as much as you do... When in fact you're totally in love with her."

fall from grace

He looked over at me with a cheesy grin. "I'll let her know one day, that she's got me wrapped around her finger, unlike Noah who spilled his heart out only to have you run from him."

I stopped smiling. "Stop. You know how I feel and why I made the choice to break up with him."

He nodded. "That burden you feel, I can imagine it's heavy but from an outsider's point of view, it's total bullshit. Your mom wouldn't want you unhappy. She loved you and it wasn't just you I saw her look after in school. She looked after him too."

I knew he was right about Mom wanting me to be happy, and I also knew she cared for Noah… at this point, the guilt I felt didn't really feel like guilt, it just left me with this confused, dull feeling inside me. I thought about what it might be like to go back home and see Noah, but that meant facing Dad again and also dealing with the possibility that Noah and I might really be over.

I didn't miss him as much as I used to. Even my obsession with checking on him through Facebook felt like a habit. He never posted anything about his life so I didn't know if he was seeing anyone. I did know that he created a Facebook page for all his wood carvings. Only these days he kept to the big stuff that he made from logs. I left all mine at Dad's when I left.

"If Noah feels the way I do lately, then maybe we've truly grown apart and we can move on from each other," I mumbled softly.

He burst out laughing and I glared at him. "You're not serious, are you? Then why haven't you dated?"

"I did go out with that Matt guy," I told him.

"Once," he pointed out. "You look like you were going to throw a punch when he tried to come inside after the date."

"Because he kissed like a blowfish," I muttered, getting all riled up that he was bringing up my lack of dating.

"Just face it, your body won't betray your feelings for Noah even though you've convinced yourself your feelings for him have dulled, they haven't. You just haven't been around him to get the full Noah-effect he has on you." I rolled my eyes at that one. "Don't even pretend, I've seen you two from the sidelines our entire lives so I know."

I grabbed an empty pop bottle on the floor and threw it at him. "Be quiet, stop pretending like you know stuff, you're *Dustin.*"

"All right, whatever you say."

These feelings I had for Noah were long gone, even when I sat on my bed with Gus on my lap and scrolled through Janet's new posts. I wasn't doing it because I wanted to be with him, I did it because it felt like I was checking up on an old friend. I jumped up when I saw that she had posted new pictures a few hours ago. They were group pictures. Maybe from a cookout. I scanned the faces for Noah and fell back when none were of him. Gus yelped, I almost killed him by squashing him. I gave him a bunch of hugs and kisses while he wagged his tail and looked at me like he was trying to figure out why he deserved to get laid on.

And it definitely wasn't Noah's face and body I conjured up inside my head as I slipped my hand inside my shorts to find relief the nights I needed it to fall asleep.

It wasn't.

————

The next few days were dull and meaningless. I went to work at Applebee's and then I'd come back to the apartment where the only one who greeted me was Gus, and it was Rachel's cries of pleasure with Dustin in the next room that kept me up at night.

I didn't go home at all. I stayed here even in the summer months. Every summer before now, it never felt like this because I knew I'd have college that would start back up in the fall and I'd have a reason to still be here… Now everything was over and I was scared.

fall from grace

It was a lot easier staying away then it was going back to see the father that rarely called. I'd call him sometimes too but we were the two most awkward people on the phone with each other. It was like we lost how to be ourselves when Mom died. Then I felt even worse because I haven't gone to see Mom's grave once since I left town.

I also received a message from Janet, asking if I was finished with all my classes, which wasn't unusual. She still checked in on me occasionally and even called despite the fact that I wasn't with Noah. I had been finished with everything since last week, and that was why I was in such a funk with my life. I could stay here, I was offered a job already but I was so antsy. I didn't feel contented and I couldn't relax. I felt like I was a giant spring that was being held down, close to springing free—aka, me going bananas if things didn't start to feel better, normal, or more accurately, *right.*

My phone woke me up super early the next morning. Instead of answering it though, I hit the ignore button but whoever it was called straight back. I groaned and pushed Gus away from my face because he kept wanting to lick me. Apparently, he thought I should get up too. It took me a minute to see who was calling because my eyes were blurry from sleep, but they widened when I saw that it was Janet.

"Hello?"

"Grace." She was crying. I raised up, feeling completely awake with her muffled voice crying in my ear.

"What's wrong?" I asked right away.

"It's Noah," she started.

I grabbed my chest. "What? What do you mean? Is he okay?" Of course, I knew it must be something bad when she was crying like she was. My stomach fell to the floor.

"I don't know, they haven't said anything. He was at the garage when he—" She choked up again and now I was on the verge of crying. "Can you come?" she asked.

261

"I'm leaving now," I murmured as I stumbled out of bed and hung up. My entire body was shaking as I tried to get to my door and caught my foot on the edge of the doorway. I hollered from the pain as I hopped and held my foot up. When would I ever stop doing this to my toes? I wasn't going to have any left!

Dustin stumbled out of his bedroom barely awake. His eyes were more closed than opened when he came to check on me. "What happened?" he asked.

I dropped my foot and felt my face pinch together, the thing it did right before I burst into tears. "Noah." I started crying real ugly and it seemed to wake him up because his eyes widened as he took a step back, holding his hands out.

"Eww, I can't deal with your ugly crying," he told me. "Have you finally realized how stupid you've been?"

Rachel crawled out of their room next. "What's wrong, Grace?"

I started running around in circles trying to find my wallet, keys, and shoes as I cried. "Seriously, Grace, what's wrong? You're freakin' me out," Dustin said.

"Noah's been hurt at the garage, I don't know what's going on. I have to go," I told him.

"Shit," he muttered. "Hold on, and we'll both go. You can't drive in your shape anyway."

"No," I reacted. "I want to go alone, besides we both can't leave work." I already had my shoes on when I bent down and picked up Gus. "Come on, boy," I said to him as I hurried to the door.

"Why are you taking Gus?" Dustin asked. "We can watch him."

"I'll just take him," I told him.

He lifted his eyebrows like he knew something but otherwise kept his mouth shut. "Be careful."

fall from grace

"Yeah, let us know when you make it so that we don't worry," Rachel told me and I nodded.

I was a hot mess the entire trip back to Virginia. I went from crying and swerving through lanes to nodding and shaking my head, telling myself he was all right. I got so bad at one point that Gus was howling with me, crying because he sensed my distress. The radio was doing nothing to calm my brain.

I was so stupid. Why didn't I at least talk to him? Why did I shut him out completely? *Because you knew there was no such thing as being Noah's friend, no such thing as hearing his voice, or seeing his smile without landing on his dick like the last time you encountered him,* said the crappier version of me I didn't like.

The darker part of me begged me to turn around and pull out my old cell phone hidden inside my dresser back at the apartment and view Mom's text and remind myself, she was out on the road again that evening because she was coming to get me, who wasn't even supposed to be with Noah because Dad had said no. I always got my way with Mom. She always did so much for me, and I lost her that night because of my love for Noah.

How long do I have to punish myself? How long do I have to live this way before I feel like it's enough?

Only Mom couldn't answer me. She couldn't relieve me of this burden like I knew she would.

But now, I realized I could lose Noah the same way I already lost her and it hurt so bad, I couldn't stand it. I couldn't sit still, not even for my guilt.

I just needed to see that he was okay was what I told myself, and once I saw it with my own eyes, I'd go on living without him like I knew I should because my feelings for him have calmed into a small breeze, it was settled so deep inside me that I could hardly feel its presence. Noah and I were over. I was positive once I checked on him, I'd know that I was right.

263

michelle gross
But please… be all right when I get there.

I arrived at the only hospital in Jewel County knowing this was where they had to have taken him. I called Janet to let her know I was here but she didn't answer which probably meant she was inside. It was still early, but it was already hot so I scooped Gus up in my arms and ran. I paused at the door and tried calling her again, beginning to wonder if this was the right hospital but then again, I didn't even ask if he was at one.

When she didn't answer, I ran inside and stopped at the first receptionist area I came up to. The lady looked up and her eyes hardened on Gus. "No pets," she said in the unfriendliest tone imaginable which I couldn't blame her for doing her job, but I couldn't leave Gus outside in the heat.

"I just need to know if there's a Noah Phillips that was brought in a few hours ago," I said in a hurried voice.

"And you are?" she asked as she started typing on the keyboard. When I didn't answer, she looked back up. "We don't have anyone by that name."

I sighed and back away. "Thank you." I pulled back out my phone and tried calling her again. She still wasn't picking up. Was I going to have to go to their house or brave it up and call Noah myself? I should have asked what was wrong. My brain short-circuited the moment she said, "it's Noah" in that God-awful tone that placed the feeling of dread in my system.

I called again as I walked until something smacked into my legs. I looked down to see the little boy fall because I walked into him. His cup landed between us, splattering whatever drink he had across the floor.

Gus wagged his tail at the commotion as I bent down to the little boy. "Oh, I'm so sorry," I told him as I helped him up. "Are you okay?"

fall from grace

He dusted off his butt and looked down at the clear drink trailing down the hall. "Aw, man," he mumbled before his eyes landed on Gus and sparkled. "I love puppies! What's his name?"

"Gus," I told him, fighting the urge to tell him Gus wasn't a puppy. Not that it mattered.

"Oh God, Jimmy." It seemed his mom finally arrived, dragging along another little boy and a stroller with a newborn. "What did you do?" she asked him as she looked at me and smiled like she was about to panic.

"It was my fault. I accidentally bumped into him." More like ran him over, but I didn't tell her that. She smiled and seemed much happier that I eased her worries that it wasn't her son's fault.

"Puddle," the other little boy said and laughed as he started pouring out his drink.

"Dillon," she yelled as she ran to stop him but she was too late.

The hallway was now an even bigger mess.

"I'll go tell them it needs to be cleaned up," I told her and she smiled and thanked me. The receptionist saw me coming back with Gus and gave me the death stare. I politely told her what happened then turned to leave and then never turned back around so fast in my life. The lady was clearly getting tired of my face, but seeing Noah walking up the hall scared the life out of me.

Wait a minute… I turned back around slowly and scooted off to the side as I studied his body. My God, he had grown even more. His shoulders seemed so much wider now and his chest so… *What the hell has he been doing?* He had a trimmed beard now which was a reddish-blond. "Noah," I breathed out pathetically where no one else could hear me then I also noticed he was perfectly okay. "Noah," I growled his name this time.

My eyes landed on Janet and Dean next to him. My eyes hardened on her… That sneaky old woman, she totally fooled me and I

265

didn't even take the time to ask questions I was so scared for Noah. But why were they at the hospital? Or was something truly wrong? Maybe it was something that couldn't be seen?

Oh, my God, they were heading this way. I turned around and the receptionist was still glowering at me, so I ended up circling around to find somewhere to hide so Janet didn't know that I was here. "You and your dog have to leave, or I'll call security," the receptionist told me.

I nodded. "I'm leaving," I whispered, looking down at what I was wearing. I was still in what I slept in! And I didn't even want to know what my hair looked like. I looked up and saw Janet eyeing me with a smile.

Oh, dear Lord, why did you make me such a flustered and awkward mess of a person?

"Grace, you came." Janet beamed at me, and I watched in horror as Dean and Noah both turned this way.

I brought Gus up to my face and turned around. "Grace?" Noah sounded surprised to see me. "Grace!" I turned back around that time and saw him coming toward me. I eyed the place in the floor where I knew all the liquid was. Noah was picking up his pace.

I held out my free hand. "Wait, Noah, don't."

"Don't tell me to fucking wait," he growled, and I felt the unexpected, heated rush in my system from his words alone. Then Dustin's words hit me, *you haven't been around him to get the full Noah-effect he has on you.*

I backed away and gasped as he slid and fell into the drink on the floor. He hollered like he was in pain and I started running to check on him. "Are you okay?"

He grabbed his hand. "Ah, shit. I think my finger might be broken."

"How did you break your finger sliding through someone's drink?" I couldn't help but ask.

He stood up, still holding his hand as he glared at me. "Because it was my finger that caught my fall before I could move my hand the right way."

"Noah, are you okay?" Janet asked as they walked up behind him.

He ignored them. "What are you doing here?" he asked me quickly. "Are you finally back?" I couldn't tell if he was hoping or asking.

Now it made it hard to confront him even more. I held Gus nervously as I looked at Janet. "Janet called crying, saying something happened to you while at the garage." Her husband and Noah both looked at her at the same time. She grinned without a care at all.

"I didn't expect you'd get hurt for real when I fibbed a little…" she mumbled sheepishly. "My soaps have really been paying off, it was so easy to get emotional after watching an episode this morning…"

Noah sighed. "So, that's why you wanted me to come with you guys here, I thought it was weird."

"What are you doing here?" I asked.

Dean smiled. "I'm having my gallbladder removed."

Great, I drove all this way for Dean's gallbladder. I tugged on my hair self-consciously, hoping I didn't look as bad as I felt. "I think you might have broken it, by the looks of it," Dean told Noah as he held out his hand.

"You're already at the hospital, go get it checked out," Janet told him.

"It's just a finger." He shrugged his shoulders like it was no big deal.

"Nonsense," Janet said.

"I also think you should get it checked out," I added as he lifted his gaze and held mine, "too."

"Grace can go with you," Janet said with a sneaky smile.

"I don't need her going with me," Noah muttered, which made all of this even more awkward. As I thought, we weren't what we were. Why did my chest feel this tight?

"Miss, I've asked you time and time again to take the dog outside," the receptionist found her way outside of her area and said.

"Here, I'll watch him while you go with Noah," Janet told me as she took Gus from my hands without letting me reply. She looked to Dean. "You'll be fine without me."

He laughed. "I reckon I don't need you to hold my hand," he said, placing a kiss on her cheek before looking to Noah and me with a smirk. "But, Noah's not of age yet, so I believe you should go with him." He winked at me and I had no idea what to do.

Noah walked off and Janet waved for me to follow him as she walked outside with Gus. "Go on now," Dean urged me. "Put him out of his misery, at least." And with that, he walked off and I turned and followed after Noah.

Once I caught up to his long strides, I slowed down. "How does it feel?" I asked him.

"Broken," he answered, then he turned and met my eyes as we walked. "It feels broken." Now I didn't feel like we were talking about his finger anymore.

I waited in a seat while he checked himself in. I was sending Dustin a text when he sat down and he must have seen his name because he muttered, "I can't believe you lived with Dustin the last four years," and turned his head the other direction.

"As roommates," I told him as I pulled out a picture of Dustin and Rachel on my phone. "Here's his girlfriend." I showed him and waited for him to look better or something.

He just arched an eyebrow. "I have Facebook, remember?" Whew, he was being an asshole. I deserved it, but I couldn't help but want to make it better. I couldn't stand him being so not Noah with me.

When we were quiet again, he finally turned his head back to me. "Are you going back?" My stomach swam with butterflies.

"Noah Phillips," a nurse called his name.

He got up and I did too. "What are you doing?"

"I'm going with you," I replied. "I don't want to sit out here and wait," I added so he wouldn't object.

He sighed, and I followed behind him again. The nurse checked his weight and things and we were placed into a room to wait for the doctor. "So, you're only here right now because you thought I was hurt?" he asked. And before I could answer he said, "You don't have to answer. I can tell by the way you look, like you rushed here without any thought… How fucking sweet of you to come back only when you think I might be laid up in the hospital."

"I think I should go," I said quickly as I stood up.

"Yeah, please," he dared to say.

I took a deep breath and sat back down. "I'm staying."

"You do whatever the hell you want anyway," he muttered seconds before the doctor walked in. The awful mood between us was thick as they x-rayed his hand and diagnosed his finger broken. He was sent on his way with a finger cast.

Even the way he walked ahead of me looked angry, like he was pissed at the world or just me. I tagged along behind him in silence admiring the shape of his butt in those jeans and the way my body felt despite the fact that he was angry as hell.

269

He stopped and I bumped into him. I backed up as he turned around and glared at me, his eyebrows in angry slants. "Are you with anyone?"

"What? No." I shook my head. "Are you?" He didn't answer, instead, he turned around and started walking away from me. I watched him go before I started running. "Noah." I grabbed his arms but he kept walking out of the hospital door. "Fine, whatever. I don't care."

My insides were crying out.

I spotted Janet sitting on a bench feeding Gus ice cream. She saw us and smiled then frowned as she spotted Noah hauling his butt into the parking lot and leaving me behind. I didn't know what else to do other than to go grab my dog and leave.

"This didn't go like I hoped," she told me with a frown as I picked up Gus. "I'm sorry for what I did, if that counts for anything. I just wanted you to see where he is in life. You'd be surprised at how far he's gotten. He's doing good for himself."

"It's okay, really… I just didn't think about what might happen if I had to lose him even as a friend one day."

"Noah's feelings for you are beautiful, something so precious and big that I hate to see it ruined because you think that you don't deserve to be happy. You do, believe me, moms want their children to be happy. Yours is probably crying as she watches over you."

I blinked away tears as I nodded and walked away.

"Come to the house tomorrow," she told me.

I looked back and shook my head. "I don't think that's a good idea."

"Nonsense… It's a good chance to make peace with Noah. Besides there's something I want to show you." She winked as she got up. "I better go check on Dean."

36

She's so fucking good at it… showing up unannounced or unexpected, sending my heart, mind, and body into a state of panic. With no call or text—nothing, she pops up where I can see her before I can go get her.

Whether she's sixteen or twenty-two, she has a knack for making me act a fool. I lost a touchdown, now I broke a finger.

I'm angry. I'm so damn angry because I was so happy to see her standing there, rosy-cheeked and cuter than she was the months she left me in sleeping clothes with Gus in her hand… only she didn't come back to me, she came back for the fear of losing me. I'm happy that she cares, but I'm pissed that it takes her thinking I'm hurt to get her to finally come back, right when I was days away from going to get her.

So typically… Grace wouldn't be Grace if she didn't corrupt my well thought out plan to seduce her into coming back home with me.

Regardless that I stormed off on her, I already knew I'd make my way to her.

She wasn't going anywhere, at least, not without me.

N.P.

It took forty-five minutes to get to Dad's. I spent the entire drive rehearsing what I should say to him when I randomly show up for the first time since I left.

At least, Gus was happy. He jumped out of the Escape when I opened the door and started sniffing everything before he ran up on the porch and waited for me by the door. I didn't knock, I just stepped on in. His truck was home.

I was taken by surprise when I saw the shape the house was in. The sink was overflowing with dirty dishes and take-out was everywhere. I heard Gus barking. "Gus?" Dad's surprised voice came from the living room. I stepped back out of the kitchen and made my way to where he was. He saw me the same time I saw him. "Grace, why didn't you tell me you were coming?" he asked as he started picking up dirty plates and bottles in a rush.

I took in his unshaven face and tousled hair. He looked horrible to me. Dad was a man that was clean shaven and well-kept, he had been my whole life so it was weird to see him this way. Noah looked clean and groomed to perfection with his facial hair and while it suited him and added to his rugged looks, I couldn't say the same about Dad. His case was completely different. He was letting himself go.

"Why because you want to hide how you've been living from me?" I asked as I snatched the empty bottles from his hand. "Just leave it, I'll clean it up."

"I can clean up after myself," he started.

"I said I got it Dad," I muttered, meeting his eyes with a stern look that told him I meant it. He backed away and ran his hand through his hair. "Why aren't you at work?"

He sighed as he walked over to the couch and sat down. "I took the week off, I was actually coming to visit you for your graduation. I thought about it…then changed my mind at the last minute."

I paused at the door. "Why didn't you?"

"Couldn't convince myself to go through with it," he told me honestly.

fall from grace

I carried the trash I had in my hands to the kitchen to throw away but had to set it down on the counter so that I could empty out the trash can that was overfilled. Once that was done, I just grabbed a black bag and went back into the living room and started picking up.

My chest hurt. I hated this. Dad wasn't this person, he wasn't a slob, neither of my parents was. I leaned more on the slobbier side than they did. It made me wonder if maybe Dad hadn't needed me to leave when I did but to stay. I couldn't take back the four years I was gone, so much was left unsaid between us. This time apart made me stronger and I wasn't afraid of his disappointed frown like I used to, which told me that leaving might not have been best for everyone, but it had been for me. I had grown, if you ignored the fact that it took Janet lying to get me back home but now that I was here, I realized how much I needed this.

I wanted my father back, even if he still looked at me in disappointment. He needed me and I realized that some part of him knew that or he wouldn't have made plans to see me, even if he backed out on them. That was the most beautiful feeling I felt in a long time when thinking of my relationship with him.

Maybe we could learn to heal ourselves without Mom.

"Why do you look like that?" he asked me, staring at my sleeping clothes.

"Why do you look like that?" I countered back, and he just nodded, knowing he walked into that one. "Dad, why don't you go get cleaned up and we'll go visit Mom's grave once I'm finished cleaning up?"

He got up. "I'll help," he said, and quickly added, "then we'll go see her."

We cleaned up in silence, not an uncomfortable one though. When we were finished, we both went our separate ways to clean ourselves up. I was stuck rummaging through my old clothes until I found something to wear. The clothes had a slight smell to them where

273

they had been tucked away in my closet the last few years but I changed into a pair of shorts and tank top anyway.

I couldn't help but nod my approval as Dad stepped out of his bedroom clean shaven and showered. "Much better," I told him and he smiled slightly.

Dad took us to the cemetery in his truck, and I laughed at Gus most of the way there as he hung his head out of the window. Dad watched us from the corner of his eyes, and I thought I saw the crinkle of a smile appear on his face.

"Did you become a teacher because you wanted to, or because it was your mom's career?" he randomly asked.

I shrugged my shoulders. "A bit of both. I started out choosing education because of Mom but in the end, I stuck with it because I realized I enjoyed it."

"You're a lot like your mom," he mumbled then looked at me. "A lot like me too, though, not that that's a good thing." I arched an eyebrow at him. "We're both hard-headed and you've always gone after what you wanted just like I did with your mother when I first saw her… But now, you're at a standstill." I felt like his words were off, I was anything but still.

"I was offered a teaching job back in Kentucky," I said softly.

"Are you going to take it?"

"I don't know… What do you think?"

He exhaled. "Don't make your choices on anyone else's opinions, only your own. I thought I taught you that. It's what you want, not what I or anybody else wants."

Couldn't he see that I wanted him to say that I could come home? That he wanted me to be here like I wanted to be here?

I looked out my window in disappointment. My chest tightened when we arrived, the thought of facing Mom in this way again brought back the sadness. Gus jumped out when I opened the door and he followed alongside Dad and I as we walked up the hill to Mom's tombstone.

"We should have brought her flowers," I mumbled to him once we were there.

He held his hands out and looked around like he was thinking the same thing. "You're right," he added. We were both hopeless, I'd admit.

"Who brought those flowers?" I asked as I pointed to the fake flowers stuck into the ground. There were two different sets.

"I brought roses up here on her birthday last month, but I don't know who brought those up here," he told me, and I already knew who it might be. Dad saw my expression but didn't comment on it.

"Do you think she's disappointed in me?" I asked abruptly.

He stood still for a while. "Why would you ask that?"

"Because... I don't remember ever being a good daughter."

"If you were never a good daughter to us... then I was never a good husband or dad... But I happen to know that your parents never once thought of you as a bad daughter, you happen to be their entire world." He wiped his hand across his mouth and stopped talking.

He couldn't say things outright to me anymore, that was the way things had become between us... But what he just gave me was enough for me to show Mom a smile.

As we walked back down the hill, Dad asked again, "Why did you come back?"

I tightened my ponytail before I answered, "I thought Noah had been hurt."

His eyes widened as he took in the news. "Well, is he okay?"

I smiled. "He's fine, besides a broken finger."

275

"Have you two kept in touch?"

"No, we didn't." I sounded depressed about it, and I was. I really hurt him this time, even though my goal had always been to break away from him. Now that I was truly doing it, I couldn't stand myself.

"And you came back early in the morning… without even changing out of your pajamas for Noah's broken finger?"

I groaned. "I didn't know anything," I muttered, then sighed. "He's stuck in here," I pointed at my chest, "and he ain't ever coming out. I can't pull away from him completely."

"If you loved him, you wouldn't have been able to leave him like you did, would you?" he asked me.

"Oh." I started laughing. "I love him, that's always been the problem. I love him so much that it consumes me and I become reckless… That day, I begged her to let me see him, and of course, she agreed. I didn't think she'd come to get me, not when she knew Noah was going to bring me home."

"Stop, Grace," he snapped. "Don't bring up that night, don't bring up the past, please."

"Dad…" I met his eyes and hoped he saw my despair. "You blame me too, like I do myself, though!"

"What?" He genuinely seemed taken aback. "What are you talking about?"

"You blame me for having Mom out on the road that night, don't you? That's why you ignored me after she died and wanted me to leave the house?"

"Grace," he uttered my name as he grabbed my shoulders. "Why would you even think that?"

"Because that night you told me she was coming to get me!" I yelled, tears burning my eyes.

fall from grace

He let go of me and brought his hands to his hair. "So… this change in you… you breaking up with Noah, all of it was because of what I said?" he asked in disbelief.

"Because my feelings for Noah always came first, and because of that, we lost Mom!" Dad looked seriously disturbed. "You distanced yourself from me because of it, how could I not feel guilty?"

"I want you to stop," he told me. "If you've been living all this time feeling the way you have, your mom won't ever forgive me, and I won't be able to get back my relationship with my daughter."

I opened my eyes and looked at him. "I wish it were that easy, but I can't just ignore this ugly feeling, not when Mom could still be here if I had just listened and stayed home and spent the weekend without Noah," I hiccupped. "I need you to forgive me. I need Mom to forgive me. I need Noah not to love me anymore… But what if he already doesn't? What am I going to do then?" I dropped to my knees and cried into them. Gus started whimpering and sticking his nose between my legs.

Dad pulled me up by my shoulders. "Let's go home."

On the drive home, I managed to pull myself together within seconds as if I hadn't just broken down over the guilt that had been haunting me for the last few years. What was even worse was Dad's lack of words. He still had nothing to say. I scooted up in the seat as we pulled into the driveway and spotted an old truck. My eyes moved toward the porch where Noah sat on the steps. He lifted his head up from between his knees when he saw us pull in.

"Looks like Noah," Dad said.

I felt nervous. I thought he had been upset with me? He had every right to be… yet he was here. "Yeah," I mumbled as I unbuckled and let Gus out.

"Why do you look so scared?" Dad asked me with a hint of a smirk I couldn't decipher. He was just as hot and cold as I was.

277

"I'm not," I huffed, low enough so that I couldn't be heard by Noah. "I just don't understand why he's here…"

"He's damn frustrating, that's for sure," Dad said with a sigh as he climbed out of the truck. "Noah knows what he wants and he gets it, he isn't swayed… Which makes one wonder why he let the one thing he claimed to care about so much go? I wonder… is he gonna let you get away so easily this time?"

"Dad…" I mumbled.

"Go see what he wants," he told me as he shut the door. I climbed out and followed behind him. Gus was on Noah's lap and he stood up with him when we approached him.

"Hey, Steven," Noah began, "it's been a while."

"Yeah, it has," Dad agreed. "I heard you have your own garage now?"

Noah nodded, and my eyes widened as Dad's words sunk in. "Garage?"

"Heard it had a real funny name, too," Dad added with a smirk that I could have sworn looked like he was messing around with Noah.

"Ah, I don't know about that," Noah muttered quickly, eyeing me as he did.

"When were you going to tell me?" I asked to either of them.

"When you came home and saw it for yourself," Noah retorted. I bit the inside of my cheek and sighed.

"Guess I'll head inside and let you two talk," Dad informed us.

"Wait," Noah called out. "I was going to take Grace for food, how about you come with us?" Noah was so much braver than me to ask Dad out when it took me over five years just to ask him to go somewhere with me again. I also noticed how he said "take" instead of "ask" like I had no choice in the matter.

278

fall from grace

Dad smiled sadly and shook his head. "Y'all go on ahead," and with those words, he walked inside hollering for Gus to come with him.

I crossed my arms when Dad left and even Noah dropped the good guy façade when it was safe. "What? I thought you were mad?" I couldn't help but taunt him.

"Come on," he muttered. "I'm starving."

I turned and followed after him as he walked to his truck. "How is that my fault?" I studied the red Ford. "Where's your Jeep?" I asked.

"Had to get a new one," was his answer as he climbed inside.

I ran around to the other side and got in. "You mean, you had to trade it in for another beat up one?" I already liked his truck though, it only had one long seat… If we had been dating, if we were together, I could scoot over right now and link my arm with his as he drove. The idea was so tempting, I jerked the seatbelt over me and focused ahead.

"I don't recall you ever having a problem with the Jeep," he hummed.

"What are you over there thinking about?" I blushed.

He smirked. "You never made any comments about my Jeep before is what I mean. Why? What are you thinking about?"

"Where are we going?" I redirected the conversation to something safer.

"Ribs?" he offered and I simply nodded with a smile. As he pulled out of the driveway, he glanced over at me. "Grace."

"Hmm?"

"Your cheeks are red," he teased. "You're still thinking about the Jeep?"

"Leave me alone," I grumbled, looking out the window.

He laughed. "We can make new memories in this one."

I turned my head. "I don't know what you're talking about but leave me out of it. Besides, you left earlier without even telling me goodbye, and now you show up and expect me to go eat with you?"

"You're in my truck, you're with *me*, ain't you?" he grunted.

"Because I'm starving."

"I was going to wait it out and let you come to me, Grace, and remembered that this is you I'm talking about. I couldn't wait and let you leave town again."

I tucked my hair behind my ear and looked down at my legs. "Are you seeing anyone right now?"

His eyes looked so soulful and earnest when he looked at me. I felt it breaking me down, pulling and tearing me apart, or *open*. "I promised, didn't I?"

I looked ahead and fought the urge to touch my face as the emotions overwhelmed me. I couldn't sit here and believe that this giant, beast of a man Noah had become hadn't lain with anyone else since me. Did he really keep his promise when I told him not to wait for me? My chest felt like it might burst.

I felt hot. I mean, really hot. My face and stomach, my entire body was burning, completely aware of the man next to me.

"You're always storming back into my life when I least expect it, just like when I saw you on the football field, and earlier at the hospital. You make me lose my damn mind," he muttered, raking his fingers through his hair as he drove. "I'm so pissed that you're only back because you thought I was hurt but not pissed enough."

"What's that supposed to mean?"

"You're not running away," he informed me.

"I have nothing to run from."

He smirked. "Good."

fall from grace

Despite our tempers with each other and Noah's body mass, nothing had changed, yet everything *had*. I couldn't explain it… or maybe I could, if it was even possible everything I felt for him was even more intense, so out there and around us, choking me with its presence like it refused to let me ignore it any longer. Even with the intensity, I still found the same comfort I always did when I was with him though. I propped my feet up in the window as I sucked the bones clean as we ate ribs in his truck. I didn't know why we always chose to eat alone than going inside places, but this was what we preferred. The intimacy was still what I loved.

"I see you're still a messy eater," he noted as I slurped on my drink. I looked down at my barbecue fingers that were now all other the cup before glaring at him. "Have you been with anyone?" he asked abruptly.

I almost choked on my pop. I moved my legs and dropped them to the floor as I raised up. "I've dated…" *I've been on one date.* "Yeah, I've dated." We would leave it at that. No need to let him learn the truth and piece together that he was still my only partner. I was too afraid of what might happen if he knew. I wanted him, I shouldn't want him. I loved him, I thought my feelings could simmer into nothing, but that had been a mistake. Noah was my kryptonite. He made me weak and wild with his touches, but he was also the kindest, most loving human I'd ever met. He was the kind of person you strived to be and for some crazy reason, he loved me. I was the lucky girl that moved to the neighborhood and placed myself into his world without realizing how much I'd get in return… Something that beautiful, I'd wish on a billion stars to have it back without the guilt of Mom's death looming over it.

"That's good." It felt like his eyes were caressing my skin. I broke into chills. "Now you know no one can love you like I can. No one can give you what we are when we're together because that's for you and me. Nobody belongs in our lives."

I looked away and sucked in a shaky breath. It felt like a live wire in the truck, the tension between us was so thick and full of life that I knew I had as much as I could take of Noah for today before I did

281

something that would break us more. I didn't want to hurt him or me anymore. I needed to break free of what we had, and hope that when he finally let me go, I wouldn't regret it.

Who was I kidding? I already regretted having to leave him with every fiber of my being. Regret was a long time best friend with my pal, Guilt, over the years. I was so used to both of them that their presence was so dim until these moments that shoved them in my face.

"Can you take me home?" I asked a little too shakily.

Just when I thought he might push me further, he didn't. He started the truck up. "Yeah, as long as you don't leave town."

"I'm not leaving," I told him, but when his eyes lit up and darkened over me, I felt like he misunderstood me.

What was even scarier, was the way I was almost begging him to end my guilt in some sort of way—any way.

Back and forth, back and forth, my brain and body decided for me. What a mess my mind was.

37

She's so aware of me, just like I am of her. The willpower it took to act like I didn't want to forget the world and get lost in her was because of my love for her. I want her always and forever, not just for an hour or a day. I won't take bits and pieces. I'll take her whole because it's what she needs and deserves, and that's everything to me.

She can't pretend not to know that she's everything to me. If she's forgotten, guess I'll have to remind her.

*Any hands that have touched her will be erased, **forgotten,** gone until there's only mine.*

I've planned and waited for us to grow up, to win her heart and accept mine, and live happily ever after. Even as a boy, I knew the kind of man I was. I don't give up. Ever. Not on the things I hold dear. Not on the one that holds my heart in the palm of her dainty hand.

N.P.

I went up and down the stairs a hundred times that next day, telling myself not to go to Janet's house. I called work and fibbed, and suddenly feared my own choices. I had no idea what I was doing but staying here and calling into work weren't smart choices…

But they felt like the right ones.

michelle gross

Dad finally got tired of me pacing around the house and just told me to go see or do whatever it was that was causing me to wear down the floors.

Even on the drive to her house, I kept telling myself that this wasn't a good idea then I remembered that I already drove this far because of Noah so anything else I did, couldn't hurt. I was invited, and I told myself I was only going to see what she wanted to show me. But that was kind of worse because I knew the only thing she would have to show me would be about Noah.

Did he still live with them? Or did he move out?

I didn't see his truck when I pulled in and the disappointment was thick in my throat. I also brought Gus with me because I didn't want to leave his care on Dad. I didn't think Janet would mind, considering she watched him at the hospital while her husband was going in for surgery.

The bad idea got even worse when I knocked on the door and a younger version of Dean answered the door, holding a baby in his arm. "Um," I started, not sure what to say as I held Gus, "is Janet home?"

He looked me over once then smiled. "You're Noah's Grace, right?"

Noah's Grace? "I am Grace, I don't know about being Noah's," I corrected him, and he smiled, although I wish my heart would stop fluttering like it enjoyed the sound of being Noah's.

"I'm Janet's son, Jeremy," he told me, extending his hand out to take mine.

"The army, right?"

He nodded. "Yeah, one of them." A petite blonde moved in the doorway with him. "This is my wife, Sarah," he told me then smiled at the baby in his arms. "And this is our little miracle baby, Sammy." They looked so perfect, the three of them together, that it made my teeth hurt.

"Come on in," Sarah offered.

284

fall from grace

I didn't make it one step when Janet yelled, "Keep your shoes on, Grace, we're leaving."

Oh, boy.

I stood there awkwardly as they both smiled at me. Janet shoved herself between them. "Mamaw will be right back," she cooed to the baby as she kissed him on the forehead.

"It was nice to finally meet you," Sara yelled as Janet hurried me to her car.

"It looks like one of your sons and his family are in to visit. Are you sure you want to leave?" I asked, then watched as she opened the car door and climbed in. "Wait, where are we even going?"

"Both of our sons are in, and they will be for two weeks, so stop making excuses not to be here," she mumbled as she looked up at me from the seat. "Well, come on, I have a husband laid up on the couch that wants to be petted after his surgery so let's make this quick."

"I brought Gus," I went on.

"He's fine."

I ran around and got into the passenger side seat. "I wouldn't have come if I knew I'd be bothering you guys," I said again as I buckled up.

She started the car and grunted. "Stop. You're still trying to make up every reason as to why you shouldn't have come to see me today but guess what, Grace?" She was grinning as she pulled out of the driveway.

"What?"

"You came anyway."

"If there's something you want to ask me about Noah, ask away," she said softly. "We have a few minutes before we get there."

"Where are we going?" I asked.

"The garage."

Now I really was nervous. "Why? Is Noah there?"

She turned and smiled at me. "Why are you being so nervous? He's the reason you came all the way to see me, right?"

I wiped my face nervously, placed my palm on my knee, and held Gus with my other hand. "I came because you said there was something you wanted to show me."

"And I am," she replied with a smirk. "Noah's never stopped waiting for you despite knowing that you were trying to run from everything you had with him."

I glanced at her apprehensively. "It sounds like he's told you everything."

"You're not the only one that felt horrible about the way your mom passed away. Noah felt the same things you did, and with you pulling away from him, he needed someone to listen."

"Noah... he felt the same way I have?" I asked quickly. "He never..."

"Because you were clinging onto it so hard, he knew that if he did too then neither of you would fight for your love because you'd both be trying to figure out if you should blame yourselves for your mom being out that night." She went on, "I'll tell you the same thing I told him and what I told you yesterday... let it go. I never met your mother, but some things you just know, and she wouldn't want you this way no matter what reason she was out on the road that night. It's crazy the way humans will cling so hard onto the bad things than focus on the good ones."

"You don't understand," I muttered. "My dad has been steadily pushing me away since she died, and no matter what anyone says, I feel like he blames me and can't even stand to be around me. He loved me so much... and just like that, he can't stand me. I hate it! This man that I've loved my whole life suddenly being cold to me. What if the same thing

286

happened with Noah? What if one day he was so disappointed in me that he became the same way?" I shook my head violently. "There's no way I could handle that. I'd rather live with this guilt and leave him than for him to one day look at me the way Dad does!"

Janet slammed on the brakes, and I looked up to see that she had pulled off beside the road. She looked so sad when she faced me that I placed my face in Gus's fur so I didn't have to face it. She pulled me into her arms and I stiffened. "You've been having all these thoughts without anyone to talk to?" she whispered. "You must miss her so much. I still miss mine, they were always the ones we could go to when things were tough, whether it was with life or just the thoughts inside our heads. Sometimes a girl just needs her mom." With her words, I broke down and cried into her shoulder.

Janet's shoulder was so comfortable that I found myself crying for the longest time before I finally settled down. I had so many tears, so many emotions, so many choices, so many things I wanted that I thought I couldn't have, and things I wanted but was afraid of one day turning uglier than I felt now.

I finally pulled away from her when I felt better, also a bit drowsy now that I had cried to my heart's content. "I understand why you're hurting but believe me, there's nothing you can do that can ever disappoint Noah. The worst thing you could have done to him, you already have by leaving him, and he still hasn't lost sight of you." I wiped my face. "Time to let it go. It's time to live," she said before getting back on the road.

I cleaned my face up but it was still obvious that I had been crying. I felt strangely better, but still nervous because I didn't know what I was doing. "I'm not much, and I know you don't know me well enough, but that can change and I can always be a listening ear or shoulder to cry on… Never let yourself suffer alone, you were only eating yourself on the inside."

"Sorry about that breakdown," was the only thing I could say to her. Twice in two days. Maybe I tried too hard for so long and kept it bottled away to the point that I truly was falling apart.

When we arrived at the garage, I immediately knew that it wasn't the same. My eyes took in the new name and I was completely speechless. In italicized gold lettering, *Prissy Auto Repairs and Services* was plastered on a sign at the entrance and again on the newly painted garage. Black and gold paint job. This place looked amazing.

"What?" I finally mumbled.

Janet was grinning. "Dean sold the garage to Noah." I looked over at her. "It was time. He was ready to rest and he knew Noah would be the perfect choice. Neither of our sons wanted it and they don't live around here anyway."

I looked at the garage again. "You're grinning," she informed me as she watched me. "Are you that happy about Noah getting himself a garage or is it something else?" *She knows.*

Of course, I was. My skin felt like bursting. The only boy I ever loved was now a man who made his garage's name the nickname he called me. After a good cry, all of these good feelings were hitting me as I stared at the title, and there I was smiling again.

"I can't go in there with the way I feel right now," I said immediately as I clung to Gus in my arms. He knew the car was parked so he was restless to get outside.

"Why not?"

"Why did you bring me here?" I dragged out a sigh. "Why did you show me this?"

"I brought you here because with him is probably where you want to be, but you don't want to admit it because of this pointless guilt and fear. I knew if I brought you here, you'd be left without a choice." She touched my arm. "I brought you here because Noah's my family now, and there's this other thing I'm doing."

"What?" I met her eyes.

"I'm saving Grace," she answered, "I'm saving *you*, from yourself."

"Wait, Janet," I whispered quickly as she opened the door. Noah stepped out of the open garage doors wiping his hands on a rag as he saw her and smiled. He took my breath away even greased up, maybe even more so. He was so handsomely sculpted, and it wasn't just his appearance that was rich and vibrant.

"What are you doing here?" he asked her then when Gus started barking, his eyes fell on us.

I was so fidgety and nervous for some reason as he smirked at Janet before walking over to my window as I rolled it down. He peered down at me with a smile. "Might as well get out," he told me as he opened my door.

"We can leave if you're busy," I rambled as I got out and stood beside him anyway.

"I'll never be busy enough when it comes to you," he said effortlessly, and I looked away, lowering my gaze to the ground instead of at his alluring smile.

"Come inside, it's a little cooler," he told me as he grabbed my arm and pulled me forward. "There's a little office inside, I'll show you."

I smiled, thinking that he might be anxious and a tad excited to show me the garage that was his now.

"I like the name you picked out," I found myself saying.

He turned and cocked an eyebrow at me before grabbing his neck and smiling almost like he was embarrassed. "I thought you'd like that." Then he turned back around as we slipped inside. Two other men were inside working and they nodded and grinned at us as we walked past them. "It was only a matter of time before I went and got you and brought you home myself to show you."

Home. Where was that for me anymore?

I thought I heard Janet's car starting up and pulled away from Noah as I ran back toward the garage door. Noah took Gus from my hands as he moved beside me as we watched Janet drive away. "She left me," I muttered.

Noah laughed. "Guess you're stuck here with me until I bring you home." He turned back around and I followed, silently thanking Janet for taking my choice away but at the same time, the fear kept me on edge, reminding me of the guilt.

He took me to a back room which was a small office. *His* office. I eyed the rolling chair right before he said, "Go ahead and sit down."

"What time do you get off?" I asked as I plopped down in the chair and started spinning myself in it.

"Are you going to play at your teacher's desk when you start teaching as well?" he asked, leaning against the desk with his arms folded as he watched me. When I tilted my head back at him, he added, "You might have tried your hardest not to find out about me, but I tried very hard to keep up with you the last few years. You're suited to be a teacher."

I started spinning again. "You never posted much online, so of course, I never knew what was going on in your life."

He kicked his foot out and stopped me from spinning. I swallowed as his gaze heated me up with a smirk. "So, you were curious?" he asked. "You could have just called, even better, you could have come home to me already."

He pulled me closer with his leg until my knees hit his legs. "Why do you keep expecting me to come back when I said, 'don't wait'," I whispered, trying to dispel the mood between us. It wasn't working, and with the heavy-lidded gaze he was caressing my body with, it only seemed to have made him worse.

"You're here, aren't you?" he caught me with his question. "How did you end up with Janet? You drove, didn't you?" He leaned over me, placing his hands on the arms of my chair. I leaned back, trying to make myself a part of the chair. "You're asking to be caught, Priss. No, you're begging me to keep you… you just don't realize it yet, but don't worry, I'm not letting you go this time."

He loomed closer, his azure eyes calling me in as his breath fanned my neck. I shuddered and leaned away. He followed until his lips were at the pulse thrumming in my neck. A single light kiss made me shiver. I placed my hand between his mouth and my skin. "What are you doing?" I mumbled.

He didn't pull away and it was killing me. "It's been a long damn time since I've had your body right here for the taking, instead of my hand, Grace, and I'm coming unglued because of it, especially with you right here stuck in my office…"

I let my head fall back as I closed my eyes. "It's been so long," I agreed.

I gasped when he scooped me up unexpectedly and tossed me onto the desk. I looked at him stunned as he placed his forehead against mine. "You haven't even been with anybody else, have you?" It wasn't a question—he knew. "I know just what I created inside you when we were only thirteen, why didn't you sleep with anyone else?" he whispered into my neck. "I can tell, I just know. You keep giving yourself away." I'd been exposed beneath the heated gaze and his long eyelashes.

I pushed him barely. "This is inappropriate."

"I'll be inappropriate every damn time I'm with you for the rest of our lives because I'm going to keep you by my side and smother you with all this you've made me hold onto for the last few years."

He cupped my cheek and met my eyes. He kissed my nose, my forehead, my cheeks, and my chin. By the time he was finished, I was shaking with this strong, intense emotion and breathing hot against his face. I grabbed his hand and leaned in.

"Noah, whoa," one of the other workers said as he stepped into the room then immediately covered his eyes. We weren't doing anything, but Noah was standing between my legs and an inch from my face when I coughed and shoved him away slowly. "We got someone out here wanting you to do an estimate… I didn't know you'd be busy," he said, winking at Noah.

"I'll be right there," Noah said, and the worker walked away from the doorway. He looked back at me when he was gone. "Are you hungry? I can make one of the guys go out and get you something. It's gonna be a few hours."

I nodded. "I'm fine. Go on and work, I'm gonna stay in here."

He smiled at me. "Everything's right with the world again."

He surprised me so I said, "What?"

"Having you by my side again." He didn't give me the chance to say anything as he slipped out the door. I stared down at the jacket beside me and picked it up. Noah's name was on the tag. I brought it up to my neck and sighed.

That comfort I felt with Noah always reminded me of Nyquil. His presence had a way of making me content with life and everything to the point that I was drowsy. Before I realized what I was doing, I laid down and cradled myself atop the desk and drifted to sleep and hoped when I woke, it wasn't the guilt that greeted me.

———

When I woke, I knew it was Noah's arms that carried me. The stream of light hit my eyes and I brought my hand up to shield them from the sun. "Finally awake?" Noah asked as he opened his truck door with me still in his arms.

"See ya tomorrow," someone called out to Noah, and I raised up and tapped his shoulder so he'd place my feet down. I wiped my eyes and mouth as I climbed into the driver's side.

"Bye," Noah said as he waved.

"Gus?" I asked, and he picked him up and placed him inside the truck with me.

I scooted to the middle and waited for Noah to climb in. I grabbed my phone from my pocket and checked the time. It was after four which meant I slept for a few hours. No wonder my neck was so sore. I rolled my neck and shoulders.

"I don't see how you slept on top of a desk," he muttered as he climbed in and shut the door. "Only you." He smiled.

"My neck is killing me," I admitted as I glanced at the garage again and smiled. "Are you getting off now?" He nodded as he pulled out. "My Escape's at Janet's," I told him. "Do you still live with them?"

"No," he answered. "I'm taking you home. I want you to see it."

"You have a place too?" I asked, amazed. "I just finished college, how do you manage to have your own garage and place already?"

I could easily afford my own place with my savings, and all I had to do was find a teaching job, so maybe we weren't so far apart or at least I hoped.

"It's called being in debt," he said with a smirk, and I smiled. "Honestly, if it hadn't been for Dean and Janet, there's no way I would have gotten this far. Running the garage is a lot more of a pain than it had been just working there, but I enjoy it despite the headaches that come with it." I nodded.

"What about your dad?" I asked casually.

"I had to cut ties with him," he answered. I couldn't believe it. "He gave me no choice. He wasn't going to change, and I know somewhere deep down, there's a part of him that loves me, but he'd rather use me than love me."

"I don't know what to say," I told him as I searched his face as he drove. "I'm sorry. I had liked John despite everything. Even as a kid, I thought he looked like a parent some days when he helped us. It just wasn't enough to make up for the bad things he put you through... I think that was the right choice."

He looked at me sadly. "Why didn't you tell me he was harassing you for money?"

My eyes widened. "It was only a few times."

"Fuck, Grace, you're my sun, you're my moon and stars; my world revolves around you no matter how much you want to deny it. Do you know how sick I felt when I found out that he'd bugged you while we were together? It's embarrassing and I can't stand the thought of you putting up with that because of me."

"I didn't tell you because I knew you'd end up giving him whatever he wanted so that he would have left me alone, and I didn't want to see that happen either. I hated to see him take advantage of you."

"It's the same for me... That's what made cutting ties with him so easy."

"Noah... you can't just make choices because of me. You can't just cut your dad out of your life because of me."

"I did it for *me*, Priss, so that I could be with you comfortably and without the burden of him making our life hard. You know I love him despite everything he is, it's like it's in my DNA to love him, but I love you more—I want you, our future, our happiness more than anything else, and I'm not going to feel sorry for it either." He looked away from the road again to look at me. "It's that easy, Grace, to be happy."

He placed his hand on my knee and I glanced down. I was letting him pull me in, I felt it, the rattle in my chest, the need for him burning into my very existence.

fall from grace

He pulled into a long driveway and my eyes took in the two-story house. It was beautiful. Simple, nothing at all grand, but it stirred the longing somewhere deep inside me. The yard was big, I could already picture him cutting the grass as I planted flowers. I could see myself on the swing on the porch, my feet propped up in his lap as we read together like we always did growing up. I could see us leaving in separate cars every morning with a goodbye kiss and smile before going to work. I saw everything so perfectly that it stung my eyes and I had to look down once again.

"Well, what do you think?" he asked. "It's us, right?"

I finally covered my eyes. "Why are you doing this?"

"Why did you come to me?" he asked back. I looked up from my hands as he placed the truck in park and met my eyes with resolve. "You came this far by coming to me today, it's time to come the rest of the way."

Noah's words were magic and chaos to my heart and body.

"Come back to me all the way," he whispered beautifully.

Then he opened the truck door, climbing out and pulling me with him. I let him lift me up slowly before he placed my feet on the ground. Static was between us as I let him take my hand and lead me. Gus followed behind us as we walked to the backyard. Noah pointed to the huge beech tree in the yard. "And that is the main reason I bought this house so that I could build a treehouse for old times' sake and for our future kids."

He grabbed my other hand and moved in close. "The future that I pictured growing up, the words I said, and the promises I made to myself are here. I'll make you happy and when you're happy and next to me for every year here on out, I'll be happy. Your mom was on my side. She said for me not to disappoint her and I haven't, but I will if I let you go again."

"Noah—"

"You made me a promise that you'd be the only girl I'd spend my time with if I'd always take you on an adventure," he spoke over me.

He was giving me the biggest swarm of butterflies in my stomach. "We were six and seven," I said half-heartedly because, in the end, I held Noah above all others from the very beginning so I knew how little our age meant. In fact, Noah was the only boy—man I ever saw, even now. I couldn't go to another man and think of him touching me without getting sick to my stomach with just the thought. That's just the way it was and after being around a ton of opportunities in college, I realized that part me was never going to change. That part of me belonged to Noah before I even knew I gave it away as a kid. My heart and body. Probably even my very soul belonged to the man trying to fix what I broke.

"You have been my dream, my motivation since the moment you climbed up that rope." He didn't relent.

"Noah."

"Don't pretend," he yelled before softening his expression once more.

"Don't pretend about what?"

"Don't pretend that you don't know that I've been orbiting around you since we were kids."

"I thought that was me with you," I dared to whisper back.

"Don't pretend that I wouldn't try my damnedest to reach up and pluck the moon from the sky if you asked."

The heat burning through me wasn't pretending either. I swallowed and searched his face, gazed at his lips before I met his smoldering expression once more. He was trying to bury me with all these words, feelings, and gazes.

"I got another adventure, one I've been planning for a long time," he revealed to me, and the fear slid into my veins as he pulled me to his chest, wrapped his arms around me, and swallowed me with his rugged beauty. "Marry me, Priss. Let's make every day an adventure. Let's go on walks. Let's take naps. Let's read and do whatever together like we always did before, and let's do new things like vacations and road trips. Anything you want. Let's be happy."

I had to get away from him. I shoved him away and turned around and started walking the way we came. "Grace!" he yelled, and my feet felt like lead they were so heavy. My heart was protesting but my mind was everywhere.

"We can leave here, we can go anywhere!" he kept yelling, but I didn't dare look back to see if he was coming after me. "My home is where you are. Nothing here means anything if you don't stay. I'll go where you go."

I covered my eyes and mouth with my hands and tried to keep the tears at bay. Noah was more than likely in a lot of debt, yet I knew his words weren't empty promises. He'd go wherever I told him to and that hurt most of all.

"Gus," I called out with a voice jam-packed with emotion.

I turned around and saw Gus standing next to Noah, who was just standing there watching me in the same place I left him. Even Gus knew my heart. He looked like he wanted me to stop hurting everyone too. I turned around and walked anyway. I walked and walked until the hole in my heart grew. I made it to the edge of his driveway. I'd held onto this guilt for so long, would it be so easy to just let it go?

Noah, my feet really don't want to leave this time. Too heavy, this burden was...

There was something beautifully tragic in the way someone fell to their knees, some held their arms up high, clawing to the surface to get back up, while others picked themselves up slowly, one leg at a time, and the ones that never got back up and drowned their hopes and dreams...Then there was Noah, who was only a kid when he centered his future around me.

And here I was walking away from him again.

So, I stopped and took a deep breath. Sometimes you had to drop all the pieces and let go of all the things that were keeping you from being happy.

I was running when I didn't want to be. I left once because I thought I should suffer. I didn't want to leave again. I didn't want to be without him any longer. My peace. My comfort. My passion. My dreams. My happiness. He was all of them.

"Sorry, Mom," I cried as I turned around. *This ugly feeling I've held onto for so long. This unwanted guilt. I'm going to let it go and trust that you'd want me happy with Noah, instead of what my mind wants me to believe.*

And just like that, in this smothering evening heat with no rain or clouds, I washed away all the things that held me down. And I ran back to where I belonged.

Typical Noah, here I was running back with tears running down my cheeks, and he was running to me so we met halfway. More like collided in a mess of tears and locked away touches. His hands were unsure as they wrapped around me. He watched as the tears streamed down my cheeks. I grabbed his arms and pulled him into me but not without whispering, "It is that easy." My lips slammed into his, and it was the most amazing sound—his soft, pleading groan when I did.

My feet were off the ground as he lifted me up while shoving his tongue down my throat. It wasn't enough, it was *never* enough when it came to him. "I love you, Noah, I love you," I breathed the words into his mouth as I continued to kiss him while he carried me away. "I love you, and I'm so sorry. I needed you the most when I pushed you away, but I didn't think I deserved to be happy with you after—"

"Shh," he mumbled across my lips. "I'm going to make you happy, Grace, I love you so damn much." His arms shook as he carried me. I pushed against his chest so he'd place my feet back down and started tugging at his shirt. He threw it on the gravel driveway as we scooted our feet across the rocks and dirt to reach some unknown destination between kisses. He tore at my shirt and I helped, then he stopped and tugged down my shorts. I stepped out of them and jumped him while he caught me by the legs and I wrapped them around him. He carried me inside where he dropped me down on an air mattress in his living room that was empty.

I made the time between his kisses to say, "Your house is completely empty."

He lifted his head and grinned. "It's a work in progress."

I laughed and brought his face down to kiss me. He made quick work of his jeans and my eyes took in his erection, the mushroom tip, and all its glory, and the need to have him inside me grew worse. He undid my bra and covered me in kisses as I moaned and dug my fingers into his hair. His beard brought on a new powerful sensation that I loved. "Noah, we have the rest of our lives for foreplay, I need you inside me now," I moaned as he covered one of my nipples with his mouth.

He looked up at me. "I'm going to explode before I even get inside you," he admitted with lust-driven eyes. "It's been a long time." I loved his honesty.

I took my hands to his cheeks and lifted his face to mine until our noses were inches apart. "I like you the most." I slid my hands down until I was touching his. "I never had to be with someone else to know that I like your hands the most, it's your touch that I love and crave. Even so, I could have tried a thousand different touches and I would have still only wanted yours." I could be honest too.

"That was overkill, am I dreaming? You can't really be underneath me right now saying words like that after leaving me for so long," he whispered.

I kissed his forehead as he placed his lips against my chest. "I'm sorry." He kissed me again.

"Are you on birth control?" he asked.

"I'm not," I gasped as he slammed into me all at once.

The pain was exquisite because of what came with it. My body welcomed the rush of him inside me. "Good to know," he groaned. "Feels like home."

He kissed, caressed, and molded me as he moved into me. It was rushed and perfect, the feel of him above me as he brought us to the peak. I could go back to who I was. The girl that wholeheartedly loved one boy, even when her friends told her it didn't make sense to be with only one guy and think there wasn't better out there.

Maybe I was completely ordinary and a simple small-town girl but to Noah, I was *everything*. And if being his everything was as far as I got in life, that was perfectly okay with me.

Then he brought us over our peak and I shattered beneath him as he pulled out and came on my stomach. He cleaned me off with his shirt before cradling me in his arms. I looked up from his chest with a smile. "Did we leave Gus outside?"

He chuckled and got back up from the air mattress. "I'll go get him. You stay there naked."

I grinned. "Can you get my shorts outside? My cell phone's inside the pocket."

He nodded and ran out the door buck-naked. I was glad he didn't have neighbors. I shook my head and fell back against the mattress. I was going to be happy with Noah. I looked around the empty room with a contented smile. It was okay to picture my future with him right here. The only person that had control over my happiness was me.

Gus came running through the door followed by Noah. He started jumping onto the air mattress as I heard Noah running water in the kitchen. "Careful, Gus," I told him as I helped him on the air mattress and covered myself with a sheet. Noah came back into the room with a bowl of water that he sat down on the floor for Gus.

fall from grace

Noah pulled his cell phone out of his pants' pocket lying on the floor and handed me mine as he sat down next to me. He pulled open a text and showed it to me.

I'm rooting for you.

So don't disappoint me.

It was the text Mom sent him the night she passed away. It hurt to think of the way she died. Her death was a wound I'd never be able to heal, but I would slowly learn to live with it… Like right now, the text made me smile instead of burst into tears and guilt. She had been rooting for us from the very beginning. I had to believe that she'd want us happy instead of miserable. "I had to take a picture of the text so that I would have it on this phone… She gave me a tough time with you but it was because she wanted us both to succeed when we got older."

"I saw that you still carved," I told him. "I think she would have been happy to have known you kept to it."

He smiled. "I have a shed at Dean's where my saw and things are, I'll have to build something here for when I get orders."

"Sounds like you've got a lot of work to do with building a shed and treehouse…"

"And not to mention time at the garage, the woodwork, and keeping you happy… I might be a busy man, but I'm going to always make time for you. Everything I do is so that I can give you a comfortable life."

I pulled him down and kissed him. "I can't believe I wasted away some of our years together."

"We'll have to make up for lost time," he said as his hand trailed down between my legs.

———

I was sitting on the top step of the porch with a sheet draped over me as I watched the sunset. Noah stepped out of the house and placed a

301

pot of ramen between us as he joined me. "It's all I had to make," he told me as he handed me a fork. "Did you call Dustin?" he asked, and I nodded. I let him know that I wasn't coming back, but he had laughed and said he had expected this outcome, and maybe deep down, I did too.

"He offered to pack my stuff for me and bring it back, but I'd rather do it."

"We can go get it this weekend," he told me.

I smiled and took a huge bite. "I wish she was still here, Noah," I found myself saying as I glanced back at the yard. "It hurts not having her to share my day with, like right now. I'm sure she would have loved this place for us. I could imagine her dragging Dad along because he would have still been giving you a hard time." I smiled sadly and took another bite. "I want Dad to be happy… and I don't think I'm going to ever have my relationship with him back."

He flicked my nose. "He loves you… I can imagine I'd fall apart the same way if I had to lose you in such a way that he lost your mom." He placed his hand over mine. "Some people cope better than others, you and your dad weren't those that could."

I gave him another tearful smile. "Why didn't I let you comfort me sooner?" I mumbled and he kissed me softly because of it. "Such a waste of years and all that unwanted guilt would have been easier to let go of if I had just let you love me despite everything."

"I loved you regardless, but I'm glad you're here now. Just promise me one thing."

"What?" I asked.

"Don't shut me out the next time something bad happens. Let me hold you and make it better. When you're thinking of your mom and missing her, talk to me like you are now. Don't shut me out like you did before. You might as well stab me with something because that's what it feels like when you put distance between us."

I placed my fork down and leaned into him with a smile. "I promise to let you take care of me, and I'll take care of you."

"Do you want a big wedding?" he asked.

"You have to ask first," I whispered.

"I thought I did earlier."

"Yeah, but I ran away." I looked up and grinned at him. "But, my heart was seriously about to beat out of my chest when you did."

He stood up, pulling me with me. I started blushing and laughing because I knew what he was about to do. He pulled me into his arms and dipped me. "Let's go on an adventure, one that lasts forever." I was laughing and he was smirking. "Marry me."

"Of course, I'd take on any adventure as long as it was with you."

He smothered me in kisses until I pushed his face away while we laughed. He lifted me back up and I grabbed my back when my cell phone started ringing in the house. "It's mine," I told him as we went inside. I picked it up off the bed and felt the same feeling of dread from that night Mom passed away. "It's Dad," I told him.

"Hello," I answered.

"I was worried you weren't planning on coming back home tonight," he responded. He was right. I was planning on staying here with Noah. "Come home and bring Noah too." Before I could say anything, he added, "That's who you're with, ain't it?"

"Yeah, we'll head over now."

"Good. Bye, Grace."

I hung up and looked to Noah. "He wants us to come over... I don't know why."

He grabbed my cheek and squeezed. "It doesn't have to be anything bad just because he called, Grace... it could be something good."

303

"You're right." I nodded, but was still afraid, nonetheless.

———

Noah had driven us to Dad's. It was almost an hour drive from his house. As we walked up the steps, he said, "Relax."

"I would if I could," I told him with a weak smile. "I just hate disappointing him."

"You are not a disappointment." He grabbed my hand and opened the door.

Dad poked his head out of the kitchen. "I, uh, ordered pizza if you guys would like some."

"That actually sounds good. We ate ramen right before you called and it didn't quite hit the spot or fill me up," Noah said with ease. I smiled and relaxed next to him.

We followed Dad into the kitchen where he moved hastily around the kitchen and found some paper plates. Two pizza boxes were on the table and something about this made my heart hurt because it looked like Dad was trying… For a moment, I just stood there frozen as I watched him awkwardly get us out something to drink almost like he had rehearsed it. "I remember you liked Meat Lover's, didn't ya, Noah?" Dad asked him.

"Yeah, I do," Noah replied.

He looked up from the table at me. "I got us bacon and banana peppers, our favorite."

I found myself smiling. "That sounds so good right now," I told him, and Noah was giving me a huge grin as if he was enjoying this for me.

We all sat down and started digging into the pizza. "You're still living over in Jewel County, aren't ya?" Dad asked Noah.

fall from grace

He nodded. "Yeah, I am. I just recently bought me a place over there. I was renting a place before that," he said, looking at me since it was the first time I heard about it too.

I smiled and he placed his hand on my knee as he ate as if to say that we had all the time in the world to catch up on the last few years.

"That's great, Noah, it really is." Dad looked down at his paper plate before adding, "You proved me wrong, Noah, and although it's damn irritating to have to admit that, I'm glad you did."

Noah and I looked at one another and grinned. "I've always known what I wanted, and I made sure I could get it," he said while staring at me.

"There's nothing wrong with that," Dad agreed. "Grace." I looked over at him and stopped smiling. "I didn't realize how much I hurt you when we lost your mom and if I had known you were blaming yourself the same way I had been, I would have spoken up instead of sinking into this sadness that's had a hold of me since your mom passed away."

I frowned. "What do you mean? The same way? Why would you feel that way?"

He gave me a miserable smile. "That night at the hospital when you showed up with Noah and your mom was still in surgery and we didn't know the shape she was in… I had been angry and scared, so I had said she had been coming to get you just to make you feel horrible for going to be with Noah when I had told you not to. She hadn't been coming to get you."

"What?" I mumbled. Noah looked just as startled as I felt.

Dad placed his fists against his head as he finally broke down, "She wanted take-out, you know how your mom was with take-out when she didn't want to cook… She had asked me to go with her, but the only thing I wanted to do was argue with her because she had taken you to meet Noah. I was so angry, but she was completely calm and cheerful as

305

I griped the entire time and when I refused to go with her to get us some food, she said she'd go herself. I kept telling her to call you and get you to come home, and I remember clearly what she said to me as she was walking out of the door that day, 'Steven, you might as well get used to it because mark my words, that boy is going to be our son-in-law one day'."

I was crying while Dad muffled his own. Noah was deathly still next to me. "She had so much confidence in you both, but I was so scared and angry, Grace, you were my baby. I didn't think someone with a background like Noah could give you what you deserve." Dad wiped his eyes. "I'm telling you this because you've been hurting for something that wasn't your fault, if anything, it was my fault for not going with her. If I had gone with her, I would have driven and it might have made a difference."

I covered my eyes and cried harder. I felt Noah's arms go around me. I'd been feeling guilty for nothing and while I thought Dad had been distancing himself because he blamed me, it was really himself that he blamed. All this time, Dad and I felt the same way.

I felt Noah's shoulders tremble and that was when I uncovered my eyes and saw that he was on the verge tears as he held me. There was something so heartwarming about it because all this time, Noah felt the same way just like Janet had told me, but he held onto me instead of letting it eat at him. But now, the truth was out and we were set free.

"I'm so sorry, I hadn't realized you took my words to heart when I spoke out of anger that night at the hospital," Dad apologized.

But I had already decided to let go before he even told us the truth of that night. I stood up and walked over to Dad. He looked up at me and I did what Mom would want us all to do. I hugged him tightly, and he placed one hand against my back as he cried. "I already let go of that night before I even came here… It's time for you to do the same. Instead of remembering Mom for who she was, we've been stuck on the day we lost her."

fall from grace

"I miss her so much," he told me. "I wish I could go back to that day and just go with her."

I pulled away and met his eyes. "Then I might have lost both my parents that day and I've missed you and her both enough the past few years already. I still need you, ya know."

"I'm so sorry," he said again. "I've missed you too. I didn't know how to be myself once we lost her."

We were only human. We bottled up our feelings and held on tight when it would have been so much easier to let go. I thought we would be better now.

We were dusting off our knees and standing back up.

38

You know what it's like to fly? To soar so fucking high and be free?

Neither did I until that heavy burden fell off my shoulders.

I got my girl, my Priss, my Grace.

I know how to love her, I know how to keep her.

You bet your sweet ass I'll give her my last name as soon as I can.

N.P.

"This is a lot harder than I remember," I said and Noah laughed behind me.

"Hurry up, Priss, I still gotta throw you the blankets before I can climb up," he told me.

We decided to spend the night in the treehouse instead of going back home. Yes, *home.* I wasn't separating from Noah ever again, as long as I have breath in me, never *ever* would I leave his side again.

Dad was fine with us staying. He actually looked happy about it. I could imagine how lonely he had been the last few years which I planned to change by becoming a part of his life again.

It's time to heal, isn't it, Mom?

Once I made it up the rope, I shined the flashlight into the treehouse and sighed. "Our treehouse is getting old age," I told him before sticking my head over the edge and shining the light in his face.

fall from grace

"Our?" he snorted. "I recall someone always calling it hers all the time. Stop shining that in my eyes." I kept shining it in his eyes anyway. "Just wait, I'll be up there to get you in a second."

My stomach tightened with anticipation. "Hand me the blankets," I told him.

I finally moved the flashlight from his eyes and he tossed me up one at a time. Once he made it up in the treehouse with me, he tackled me down and I screamed.

"Shh." He covered my mouth with his hand and I was taken back in time to when he had done it to me when I first climbed into the treehouse.

I looked up at him with a smile and removed his hand. "You've come such a long way from the dirty boy I first encountered in this treehouse."

His blue eyes were dark in the treehouse as he gazed down at me. "You've come such a long way from the polka dot priss I first encountered... But I loved that girl then, and I love her still, and I'm going to love all the many changes she'll become."

"Not just as a man that I love, Noah, you're a beautiful human inside and out, and I'm so glad you're my human."

He settled between my legs and started working on taking off my shorts. "Let's make more humans," he whispered.

I sniggered as I grabbed his hand. "I'd like to have you a few years to myself before we start growing our family... Good thing you bought a decent size house," I mumbled as he kissed his way down me.

"I want our kids to have brothers and sisters," he told me as he dipped his mouth between my thighs and I gasped.

"Yeah, I hated being an only child," I moaned. "Good thing I had you."

"You'll always have me."

Needless to say, a baby with the last name Phillips was born nine months later.

Life with Noah…

Made all the bad things better, and all the good ones so much sweeter.

Epilogue

I've loved her since we met as kids, that's 24 years.

I've been married to her 9 of those years.

I gave her time and distance for 5 of them.

She looked for me for almost 4 of those years when social services took me from my Dad.

How many years did it take to bring us back together? Zero.

It only took a second, staring at her freckled face and dark eyes to shape my future as a kid.

It only took two football games to reunite us during the first one and finally get her in my arms after the second.

And it only took two days for her give up her run and I got her back.

These days, she lets me in and doesn't push me out. She cried on my shoulder the day Gus passed away, and she grabbed my hand and kept me close by her side the week her dad had a cancer scare. We talk and talk about her mom, especially to our kids.

We don't talk about mine though. My dad still reaches out, I still push away. If he wants to change, I'll open my arms wide and accept him into our lives despite how much I was neglected growing up. That's just the kind of man I am.

michelle gross

Dean and Janet are still a part of our lives and our kids. It's crazy, even after all these years the lengths people with no blood ties will go to stay a part of your life. That was the difference between good people and bad ones. They still foster, bit by bit, I think they make a difference in kids' lives.

I still flirt with my wife, I think she's still into me. I mean, she keeps letting me rub her butt when the kids aren't looking... Yeah, I got what I wanted.

Am I happy? Hell, yeah, I am.

N.P.

I was putting clothes in the washer when someone started banging on the door. I raised up, holding my back as I waddled to the door. When I answered, a handsome blond with azure eyes greeted me, holding a box on his shoulder. He tipped his ballcap down at me. "You have a delivery, ma'am, it was on the porch."

He stepped in and I smirked, wondering where this was going. "Delivery guys don't normally step into people's houses," I told him politely.

His eyes skimmed over the swell of my stomach. "Are you expecting?" he observed with a whistle and inappropriate stare at my breasts.

"It's very rude to ask a woman that," I said as I turned around and walked towards the kitchen. I started running water to wash the dishes and felt him come up behind me. His hands wrapped around my huge stomach and he tickled my neck with his beard. I leaned back into him.

"I've always wanted to get it on with a pregnant lady," he whispered into my ear and I bit back a laugh.

I turned around to face him. "Well you're in luck, my husband keeps me this way."

fall from grace

He smiled down at me before gently lifting me up onto the counter. "Where are the kids?" he asked with lusty intent.

"Outside playing in the treehouse," I told him, rubbing my belly against him, not on purpose, it was just always there between us. "Might need to take this somewhere else, my kids might walk in." He arched a brow and scooped me up in his arms. "Also, my husband will be home from work soon, and my dad's coming to see his grandkids." He nodded as he kissed my neck.

He stopped at the window and peered outside with a strange look on his face. "Um, Grace, who's the kid with our kids?"

"What?" I mumbled as I turned my head and looked out the window to see what Noah was talking about. Sure enough, there was a little girl playing with Nate and Allison—who was named after her late grandma who would have loved her to pieces if she had still been here. Nate was eight and Allison, four. Noah sat my feet down as we walked over and peeked out the window. "I don't know who she is," I told him.

Our closest neighbor was half a mile down the road so she had to have walked a good distance to get here. "More like, where did she come from?" he asked, and I was just as curious.

When she finally turned around, I recognized her. "Ah, she's a new student," I told him. "Jessi is her name. She's a grade below Nate. She's gonna be a tough one, I can already tell."

"Look at Nate," he said, laughing. "He looks furious."

I joined in with his laughter when Jessi pushed him away from the ladder but let Allison come up with her. He stood there like he had no clue what was happening. "This looks strangely familiar," he told me with a smirk.

I leaned into him, batting my eyes at my husband. "There's something about a treehouse."

"Well, let's go introduce ourselves," Noah said, and I waddled outside with him. Jessi climbed down the ladder when she saw me.

313

She looked at Nate. "Your mom is Mrs. Phillips?" she said it like it was horrible.

"I didn't know you lived around here," I said to her.

"Yeah, I'm staying with my mamaw and papaw right down the road." She pointed toward the left even though you couldn't see anything from our backyard.

"Daddy!" Allison screamed when she saw Noah and ran up to him. He scooped her up, tugging at her blonde curls.

"This is my husband, Noah," I told her. "Looks like you've already met Nate and Allison." I looked at Nate behind her with his arms folded over his chest. "Nate's a year ahead of you."

She nodded and looked back at Nate with a rotten smirk I knew all too well. I bent down a little to be eye level with her, already regretting the decision because I knew it was going to be hard to raise back up. "Come and visit whenever you want, just let your grandparents know."

"I was wondering why no one was answering the door, you guys were all out back," Dad said, walking around the house. Nate and Allison both ran to him.

"Did you bring me anything?" Allison asked straight away.

He chuckled and squatted in front of her. "I didn't bring anything, but I did bring someone." He looked at me. "Papaw has a girlfriend and she wanted to come meet you all."

It took a long time to get Dad to date again, but I hated the thought of him being alone. I just couldn't believe he finally found someone because he disapproved of everyone I introduced him to. "Where is she?" I asked.

He pointed toward the house. "Still on the porch."

314

fall from grace

I sighed. "You need some serious dating tips," I grumbled as I started walking into the house. "Allison, tell Papaw how rude it is to leave his girlfriend on the porch."

She turned and placed her hands on his hips. "You're not a good boyfriend," she told him, then I heard her whisper, "but you're the best Papaw."

I smiled as I made my way inside and to the front door. I opened the door and came face to face with Dad's girlfriend. She was a pretty blonde lady and when she smiled, I decided I already liked her. "You're Grace. I've seen all your pictures… and the videos your mom taped of when you were little." I think she was waiting to see if I would be upset that she had watched our home videos, but I wasn't. If Dad spoke to her about Mom then I trusted that she was a good person.

"Sorry, my dad has no manners and left you out here… I didn't know he was dating but I'm glad," I told her honestly. "Your name…"

"Beth, and we've been seeing each other for a year almost and it's taken me this long to get him to introduce me to you guys."

"Come on in, everyone's out back." Dad… that little sneaky sneak.

She followed me in. "Here," she started digging through her purse and handed me a couple of tapes. "Your dad kept most of them, but he said you'd probably like to see these. They're ones of you and Noah." She smiled cheekily. "Even I thought they were cute."

Now I was curious, I made my way to the living room and went straight for the TV. When I bent down to put the tape in, Beth took it from my hands. "Here, let me. I know how hard it is to bend over when you're that far into your pregnancy."

"You have kids?" I asked her.

She smiled. "Two. A boy and girl that's right around your age. Which one do you want me to put in?" she asked.

"It doesn't matter," I said as I took a deep breath and sat down on the couch. Our third child was a boy and he was due in two weeks. I was definitely feeling every bit of this baby now.

"I hope it doesn't bother you that I came by with Steven. I wanted to meet you guys and I thought by… doing this, I could show you that I'd never try to act like your mother. I've fallen for your dad and I'd like to be part of your life too. As a friend or whatever you'd like." She covered her face immediately. "I am being too much? My daughter tells me I'm too much sometimes."

I smiled as she rambled. She was a lot different than Mom. She was extremely flustered for an older lady and I could tell that she wanted to make a good first impression. "It's okay. My dad's been alone a long time now, I'd rather him have someone."

"We aren't living together, but I hope to change that soon," she told me, and I laughed.

"Don't go easy on him or he will make you wait forever."

She nodded. "Oh, I'm quickly figuring that out."

She rewound the tape and pressed play when it was finished. She stayed on the floor and sat as younger versions of Noah and I came to life on the screen. I grinned as we fought and played together on different clips. It cut off for a moment and this time it was just Noah, and Mom was talking to him as he sat at the kitchen table, glancing toward the hallway like he was waiting for me to come down.

"I loved this," Beth murmured as she watched the screen with me.

"So, Noah…" My heart tightened in my chest every time I heard her voice in the tape. He looked up at the camcorder. "My daughter's pretty cute, ain't she?"

He blushed and looked away, shrugging his shoulders. "Yeah, I guess she might be."

"I guess isn't good enough. I guess you can't date Grace when you grow up."

He turned quickly. "Why not?"

"You guess she's pretty?" she told him.

He stammered, "You know she's pretty without me saying she is." He was blushing again, and man, I was so loving this video.

"You can't date her until you love her."

"I already love her."

"You don't know what love is."

"I do," he told her. "She's the best, most awesome person out of everyone I know, even more so because of her freckles."

Mom laughed in the background. "Ooohhh. I still don't know if I should let you date her."

"Why not?" He seriously looked worried about the possibility.

"I won't make it easy on you," Mom went on.

"That's okay too," he told her, placing his arms on the table.

"Listen to you," Mom gasped. "You think you can marry her one day?"

He turned and faced the camcorder again. "I *will* marry her one day."

"Noah," I came to the kitchen and Noah jumped. "Why didn't you tell me you were here?" I asked him.

"We were talking," Mom told the younger me.

I scrunched up my nose on the screen. "About what?"

"Nothing," young Noah said, quickly standing up and grabbing my hand. "Let's go play."

317

Once we were out of view, Mom turned the camcorder on herself and started laughing like a hyena. "Oh, I am going to have so much fun with these videos when you guys get older." She waggled her brows. "Prepare to be embarrassed."

The video cut off again.

"You look just like your mom," Beth turned around and said.

I was still smiling from the video. "Thanks."

We made our way to the backyard where Dad and Noah sat on a bench Noah had made while the kids played. When Noah saw me come back out, he got up and I already knew he was going to drag me over to sit down before he even said anything. I just stood there and admired him as he came to me. Age had nothing on him. He was like fine wine, time only made him better. I felt my body heat up as he neared. I felt a little damp between my legs but I probably peed a little... Yeah, it happened when you were pregnant.

"Come sit down, you've been on your feet all day," he told me as he placed his hand against my back and looked at Beth. "You must be the girlfriend."

"Beth," she offered her name and he gave her a friendly smile.

Dad finally walked over to Beth with a gentle smile.

"What is it?" Noah asked as we sat down on the bench together.

I shook my head and kissed him. "I just saw a little boy on TV claiming that he'd marry his best friend." I could tell that I was confusing him so I added, "Beth brought some of Mom's old tapes."

He nodded. "I seem to recall such a boy... He got what he wanted in the end."

He wrapped his arm around my shoulders as we leaned back and watched our kids play in the treehouse. "Every promise you've made, you've kept. I'm happy, Noah."

fall from grace

"Don't worry, I'm sure you're bound to be cranky the next few months when Ned's here," he muttered as he placed his hand on my belly. "I'll keep my distance when you want to throw something at me, and I'll make you smile when I need to." I rolled my eyes at him. "I'll always make you happy, Grace."

I turned my head. "You always do."

These days when I think of you, Mom, it doesn't feel like a sad thing. I can sit and talk to your grandkids about you with a smile on my face, and oh, how I wish you could have been here to meet them. I still miss you terribly and that part will never go away, but I'm truly happy with this life I have with Noah. You sneaky parent, you always suspected this would happen, didn't you? He's still a great guy all around and since I've been next to him most of my life anyway, I know that he'll never let me down. The saddest part is the fact that you didn't get to see us make it this far when you believed in us most. We're not kids anymore, and that strong bond I have with Noah as a kid is still with us today.

Life is full of bruises, to our hearts, bodies, and minds, I trust that I'll make it through them with Noah by my side.

So, don't worry, and keep smiling down on us.

The End.

About the Author

Michelle is from a small town in Eastern Kentucky where opossums try to blend in with the cats on the porch and bears are likely to chase your pets—this is very true, it happened with her sister's dog. Despite the extra needed protection for your pets, she loves the mountains she calls home. She has a man and twin girls who are the light of her life and the reason she's slightly crazy.

As a kid, she was that cousin, that friend, that sister and daughter, the talker who could spin a tale and make-believe into any little thing so it was no surprise when she found love in reading, and figured all these characters inside her head needed an outlet. They wanted to be heard, so she wrote.

The voices keep growing faster than she gets the time to write.

The stories are never going to end. That's perfectly okay, though. We never want to stop an adventure.

She writes and loves many different genres so sign up to her mailing list to keep updated on her releases. The signup form can be found on her Facebook page.

Connect with her:

Facebook: www.facebook.com/michellegrossauthor

Instagram: @michellegrossmg

Twitter: @AuthorMichelleG

Printed in Great Britain
by Amazon

20488021R00183